Silver Springtime

Written by

Cecelia Hopkins-Drewer

ISBN: 978-0-6481160-1-1
Published by CGH Literacy Institute,
Adelaide, South Australia, 2017

Acknowledgements:

Cover Photograph – Allan Schultz
Sports Consultant – Lance Hopkins

Fictional disclaimer:
All characters and events in this work are fictional, and while an effort has been made to recreate the era of the 1980s and incorporate aspects of history which are general knowledge; the story was written for entertainment purposes. The characters have no existence outside the imagination of the author and any similarity to persons or events outside the text is the result of coincidence.

CONTENTS

Prologue

By Cecelia Hopkins-Drewer

Prologue:

It was a wet day and the children had nothing to do, so young mum Allegra pulled out an old chest of knick-knacks and memorabilia. "Let's go through this!" she suggested, "There might be something interesting."

The first things that came to light were some old toys. The children had never seen these before because they belonged to Allegra. Terry picked up the teddy bear and Ellie claimed the battered Barbie dolls. They clearly found it surprising that their mother had once been a young girl.

"Where are your cars, Mum? Terry asked as they dipped deeper into the chest.

"I don't think I had a lot of cars Terry," Allegra replied in amusement. "I was a girl".

"That doesn't matter Mum," said young Terry, who had only known a society where girls and boys played with much the same toys and were offered the same opportunities.

"I still liked dolls better," Allegra said. She found an adorable stuffed dog, "Look at this one."

Terry took the toy dog, easily satisfied. Ellie, who was a little older, had found a photograph album. "What's this?"

"Just some old pictures dear," Allegra said. "That's me when I was little – and that's Grandma."

"The clothes are different," Ellie said. Her interest was caught. "Look at those lace collars, and those puffy sleeves."

"It was the 1980's," Allegra said. "I don't remember much from being a baby, but I believe that was the era of the housing boom and rising interest rates; also the period of the ladies power suit with shoulder pads - and the "leg of mutton sleeve" on wedding dresses.

"The leg of mutton sleeve!" Ellie exclaimed, "Whatever was that?"

"A fashion revival from the early 1800s, maybe even dating back to the middle ages!" Allegra explained. "The sleeves were full at the top and slimmed down to the wrist. They gave the woman a wider shoulder line. They originated in France I think..."

"What else has changed do you think?" Ellie inquired.

Allegra shrugged. "Society has changed a lot, I think, but people are still pretty much the same inside."

Terry was rummaging around in the bottom of the trunk. "A book", he exclaimed, pulling out a hardcover, floral bound journal.

"It is a diary," Allegra exclaimed. She took the notebook from her son and turned it over. "1984" she read. "That was the year Grandma met Grandpa."

"Go on Mum," Ellie exclaimed in excitement. "Let's read it! I want to know how Grandma met Grandpa!"

CHAPTER ONE: ORIENTATION

It was late one afternoon in February when Stephanie Lowood arrived at Silver Springs University on the north-east coast of Australia. Silver Springs University was an alternative tertiary institution which awarded degrees in conjunction with a prominent UK university that agreed to underwrite them academically. The Queensland campus was dedicated to the training of teachers, pastors, nurses and administrators for the private sector.

Stephanie was over a thousand miles from home, but had not yet had time to become homesick. The era was the nineteen-eighties; and the repressed rebel inside of her sensed that the youth of her generation had missed the fun and freedom of the nineteen-sixties and seventies. Punk glamour was in vogue, but aside from the influence on hair styles and electric music in the 'top ten', society was predominantly conservative and materialistic.

Stephanie reflected it seemed unfair that young people were expected to choose a career which would define the rest of their lives, and everyone hoped to buy a house, even though land prices were booming and the required deposits seemed impossibly large. Schools focused upon the academic subjects and business subjects were only offered by a few progressive public schools.

In the conservative circles with which Stephanie's family were associated, dating opportunities were also restricted for the youth, and there was a high degree of supervision by strict adults.

Stephanie paid the deposit for her key and was promptly shown upstairs to the room she was to share with another girl for the next forty-odd weeks. There were two beds, two single wardrobes, two sets of drawers, and one large desk. The back of the room was lined with shelves.

All her worldly possessions had been crammed into two huge suitcases. She heaved them both up onto the bed under the window and opened the lids. Her industrious unpacking was interrupted by a knock at the door. A pretty girl with short curly hair stuck her head into the room.

"Hi", she said, "I'm Melanie. I am the student dean for this floor, and I was sent to bring you down to assembly."

Stephanie smiled, pleased not to have to attend the first dormitory meeting alone. The idea was still a little daunting as she had yet to acclimatise to the idea of actually living at a boarding institution.

"Thank you Melanie", she said. "That would be lovely. Let me introduce myself. My name is Stephanie, and I am from South Australia".

"I am from Melbourne," Melanie said. "I am completing the final year of the Primary Teaching degree."

"Cool," Stephanie said. "I am doing Secondary Teaching. It sounds like a very interesting course."

"The subjects can be quite challenging," Melanie said. "I am sure you will do well though."

Melanie led the way down two flights of stairs and along a corridor.

"The girls' dormitory", she explained, "Has its own meeting hall. Assemblies are compulsory, and once the semester starts, a roll of attendance will be marked each evening. The boys come across and join us for assembly every Tuesday night, and visiting ministers run services on the weekends for students who are Christians."

Melanie sounded as if she enjoyed combined assembly and Stephanie wondered if she had a special boyfriend. It seemed too soon to ask her such a personal question.

Arriving at the women's assembly area, they sat down on one of the front benches. There were two other girls there already. One was called Grace and the other was called Debbie. Debbie had long brown hair, and Grace had a short stylish "bob" haircut. They were both first-years. Debbie, like Stephanie, was studying to be a teacher, and Grace was doing her Secretarial Certificate.

Assembly began with prayer. The speaker was the Staff Dean of girls' hall, their "Housemother". The Dean smiled and welcomed all of the girls to the university. She said that she hoped they would all be very happy, and they were to come to her when they needed anything. Then she began to read a list of rules.

Stephanie tensed up as the Dean read. She was naturally well-behaved and somewhat over-sensitive to rules. As gentle as a dove, she longed for nothing more than to be her natural self. Whereas other temperaments could ignore protocol or work around regulations, Stephanie's gentle personality found conventions oppressive and she yearned for freedom.

Amongst other things, there was a curfew in the evening. A security system locked the dormitory at exactly ten-thirty p.m. Each girl had a plastic card designed to work the security system, but they were supposed to apply for permission to use it. Their swipe cards could identify them if they made unauthorised use of the electronic lock and there was an implied penalty for being out late.

The security system provided the girls with privacy and protection, but it also sounded quite restrictive. Moreover, no males were allowed to progress beyond the reception area of the dormitory. There were special recreation areas in another building where guys and girls could meet to play pool and table tennis, or watch television. Similarly, no females were allowed to enter the boys' dormitory. Penalties for breaching these provisions were severe, including expulsion from the institution.

Stephanie had known as she packed that radios and contemporary music were not encouraged in the dormitory, and that due to the strong influence of the local Reform Church, dancing would not be encouraged - as either a social exercise or form of artistic expression. Stephanie had resolved that, under the circumstances, she would concentrate on study and absorb herself with the facilities that Silver Springs University had to offer. If some of her clothing designs were a little radical for staff taste that would be her one area of rebellion, as she was very proud of her skill as a seamstress.

At last the Staff Dean finished her speech and sat down. The Assistant Dean then closed with a few words. Assembly over, Stephanie chatted briefly to Grace and Debbie, making a note of their room number and promising to meet up with them sometime the next day. It seemed very likely they would be in some of the same classes.

Melanie shifted to talk to her friends. Stephanie admired the older girl's confident manner as she joined a large group of girls. They were still sitting and talking as she left to return to her room. It sounded like a lot of good natured gossip about their homes, families and boyfriends.

As she approached her room, Stephanie was surprised to hear classical music playing. She concluded that her assigned room-mate must have arrived while she was out. Stephanie pushed the door open somewhat tentatively. A slight blonde girl was busy hanging things up in the wardrobe on the opposite side of the room to mine. Stephanie saw a flash of taffeta and satin as she worked. Her new room-mate evidently had some lovely outfits.

The girl looked up and said "Hello", then suddenly exclaimed, "Hold it!" as Stephanie pushed the door.

Stephanie jumped backwards. "My name is Stephanie", she stammered, wondering whether the new girl was going to be stand-offish. "I live in this room too!"

The blonde girl laughed. "Sorry to give you a fright!" she said, "My violin is just behind the door. Let me rescue it and you can come inside."

The girl crossed the floor and picked up the carved case.

Stephanie stepped into the room somewhat tentatively. There was a pile of sheet music in her path. She picked her way around it and sat down on her bed. "Are you studying Music?" she asked.

"Yes", the girl said, "It's my major. By the way, I'm called Joelle."

"What a pretty name!" Stephanie exclaimed, "I'm a Drama major and I'm thinking of doing a Life Science minor."

"My minor will be History. It goes very well with Music. I guess we will have some Education subjects together." Joelle turned and gestured towards the tape recorder, "Will it bother you if I listen till the end of the tape?"

Stephanie shook her head, "Its lovely music, what piece is it?"

"Chopin. I recorded it on the piano myself!" Joelle smiled at her expression of surprise. "I practice for hours every day. Don't think of me as a snob if I'm not in the room much. I'll be over in the Music hall a lot."

"It's fantastic!" Stephanie said. She had honestly never heard anyone play that well outside of the Symphony Orchestra, or on a commercial record. Her own music lessons had been a severe flop.

"I'm just going to have a shower", Stephanie said, going to her drawer to get her towel and night-dress. "I will see you in the morning."

Stephanie exited the room and went to the bathroom area, when she returned the room was quiet and dark. Joelle was apparently asleep.

Stephanie woke to the sound of a myriad of bells and alarm clocks all ringing simultaneously. Tiptoeing so as to avoid waking Joelle, who somehow had the ability to sleep through the alarms, she collected her things in the semi-dark and sneaked out to the shower-block. After she had finished in the bathroom, Stephanie checked herself in the full length mirror in the corridor. She was reasonably tidy, so she wandered down to the cafeteria.

When Stephanie got to the cafe, it was empty except for two boys sitting at a table. She collected her food and was looking for somewhere to sit alone, when one of the guys waved to her.

"Come and sit with us," he called out, "We don't bite!"

Stephanie carried her tray across to the table, and sat down opposite the guys.

The one who had called out introduced himself as "David", and his friend as "Milton". They both came from Northern Queensland.

David had light brown hair and a comfortably sturdy frame. He appeared to be very outgoing, and kept on calling people over to their table until it was full. Milton was slightly older and much quieter. He had blonde hair and a short beard.

Stephanie busied myself with her food. She had not fully recovered from the self-conscious stage that hits along with the hormones of the teen years. Eating in mixed company made her feel quite shy, so she let the conversation flow around her. Finishing her cereal, Stephanie excused herself simply and said: "Nice to have met you", to everyone at the table.

David was busy talking, but Milton held her gaze. He smiled

politely. Stephanie decided he could be a nice person.

Stephanie went back to her room. Joelle was dressed and brushing her hair. "How was breakfast?" she asked.

"Okay", Stephanie replied. "Quiet. Not very many people are out yet. How did you sleep through all those alarms?"

"I can sleep through anything if I know I don't have a deadline in the morning", Joelle answered, "But if I have something to do, I'm up like a shot."

"You're lucky!" Stephanie said, "I wish I had such a good internal rhythm. I am such a light sleeper almost anything wakes me."

Joelle left for the cafeteria and Stephanie began to fill in her sheaf of registration papers.

Half an hour later Stephanie arrived at the main hall to join the line of students waiting to register for their classes. There were a number of check-points set up along the length of the hall. The Lecturers sat along the tables, waiting for students to approach them.

Stephanie walked up to the table with a large handwritten sign saying "Arts" attached.

A cheerful gentleman with short blonde hair greeted her.

"You must be Stephanie," he said, receiving her papers. "I am the English Professor."

The Professor glanced through the forms, ticking as he went, until he came to her choice of major and minor. "You cannot do Drama on its own at Silver Springs University", he observed doubtfully. "I will have to enrol you in some English subjects as well. That will make you much more useful in a school too."

"That is okay", Stephanie said. "I was hoping I could do a couple of specialist theatre subjects from one of the state universities as well."

"We will see what we can do," the Professor murmured. "There are several universities that are willing to cooperate with us."

"That is great!" Stephanie said, and the discussion passed onto her choice of minor.

At first the Professor thought that Life Science was an unusual area to combine with Drama, but Stephanie explained the connection in her mind and he observed that she had received unusually high marks in her Matriculation year. Stephanie was also quite young for university entry and considered highly talented.

The Professor, whose name-tag read "Dr. Johnson", but was rarely addressed by name, "Ummed" and "Aahed" for a bit; and then he checked her application form and confirmed that her Year Twelve score was particularly high. He said he thought Stephanie could probably manage the combination of subjects, but that he had to get special authorisation to enrol her in that manner. He went away for a few minutes and then he returned.

"There may be a few clashes to negotiate in your third and fourth years, but it will mostly be all-right", he said stamping her papers with ink.

Stephanie proceeded to the business office to make arrangements to pay her fees in monthly instalments. The queue there was very long and consequently, she was late for lunch. The afternoon was full of organised tours of the library and lecture theatres.

The next day, Stephanie attended a series of orientation lectures, where they were told how to organise their time and succeed at study. Debbie and Grace were also at the lectures and introduced her to a girl called Phoebe. Phoebe was doing English teaching so she would be in some of her classes.

Stephanie saw David and Milton in the lecture theatre. David said "Hi, how are you?" and Milton told her that he was doing English and History. That was interesting - Milton would be in English with her, and History with Joelle.

The boys were accompanied by a tall dark-haired guy called Bradley. Bradley was doing a combination of subjects Stephanie found nearly as unusual as her own - English and Geography. However, he explained to her that Geography was considered both a science and a humanities.

Stephanie filled her timetable out ready for starting classes proper on the morrow. It looked quite hectic. Her first class was at 7:30 am. The idea seemed to be for all lectures to be over by lunch, to give them the afternoon to study or do laboratory work. Her Science lab would take all Thursday afternoon.

Stephanie needed to wash some clothes so she asked Melanie to show her where the laundry and the clothes lines were located. The older girl also showed her a heated room where clothes could be dried in-doors. It was a unique idea, but Melanie said that the clothes could come back from the drying room a bit musty. Consequently, most of the girls preferred to use the outdoor lines.

Classes soon started in earnest. Curriculum and Ethics was a compulsory in-house subject for all first year students. It sounded like there would be a stimulating study of the social aspects of teaching. The Lecturer advised them to buy the recommended text to use for their assignments, and ran through a brief outline of the topics they would cover.

There was half an hour between Ethics and the first convocation program of the year. Most of the girls returned to the dormitory to check their appearance and tidy their hair. Joelle and Stephanie waited for Melanie, who was changing into a dainty sun-dress.

They walked across to the campus meeting hall, which was a two story, Queenslander-style white structure. The upstairs area was light and airy, with old fashioned theatre-style seats.

Melanie hesitated at the top of the stairs, obviously scanning the room for someone in particular.

Joelle and Stephanie waited politely, as this would be the first time they met Melanie's steady boyfriend, Jonathon.

"There you are", a male voice said from just behind them, "I was beginning to think I would never catch up!"

"Jonathon!" Melanie exclaimed in delight, and she hugged him right there in front of everybody. Then she introduced Joelle and Stephanie.

Jonathon was a clean-cut guy with blonde hair. He proved to be every bit as friendly as Melanie, shaking hands with Stephanie immediately. "Welcome to university!" he exclaimed.

Jonathon had brought a friend, whom he introduced to the girls as "Jeffrey".

Jeffrey was considerably quieter than Jonathon, but Stephanie found myself mesmerised by his deep grey eyes. He smiled, and her heart turned over with a big thump.

"Hello Jeffrey", Stephanie murmured.

"Hello Stephanie," Jeffrey replied. "I'm more often known as Jeff." He continued looking at her, and she began to blush.

Jeff was about six foot tall with brown hair, and something about him appealed to Stephanie's subconscious. Her parents had not allowed her to date prior to finishing high school, and she had no idea what sort of qualities to look for in a boyfriend. However, Stephanie imagined that if there was someone special out there for her, he would stand out from the crowd. So far Jeff fitted that scenario.

Joelle pulled at her arm, "Let's find a seat", she said. "Are you coming, Melanie and Jonathon?"

They filed into one of the pews and sat down as a group, with Melanie between the girls and the guys. Stephanie couldn't help sneaking a look at Jeffrey, and went red again when he looked straight back at her.

Joelle was looking at the organ and piano, almost measuring them for her fingers. "They've asked me if I would provide an item for some of the campus meetings," she said.

"That's great!" Stephanie whispered back.

After convocation, Stephanie attended Introduction to Education, another compulsory subject for all teaching students. It consisted of an overview of the theory of education. It was one of the requirements set by the Australian Government for an accredited Bachelor of Education program.

The next morning, Stephanie attended her first English Literature class. English Literature had always been fascinating to her. She enjoyed the drama and artistic effects in narrative, and loved the author's observations of human nature.

The Professor was very enthusiastic, and Stephanie could tell right away that he would be able to deliver the lectures in a fascinating manner. He told them that they would begin by studying George Eliot, then move on to Shakespeare's *Hamlet*, and a selection of modern poetry. The course was designed to form a complete introduction to the study of literature at tertiary level.

The Life Science laboratory Stephanie attended after lunch was a different story altogether. She found she had to learn to draw – instantly; and decipher the most puzzling things viewed under the microscope. Everything was unfamiliar, and Stephanie left the laboratory at the end of three hours discouraged and exhausted.

Stephanie knew that she would do well at the theory, or else she would have been tempted to withdraw from the subject immediately. (Brenda, who was her lab partner for the first few weeks did decide to withdraw, but we mustn't get ahead of the story.)

The Staff Deans gave Stephanie the task of cleaning women's assembly area. This was part of the 'student work program' by which they earned credit towards their fees. Stephanie was pleased, because the building was a public venue, and if she kept it looking nice, everyone enjoy the result. It was simple work, but Stephanie could take a pride in completing it thoroughly, and schedule her efforts around the special events held in the area.

Stephanie hummed and thought cheerful thoughts as she vacuumed up and down between the rows of seats. The year seemed to have a lot of potential. She had made a number of female friends already, there were males to meet, a pleasant if somewhat strict atmosphere, and challenging subjects to study.

Half way through, Stephanie had to stop and shift the extension cord. Then she continued cleaning. The women's assembly area would be used for co-ed vespers that evening.

The vespers program, besides being a Christian service, offered the students a great opportunity to socialise. It was therefore popular with students of all religious persuasions. The visiting Chaplain was from the recently formed Uniting Church of Australia and did not make heavy weather of any doctrinal issues.

Joelle and Stephanie arrived at the assembly area early, and sat down beside Debbie and Grace. Phoebe came in and joined them. Melanie, Jonathon and Jeff said "Hello" as they passed them, and sat down a couple of benches ahead. Jeff turned and looked at her. His grey eyes were eloquent even from a distance.

After worship concluded, Grace got up and went over to the fourth-year group, talking animatedly to Melanie, but actually casting her eyes towards Jonathon and Jeff. The rest of the girls were beginning to notice that Grace was quite flirtatious. It seemed harmless enough at this stage.

The next morning, Stephanie consulted the campus bulletin and was thinking about attending the Inter-denominational praise service, but Joelle invited her to attend the Reformed Church service later with her. The Reformed Church was one of the biggest movements on campus and Stephanie had heard that most of the students took an interest in their activities at some stage.

Stephanie wore a matching blue skirt and fitted top, with braid around the neck and hemline. It was one of her own retro nineteen-sixty creations, although the length had been adjusted to knee level to suit the eighties. Stephanie had no doubt that she looked smart, but she felt almost plain when she saw Joelle in her full black taffeta skirt and white lace blouse. Joelle was going to be playing the piano, and explained that the outfit comprised part of her function.

They caught up with Phoebe on the stairs and crossed to the campus meeting hall together. Joelle took a seat down the front, but Phoebe and Stephanie were invited to sit with David, who was always friendly, and Milton whom they had gotten to know better in English class.

The Reform Church meeting was a formal seated occasion.

Their service followed a basic format with three hymns and a sermon. There were no responsive readings or recitals of faith such as Stephanie was accustomed to at her home church. Someone whispered that she was privileged to be hearing one of the most polished religious speakers in the Australian region, popular theologian and television evangelist Pastor Siemens. He certainly was an interesting character.

Lunch was a leisurely affair, once they had got through the queue that formed when the various church services dispersed. After eating their meal, the students all relaxed and talked amongst themselves. Freed from the pressure of study and classes, some people even appeared prepared to sit in the cafeteria all afternoon!

Stephanie excused herself and went back to her room to write letters home. Although she had wanted to travel, the sheer distance she had moved from everyone she knew was daunting, and she felt the need to create contact. Writing correspondence also reminded Stephanie of how much she missed the familiar places, and she was busy until tea time.

After tea, David organised a group for a walk down to the suspension bridge. A number of students set off, chattering noisily, and stayed down by the river until it began to get dark.

David, who was majoring in Theology, decided to lead an informal prayer session. Then he fell into a lively ethical discussion with some of the others. Milton walked Phoebe, Joelle and Stephanie back to the dormitory. His manner was quietly friendly.

The next day was uneventful. Stephanie did some solitary study after class and went to bed with a headache. The memory of her Grandmother's death just before Christmas the previous year was poignant and she shed a few tears. Her dear Grandma had provided her with stability whenever there was trouble at home, and taught her the fine art of dressmaking. Homesickness also hit her in earnest, but she did not expect the melancholy mood to last for long with all the activities Silver Springs University made available during the week.

The excitement for the following day was caused by publication of the university news-letter which announced that the first big social event for the year would be the Reverse Tea. "Reverse" didn't mean that they ate desert, then savoury, then soup - which would have been sort of fun - it meant that the girls were expected to ask the guys out. It was also sometimes known as the 'Sadie Hawkins' or 'Ladies' Choice'.

The Reverse Tea was presented to the student body as an 'ice-breaker'. Apparently the faculty had observed that on the whole, the female students were more outgoing and willing to get involved in social events than the male students.

After classes finished, the girls gathered in Phoebe's room to talk about whom they were going to ask to the tea. Debbie had the *Student Directory* and was leafing through its pages. Joelle, to her surprise, was the most confident of them all. She had already asked a fellow music student to accompany her "as a friend". Phoebe was also approaching the event practically, and planned to ask Milton during English.

Stephanie kept quiet. She was thinking about asking Jeff, but she didn't want to be teased in an embarrassing way about him.

Debbie said that she didn't know who to ask.

"It has to be someone good-looking and single", Stephanie said. "Why don't you ask David, he is really friendly?"

"I don't know," Debbie said, "David talks to everybody, but he never pays attention to any girl in particular. I would want someone who is interested in me".

"You can't always get that on schedule," Phoebe remarked. "Although it would be nice to be vaguely compatible."

"Why does the person have to be single?" Grace chipped in challengingly, "I am thinking of asking Jonathon."

Stephanie shrugged her shoulders, barely taking her comment seriously. "It is a waste of time asking someone who has a girlfriend. Anyway Jonathon will already be going with Melanie."

Grace looked sulky. Apparently she had meant it, and didn't want to be convinced that some young men were out of the running. The rest of the girls ignored her attitude and went on with their conversation.

Stephanie was both excited and nervous about asking Jeff to the Reverse Tea. 'Asking out' was traditionally the males' prerogative, and the liberty of women to develop a career had little impact on social attitudes in the nineteen-eighties. Stephanie had observed some girls knew how to flirt and drop hints to get what they wanted, but she wasn't one of them.

Stephanie got through her classes somehow, read an English novel throughout the afternoon because it was the easiest type of study to concentrate upon, and then changed into a tropical print shift dress for combined assembly. The design was brighter than the current fashion, but she liked bold colours and felt they were flattering to her complexion.

Arriving at women's assembly area, which was the venue for many combined meetings, Stephanie scanned the congregated students for Melanie. She was sitting near the centre of the hall with Jonathon. Stephanie sat down next to her and said, "Hello".

"Hello, Stephanie," Melanie replied. "How have you been settling in?"

"Good thanks, Melanie", Stephanie said. "How have you been?"

"Pretty good," Melanie said, and it was obvious she was content. Jeff arrived just then, and as the other side of Jonathon was already occupied, he sat down beside Stephanie.

Having Jeff sitting right next to her made her feel quite self-conscious. Stephanie tried to sit in a lady-like manner, and not fidget. After a few minutes, she began to relax, and the cheerful strains of items performed by senior music students surrounded them. Assembly had commenced.

After assembly, Jonathon asked Melanie to go for a walk (they were allowed to go outside at night, if they stuck to certain lighted paths and came inside before ten o'clock) and Stephanie was left sitting with Jeff.

"What are you studying?" she asked to break the silence.

"Maths and Computing", Jeff answered. "It's my final year".

"How fascinating", Stephanie said. "I am studying English Literature and Life Science."

"Very intellectual," Jeff commented. He obviously meant to be complimentary, but Stephanie was vaguely uncomfortable because she made every effort to keep up socially and did not want to be perceived as a nerd, despite being younger than many of her classmates. She much preferred to identify as a poet and artiste with an insatiable curiosity for entertaining forms of knowledge.

Stephanie asked Jeff how long he had known Jonathon, and found out that they had attended high school together in Sydney. She commented that Melanie was very nice and had been showing her around the university. Stephanie said that she had met some other nice people, and hoped to make a lot of new friends during the year.

Then they ran out of easy conversation and fell silent.

Although it was Jeff's turn to speak, he seemed to be waiting for Stephanie to say something. 'He has guessed I am going to ask him to the Reverse Tea', she thought in sudden panic. 'I had better do it now...'

"Jeff," Stephanie said very carefully, "I was wondering if you would come to the Reverse Tea with me, you know - to get to know someone new?"

There, it was out! Stephanie sat still, hardly breathing, waiting for an answer.

"I don't know". Jeff said, cryptically, "I don't go for those functions much... so maybe not this time."

"That's all right", Stephanie said, as graciously and quickly as possible. His answer was confusing, but it mostly sounded like a 'No.' Moreover, she didn't have the knack of persuasion to turn it into a 'yes' if that was what was needed. "I hope you have a nice week."

Stephanie excused herself in embarrassment. Jeff had turned her down for no good reason, but he had thrown in some mixed signals as well. She went straight to bed, and pretended to be asleep when Joelle arrived in case her room-mate asked questions Stephanie could not answer comfortably.

"It always rains in March", commented the Biology Master the next day. He was something of a local expert, and had published some papers on insects in the area. His real name was "Dr. Webb", but like the other professors, he was rarely referred to by name. He had kept charts of the rainfall ever since commencing lecturing at Silver Springs.

The rain matched Stephanie's mood - blue. She had been forced to duck around between buildings to get to classes. An umbrella covered her about to the waist, but her feet got soaked every time. Someone told her that they wore out a lot of shoes in the tropical climate. Stephanie could see why.

Stephanie spent the afternoon in the library analysing poetry for English Language, the literacy subject recommended for all students of the Arts and Humanities. Then it was time for tea, and a bit of a break before worship. Stephanie dropped by Melanie's room, confident that she would be there. "Can I talk to you for a moment?"

Stephanie asked.

"Sure, if you don't mind me doing my hair", Melanie replied, busying herself at her mirror.

"I asked Jeff to the Reverse Tea..." Stephanie began.

"That's nice", Melanie said. "I'm glad you like him. What did he say?"

"He sort of said no," Stephanie answered.

"Jeff's a pretty quiet guy," Melanie commented. "I'm sure you two will be friends. Just give it some time."

"But why did he say no?" Stephanie asked. "I only asked him to a simple tea! Is there something wrong with me, or maybe with the way I asked him?"

"Well, some guys don't like the girls making the first move," Melanie said. "Sort of old fashioned like. Why don't you ask someone else for now?"

"I'm not sure I'm brave enough," Stephanie said.

"Of course you are!" Melanie assured her, "And now you know what it's like for the guys to try and ask us. We could always be going to say no to them."

"I hadn't thought about it that way!" Stephanie said, much cheered.

Stephanie decided to dress up and take a positive approach to university life. She had a cute little white top that she wore with her jeans, and Debbie said Stephanie looked very nice when she came to class. Debbie always looked very smart herself, so Stephanie took that as a sincere compliment.

As Stephanie was walking across to the cafeteria lunch time, she noticed a boy with short sandy hair who looked very much like someone she knew at home. He was a country boy, so Stephanie only saw him when he came down to state-wide meetings, but he was a friendly person. She couldn't be sure that it was him, but just in case, she waved. The boy smiled and waved back.

Stephanie sought out two girls who had also come to university from Southern Australia, and sat down next to them. "Hi", she said.

Mandy and Lisa both said, "Hello". They were almost finished their lunches. Both girls were doing Nursing, and their timetables were very different than Stephanie's. Nurses were only on campus for one semester. Then they moved to the hospital to gain ward experience, and continued their lectures from the Brisbane campus.

"Do you see that guy over there?" Stephanie whispered. "Two tables away? Doesn't he look like Jason Karper?"

Mandy turned around to take a look. "Yes!" she exclaimed. "He does!"

"It wouldn't really be him, would it?" Lisa asked.

"I hadn't heard of him coming to the university," Stephanie said doubtfully.

"I tell you what", Mandy said, "I'll go and ask him".
Mandy was really out-going, so she could perform this feat without embarrassment. Stephanie tried not to look across the cafeteria as she did it, but she was bursting with curiosity.

Mandy returned to their table. "His name is Arthur Mason," she reported, "He is doing Maths and Commerce."

"Thanks," Stephanie said, wondering how she was going to live this down. But at least she wasn't going to accidentally call the guy "Jason" the next time she saw him.

Arthur happened to arrive at the cafeteria for breakfast about the same time Stephanie did the next morning, so she said: "Hello, I'm Stephanie Lowood".

Arthur said "Hello" and seemed interested in talking to her. He had obviously gained the impression that she liked him.
Stephanie was a bit embarrassed, but it turned out that Arthur, being new at Silver Springs University, was also interested in meeting new people. Before Stephanie knew it, she had asked him to the Reverse Tea and he had accepted!

Stephanie left the cafeteria feeling satisfied that she had joined the privileged group of girls who had organised their dates, and knew with whom they were going. Stephanie made sure that she said "Hi" to Arthur and his friends whenever they passed each other between classes.

Lunch time Stephanie found herself walking across to the cafeteria with Phoebe and Debbie. David passed by, and invited the girls to meet him at the side of the cafeteria at two o'clock. He said that he had heard about a heritage walk which passed the house one of the early settlers and an old building that opened to the public as a museum on weekends.

"Bring all your friends", David said, "And we'll go as a group".

They managed to find Tess, who was in Education class with them, and Joelle. Grace was busy talking to boys and didn't want to come, Mandy was exhausted and wanted to sleep, and Melanie (whom they invited, but didn't really expect to join them) said that she had seen the museum before.

There were five girls, and David had four boys with him. He introduced Larry as a fellow Theology student. The other guys were Bradley, Milton, and Luke.

They walked past some cow paddocks, and down a bush track. The ground was damp and they passed a creek. After a while they came to an old fashioned "style" set in a fence.

Luke helped Tess and Stephanie over the fence because they were still wearing their dresses. He was quite polite about it, and Stephanie was impressed by his behaving like a gentleman. She also suspected that Luke liked Tess.

The early settler's home was white board Queenslander-style and the students couldn't go upstairs because that area was roped off and marked private. There were some old fashioned pieces of wooden and wicker furniture placed carefully around the main living room.

It reminded Stephanie of other colonial homes she had visited, although it was more Federation in style due to the American influence in that period. The most remarkable thing was the rose garden out the front, which was extremely well maintained.

A few meters down the road from the early settler's house was an old butter factory. This had been in operation since around 1930, but had closed in recent years. There had been some talk about the council re-opening it as an Arts centre, but at present all the students could see were the external buildings.

Beyond the old factory was a building called "The Northern Queensland and Island Museum". It was full of artefacts and things imported from the Cape York, Papua New Guinea and the Pacific Islands. There were beads and chains, and even a huge canoe! The printed explanations of the exhibits told some fascinating stories.

They spent an hour in the museum, and then David looked at his watch.

"It's about time to start back", he said. "If we leave now, we will be just in time for tea!"

David walked ahead with Debbie, Bradley and Larry were talking to Joelle, and Stephanie joined Milton and Phoebe. Luke and Tess lagged a little way behind.

Stephanie woke early, dressed in a blue crepe suit, and attended the Inter-denominational praise service held at seven thirty a.m. in the women's assembly area. It was less formal than the later services, and included a great deal of singing. The devotional message was provided by a couple of students who had spent time over-seas doing mission work for their churches. Their experiences were fascinating, and it sounded as if they had developed a lot of emotional maturity working as volunteers.

The student services office had organised a bus trip to a beach near Noosa Heads on the coast. Stephanie wasn't planning to go, because it cost ten dollars and her student allowance had not yet been granted. However, when Joelle and Debbie found out Stephanie wasn't going, they told the Deans. The Deans got her a ticket, and talked her into going.

The bus drove along the State Route, although it took a slight detour along Creek Road, to show the students Silver Springs Mountain. It put the students down at a wharf and they walked some distance to the beach, where they changed into their bathers in the public conveniences.

Some of the guys swam and surfed, but most of the girls merely sun-baked and tried to look like fashion models. The staff set up a barbecue, and served some vegetarian sausages that came in red skins like real sausages, with bread and sauce.

Stephanie found herself talking to Arthur a lot, and she sat with him on the trip back. He was telling her about his home and what he thought of the university so far. He had some strong opinions and seemed like a fairly earnest person. So far Stephanie was finding him to be a pleasant and equitable companion.

Following that outing, Stephanie had a busy day with classes and study. After tea, Stephanie was invited to visit Debbie and Grace in their room. It was Phoebe's birthday, and Debbie had bought a cake from the tiny general store down the street. The girls were laughing and relaxing when there was a knock at the door and Melanie stuck her head in.

"Is Stephanie here?" she said. "Ah good! There you are. You are needed to help set something up in the women's assembly area."

"Okay," Stephanie said, getting up to follow her.

"Hello Melanie", Grace chirped, "Won't you stay for a piece of cake?"

"No thanks", Melanie said stiffly, "I have to go".

Stephanie followed Melanie down to the women's assembly area, and they began to shift things around. Melanie didn't look like her usual cheery self, and Stephanie was somewhat puzzled.

"Are you alright?" Stephanie asked gently.

The older girl sighed. "Yes... pretty much. It's just that your little friend Grace asked Jonathon to go to the Reverse Tea with her."

"She didn't really do that, did she?" Stephanie exclaimed. "Isn't Jonathon YOUR date?"

"Well...we had assumed we would be going together," Melanie said. "I hadn't thought to confirm it with him. So, when she asked him, he came and asked me what to do."

"You told him to say no, didn't you?" Stephanie queried.

"No, actually," Melanie said, "I don't think you can own another person. I gave him a choice. If he says yes to Grace, I'll ask a first year too, and we will both be helping new students get involved in the social scene."

"That is very generous of you," Stephanie said. "But wouldn't you rather go with Jonathon?"

"Yes, I would!" Melanie said, "I don't know what to do. This hasn't ever happened before."

Study was getting intense. All her tutorial dates were set, and Stephanie had started working on her first essay. There was heaps of work involved, and it would take careful planning to get it all done on time.

Stephanie rang home, and talked to her Mother and her Aunt Moira. They asked her all about what was happening at university. She was telling them about her study, and the gossip about who had asked who to the Reverse Tea. Because Stephanie knew that her Aunt Moira would never tell anyone, she told her that Grace had asked a guy who already had a girlfriend to be her date.

Aunt Moira surprised her by exclaiming: "Naughty girl!" quite sharply.

"Why?" Stephanie said puzzled, "I honestly thought it was silly. Melanie should have just told Jonathon to say no to Grace. That's all. Then it would be all over and done with."

"It's not that simple," Aunt Moira said. "That Grace could make a lot of trouble. Especially if she keeps looking at men who are not single. What if Melanie and Jonathon were married?"

"Aunt Moira!" Stephanie said, "We are all young. None of us are likely to be married yet."

"But still", her Aunt Moira said, "Melanie and Jonathon are serious aren't they? And now Melanie is hurt isn't she?"

"She doesn't seem very happy," Stephanie admitted. "She didn't even sit with Jonathon at combined assembly. She sat with a lot of her girlfriends."

"There you are my dear. You girls should start the way you

intend to go on, and respect the uniqueness of each other's friendships with boys. There were lots of boys without girlfriends that Grace could have asked, weren't there?" Aunt Moira queried.

"Oh heaps! And Grace is really pretty. I'm sure they would have all said yes to her!" Stephanie said.

"There you are dear," Aunt Moira agreed. "Now tell me about this boy you are going with. What is he like?"

Curriculum and Ethics finished a few minutes early the next morning, so Stephanie hurried back to the dormitory to change into something nicer for general assembly. As she went through the foyer, Stephanie saw Jonathon at the front desk looking very tidy. He had managed to get his hair cut that morning, and was obviously waiting for someone.

As Stephanie passed, he called out to her: "Hello Stephanie, if you see Melanie, tell her that I am here."

Upstairs, Stephanie knocked on Melanie's door. "Jonathon is waiting for you", she said.

Melanie flushed. "Hi Stephanie," she said, "Do come in. You know, last night Jonathon told Grace that he would prefer to go to the Reverse Tea with me! He phoned the dorm this morning to tell me the news."

"He should have told her that straight away!" Stephanie said.

"That would have been nice...", Melanie said, "But sometimes guys have to work these things out. Especially when there are lots of other girls around they could have. Now I can be absolutely sure that it is me he wants!"

"How romantic!" Stephanie said. "And you are looking very nice."

"Go and get changed," Melanie said, noticing Stephanie's old blue tracksuit. "I'll wait for you."

"What about Jonathon?"

"He won't run away - if you are quick!"

Stephanie changed at lightning speed, and she and Melanie and went downstairs together. Jonathon leapt forward when he saw Melanie. She gave him her hand, and they all walked across to the meeting hall.

CHAPTER TWO: JUST FRIENDS

On the way to her Life Science laboratory Stephanie saw Jeff. He was leaning nonchalantly against the wall in the archway between the central buildings. He didn't seem to be doing anything, just standing there as if waiting for someone. Stephanie thought for a minute that it might be her for whom Jeff was waiting, but concluded that would not have been logical behaviour on his part. It was still an outside possibility, however.

Stephanie briefly considered going around the other way and cutting across the lawn, but the grass was soggy and mucky with all the rain they had that morning. Stephanie also figured that was too much effort to make just because she was embarrassed someone had turned her down for a social function.

That decision made, Stephanie plastered a bright smile on her face, cruised forward and said: "Hello Jeff".

"Hello Stephanie", Jeff said. "How have you been?"

"Good thank you," Stephanie replied. "How are you today?"

"I'm okay", Jeff drawled coolly, stepping out from the wall and blocking her path. "I've got a basketball match this afternoon. It is just before tea."

"Oh, I hope you win," Stephanie said.

"You know, basketball is a really big deal around here," Jeff remarked. "You should come and watch some time."

"I may do that," Stephanie said. "But it can't be on a Thursday. I have a Life Science laboratory which runs right up till tea."

"I'll be seeing you around then," Jeff said casually, and turned to saunter off.

Stephanie started to say "Goodbye", but she found myself talking to thin air. Stephanie was flushed and flustered. It was obvious Jeff felt he had achieved something in talking to her; and while she was flattered by the invitation, she was also puzzled by the abrupt end of the conversation.

Stephanie studied in the morning, and then began to sew her costume for the Reverse Tea. Arthur and Stephanie had decided to go as a Roman couple, although it had taken some persuasion on her part to get Arthur to wear a toga.

In the end Stephanie had said that if he wore a white shirt and draped a piece of cloth over his shoulder like a sash, she was sure that he could wear light coloured shorts and still look like a pretty good Roman. Stephanie would keep her costume correspondingly simple. She was a bit disappointed that Arthur did not like the idea of dressing up as much as she did. Other couples were going to elaborate lengths and appeared to be enjoying it immensely.

It was also a chance to do something dramatic for a change. Stephanie had asked around, and while there was a choir, there was no serious drama group currently functioning at Silver Springs. This was a disappointment to her, as her shy personality dropped away and she became whoever she was pretending to be once she was in character. Stephanie also preferred classical plays to the skits occasionally presented by Christian groups on campus.

Stephanie borrowed a suitable dress pattern from one of the girls, and made some adjustments as she cut it out, to make sure the result would be flowing and draped. Stephanie decided to make an actual bodice and not risk having something tied onto her and possibly coming adrift. It also allowed her to work on some non-traditional decorations. She attached two soft flounces on each side of the shoulder in the place of sleeves, and made a folded fabric flower to pin on the bodice. Stephanie finished with a large sash to tie below the bust. It was probably no more authentically Roman than Arthur's costume would be, but it felt exotic and different.

The evening program hosted by the Uniting Church was going to be a unique gathering called the "Fellowship Tea". This was a combined buffet and worship, followed by communion for those who were church members. This event caused much excitement amongst the first year girls, who helped beautify each other for the occasion.

Stephanie had been reserving her few fancy outfits for really special functions, but Phoebe and Joelle insisted that this evening was sufficiently significant to warrant her wearing the little black suit Stephanie had made for herself. The skirt was long and straight with a split up the side as Stephanie's concept of glamour was taken from brief glimpses she had seen of the prime-time soap opera *Dynasty*.

Stephanie had dared to anticipate a coming change in the current middling hemline fashion and the skirt reached down well below the knees to maxi length. Stephanie teamed it with a lacy blouse that would have been revealing but for the neat waistcoat which completed the ensemble.

Phoebe used her blow drier to coax Stephanie's hair into a smooth style. Everyone told Stephanie that she looked very smart, and some people even said that they could not recognise her from a distance.

The worship discussion centred upon the different types of love described by the ancient Greeks. Apparently they recognised "Phileo" (family love), "Eros" (romantic love), "Platonic" (or friendship) love and "Agape" love, which represented a selfless compassion for other people. Coming from an undemonstrative family background, discussing all the various types of "love" in a public venue was new to her, and Stephanie became quiet and thoughtful.

The rest of the evening was tastefully orchestrated with grapes for the "wine" and squares of wholemeal biscuit substituted for the "bread" of Christian communion. The entire cafeteria was lit by candelabra with the tables pushed aside to make room for rings of seats. After the service, Phoebe, Joelle and Stephanie sat around talking with David, Debbie and Milton.

A number of people moved from group to group, mingling. Melanie came up to their circle with Jonathon and Jeff. She sat down and talked for a few minutes, then she moved on to greet Mandy and Tess. Jonathon moved on with her, and after a moment's hesitation, so did Jeff.

When there was a gap next to Stephanie, Arthur appeared and sat down to talk for a while. Then Dylan and Garry (from her Life

Science class) stopped by to chat. Dylan was short and stocky, while Garry was faired haired and athletic. Stephanie felt flattered by so many people approaching her in particular, and pleased that she did not have to seek them out.

Stephanie decided to overdose on worship and attended both the early Inter-denominational praise service and the Reformed Church meetings. The sun shone and things dried out a little, but not enough for walking in the bush, so in the afternoon a number of students played card games and quizzes in one of the recreation rooms. This had been suggested by Milton and organised by David.

Stephanie was surprised when Grace decided to join them. Stephanie had gathered the impression the other girl hadn't been talking to the other first years for the last couple of days. Now however, she made a big fuss about helping David, who was the group's natural spokesperson, adjudicate the quiz.

Somewhere between rounds of the quiz Grace asked David whether he would escort her to the Reverse Tea. The rest of the girls held our breaths at this, because the embarrassment value if David said 'no' in front of a group was quite high, but Grace had picked her target well.

David was too nice a guy to let a girl down like that. He looked briefly at Debbie, to whom he had been paying more specific attention lately, and she shrugged slightly. Then he looked back at Grace and said: "Of course I'll go with you."

The card game did not last long after that. The atmosphere had changed, and all of the girls were secretly eager to talk about what had happened.

David and Milton decided to pack up their cards, and left with Grace skipping along between them, talking animatedly. She was obviously no longer interested in the company of females.

Phoebe and Stephanie turned on Debbie immediately. "I think that David was hoping YOU would ask him to the Reverse Tea," Phoebe exclaimed.

"I believe he really likes you", Stephanie added.

Debbie looked unconcerned. "I am beginning to like him too", she confessed. "But it is the beginning of the year and there are so many people to get to know."

Debbie gestured with her hands to indicate the infinite possibilities offered by campus social life. Phoebe and Stephanie remained unconvinced.

"What if David is the right guy for you?" Stephanie asked.

"As I get to know him, that will become clearer," Debbie answered. "I know I would regret not having circulated a bit while I am young and single. I have decided to ask Garry - he has a very nice manner."

"And David is probably going with Grace BECAUSE she is your room-mate and it gives him an excuse to stick close," Phoebe said with sudden insight. "Grace has done it to herself again! She won't get a guy's full attention until she picks someone who is truly available."

Debbie shrugged, "Grace has a date for the Reverse Tea, and

that is all she seems worried about at this stage. I am sure we will all have a nice time."

Stephanie had a Life Science field trip in the afternoon. The entire class piled into the Biology Master's well-worn four wheel drive, and drove out to a beach on the coastline just above Brisbane. As Stephanie was used to lovely sandy beaches all along the coast in Southern Australia, it was a shock to find that the entire beach in question was composed of rock. However, she cheered up quickly as The Biology Master showed them how to find sea stars, sea urchins and sea sponges in shallow pools. These were all fascinating sea creatures that Stephanie had seen pictures of, but never touched before.

The other part of the field trip was harder work. The class was divided into pairs, and assigned a strip of beach stretching from the shore to the water to map and analyse. Their "maps" were designed to record the various species of barnacle living in close proximity to the water.

Brenda was working with Stephanie, and neither of them had done this type of study before. Apparently it was a special discipline called 'Ecology'. Garry and Cara were familiar with the topic from year twelve extension projects performed in New South Wales and Queensland, but Stephanie had learnt more about physiology and cell functions during her Matriculation year.

On the whole, it was fun to get off campus with a group of students and a very smart Lecturer. The guys all had really great senses of humour, and Stephanie could see that the members of the class were fast becoming friends. They seemed like a dependable bunch - which was important if they had to go hiking and camping together throughout the course.

Stephanie got a bit of a surprise in combined assembly that evening. She was sitting with Phoebe, Joelle, Mandy and Tess. It was basically a whole row of girls, and no guys whatsoever - when Jeff came in and sat down right alongside her. Jeff leant against her, and Stephanie felt herself prickle with nervous tension. Stephanie turned to speak to him, but he wasn't looking at her that particular moment. Stephanie waited for a while, and listened to the devotion. When she next glanced at Jeff, he grinned at her, but did not say anything.

After assembly concluded, Jeff sat there fidgeting until Stephanie got the impression that he wanted to talk to her in particular. However, he was not intending to initiate the conversation. Stephanie thought this was a bit odd, but decided to give him the benefit of the doubt. Perhaps as Melanie said, he was just a very quiet young guy.

"Hello Jeff," Stephanie ventured. "How are you?"

Jeff said, "Hello, Stephanie," and relapsed into silence.

"What have you been doing?" Stephanie asked in an attempt to draw him out and make conversation.

"Working and things," Jeff finally answered. "What have you been doing?"

"Study, and getting to know the place," Stephanie said. "I had a Life Science field trip yesterday. The beaches are real different around here."

Stephanie relaxed and launched into a description of the coastline. It was fun to be able to tell someone all about her field trip, and so far no one outside her Life Science class had seemed interested.

When Stephanie had finished, Jeff laughed. He said: "You'll do all right around here. You notice things."

"Thanks," Stephanie said, feeling pleased.

Then Jeff said, "I'd better be going now."

So Stephanie said "Goodbye", and Jeff stood up.

"I'll be seeing you next time," he said.

Stephanie sat there for a few minutes and pondered the encounter. She had noticed Jeff's approaches toward her were somewhat convoluted, whereas Stephanie had been hoping for something more straight-forward, a friendship did appear to be developing. Stephanie had to admit she did still like him. Hormone based emotions are not always under an individual's intellectual control, and she still found her veins filled with endorphins at the sight of him.

When Stephanie turned around, Arthur was standing by the door. He appeared to have been waiting for her too. Stephanie got up and said "Hello" to him. They talked for a few minutes, but he didn't seem as gregarious as usual. Stephanie wondered what could be wrong. Being a modest person, it did not occur to her that he could have been mildly disapproving of her conversation with Jeff.

Then Debbie and Grace came up with David and Milton, and

the students went for a quick walk across to the gymnasium, where they casually checked out all the equipment.

After tea Stephanie went over to boy's dormitory and waited in the reception area for Arthur to descend. Stephanie primarily wanted to check that he was managing to put a costume together for the Reverse Tea. He said that it was all under control. Stephanie accepted that he was not as keen on theatricals as she was, but he also said that he was busy with assignments, and sent her away quite quickly. Stephanie thought that wasn't like the talkative Arthur she had been getting to know.

Stephanie sat with Arthur once again lunch time the next day, and made a brave effort to talk to him. He was polite, but very reserved. No matter what Stephanie asked him, she received a short answer like "Yes", "No" or "All-right". This was quite puzzling. He used to tell her a lot about his course work, and they would talk for quite some time.

Melanie came down to women's assembly hall to help her clean the windows, so Stephanie took the opportunity to ask her advice about Arthur.

"He is not talking to her the way he used", Stephanie said as they were polishing the glass doors. "It has come on all of a sudden. Arthur used to be really outgoing."

"Oh, that is probably because he is jealous of Jeffrey," Melanie said.

"What?" Stephanie exclaimed.

"You two have been seen around together a bit lately," Melanie said carefully.

"Once or twice," Stephanie said "and we were just talking. There is nothing happening".

"But Jeff was your first choice for the Reverse Tea, wasn't he?" Melanie asked, spraying a big splotch of window cleaner onto the upper panel.

"It is true I asked him first. However, he turned me down and Arthur shouldn't know anything about that," Stephanie answered.

"I think he does know," Melanie murmured.

"How would he have found out?" Stephanie queried.

"I don't know," Melanie said. "I haven't told anyone. Maybe someone overheard you asking Jeff, this place is full of gossips! Or maybe Jeff even told Arthur himself."

"Why ever would he do that?" Stephanie exclaimed.

"Just being matey," Melanie said. "Males do chat. Although guys have also been known to mark their territory that way."

"I'm nobody's territory as yet," Stephanie said, "And I am not sure whether it is flattering or insulting to be viewed that way. I'm not an object - or even worse a place."

"Of course you aren't! That's just men for you." Melanie finished drying that panel and moved on to the next: "If you are worried you could try speaking to Arthur. You know, tell him that you are really happy he is the one you are going to the tea with."

"I could, but I won't!" Stephanie exclaimed. "If what you say is true, it sounds like Arthur is trying to sulk me into re-assuring him. I don't think that is a very mature response." Stephanie was rather positive about this issue, as she valued open communication, preferably initiated by both parties! "Besides, he and I are just friends, so he has no grounds to be resentful."

"What are you planning to do then?" Melanie queried.

"I am going to be as normal and friendly to Arthur as I can be," Stephanie said. "I would prefer he took the time to get to know me as a person, and sorted out what he thought for himself."

"That is a good attitude," Melanie agreed, "Just bear in mind that it works better with some guys than with others".

Stephanie sighed, "I hope that Arthur and I can still have a nice date, but I am not going to jump through hoops just to please him."

The day of the Reverse Tea dawned fine and clear. It was also the day of the New South Wales state election, so any students from NSW had to travel into Northcoast to place their votes, if they had not already done so using the pre-poll voting booth that had been set up on campus during the week.

Around breakfast time Stephanie consulted the seating plan for the Reverse Tea, and carefully placed Arthur and her names between those of Phoebe and Milton, David and Grace. That way Stephanie hoped, she would have some friends to talk to, and David who was very outgoing, would help her include Arthur in the conversation.

Most people decided to have an afternoon rest, and a muted atmosphere of excitement hung over the girls' dormitory. The Reverse Tea was scheduled to start at eight o'clock in the evening, after the sun had set, and the romance of evening had commenced.

Arthur did the gentlemanly thing and picked her up at the girls' dormitory just before eight. However, that was where the gallantry ended. He was wearing a white shirt and fawn trousers, with a piece of material draped across the shoulder and tied around the waist with an orange cord, as they had agreed. Stephanie complimented him on the costume, but he did not respond. Nor did he mention her outfit, even though Stephanie felt she looked quite elegant, and would have liked to get a positive reaction from her date.

They walked across to the cafeteria making polite and meaningless small talk. Stephanie was surprised to find that David and Grace had been moved, and Arthur's friend Michael was next to them with his date instead. Arthur spent the entire evening talking to Michael and Michael's date, a second year called Danielle. They began to talk about the restaurants they had gone to in Brisbane. Stephanie was lost and could not join into the conversation.

Stephanie spent the evening bravely talking to Phoebe and Milton about the food and the variety of costumes. Stephanie had to be careful because she didn't want to interfere with their date, however they were together as classmates and not a romantic couple and said they were happy to include her.

Half way through the evening, Phoebe and Stephanie got up and went to the ladies' toilet block. When they were there Phoebe turned to her with sympathy.

"You poor thing!" she said, "Isn't Arthur being rude ignoring you like that?"

"It's okay," Stephanie said. "That is just the difference between Arthur's attitude when he thinks that I might fancy him - and when he realises I just want to be friends. I am glad I've found out now."

"I'm glad Milton is not like that!" Phoebe exclaimed.

"Perhaps he thinks you like him too," Stephanie suggested.

"I certainly hope not! If he does I'll sit next to someone else in English Literature on Monday. Milton will work it out quick enough...", Phoebe said firmly.

Stephanie laughed.

They went back to the table and sat down. Dessert had arrived. It was white chocolate mousse, which Stephanie could enjoy whether her date was going well or not.

After dessert people got up and started moving around. Debbie had a camera and wanted to take photos of the couples in their costumes. Stephanie asked Arthur to pose with her and he did so, giving her a funny look. Stephanie saw the photo after it was printed and there was a mile of space between them, whereas other couples had looked cosy, but by that time, Stephanie didn't care that much.

Milton came to her rescue at the end of the evening, and told Arthur that he would be happy to escort both Phoebe and Stephanie back to the dormitory. Arthur looked relieved and went off in the opposite direction with Michael and Danielle.

Reformed Church and the Inter-denominational praise service passed by quickly. Stephanie thought everybody must have slept late as attendance at the services was low. During lunch the conversation turned to the outcome of the New South Wales election. According to morning news reports, someone said, Neville Wran, who represented the Australian Labour Party had been elected into government for a record fourth term. The topic of politics interested the boys more than the girls, who were inclined to be bored by current events.

Returning to the dorm, Stephanie discovered her friends had finally risen, and they agreed to meet in Debbie's room for a chat. They all reported having a great time at the Reverse Tea. Luke and Tess had been seen holding hands this morning, and were now a confirmed item!

Grace was sure that she and David, "Had the most fun!" She looked rather pointedly at Debbie, who valiantly took no notice.

Joelle said that she and Craig were getting on very well, and she was planning to accompany his violin solo on Friday night. "He is a great musician," she concluded.

"What sort of man is he?" Stephanie said teasingly.

"He is a nice guy too", Joelle said, "For someone else.... I hope he finds someone special here at the university."

"Why not you?" Phoebe queried.

"I'm not looking for a boyfriend," Joelle shrugged. "I need to concentrate on my music this year."

That was a unique idea for most of the girls. They would have liked to have boyfriends AND careers, both starting this year if possible.

"If you are well organised, you should be able to manage a social life as well as study," Stephanie suggested gently.

"A social life, yes," Joelle said firmly. "I am not sure about anything serious though."

"That is up to you, I guess," Debbie said. "But we can't always predict these things. My sister met the loveliest man when she wasn't even looking..."

"I'm sorry about you and Arthur," Grace broke in suddenly. The tone she directed toward Stephanie was more spiteful than sympathetic. "Perhaps you should have gone with Jeffrey Mannington. They say he didn't go with anyone!"

There was a short silence during which Stephanie felt myself going red. "I had a good time with Phoebe," Stephanie said finally. "It doesn't matter which guy I went with. Besides it won't be the most serious social event of the year."

"Yes", Phoebe agreed. "There are other things coming up. And the other social events are different. We have to wait for the guys to ask us!"

Grace sniffed.

Stephanie just managed to grab a hasty breakfast before the

cafeteria closed, and then she went down to clean the women's chapel area, which was always especially dirty after the praise services.

Stephanie saw Arthur in the cafeteria and stopped to say "Hello" to him. He said "Hello" back very politely, but made it clear that he was busy with Michael and his mates.

Stephanie didn't think that their friendship was going to grow from this point. Well, at least she had tried - even after the way the Reverse Tea turned out.

Joelle asked Stephanie to come to the Music rooms and turn the pages for her as she played. The musician was preparing a very complicated piece to play for a test.

When she had finished, Stephanie asked her opinion on something that had been on her mind. Namely, whether she thought Stephanie ought to have waited for Jeff to decide to go to the Reverse Tea with her.

"Definitely not!" Joelle said. "Grace just said that to make trouble. She likes to point out that other people's dates haven't gone as well as hers."

"Why do you think she does that?" Stephanie wondered.

"Being attractive to guys is important to her. She puts more work into it than into her studies," Joelle concluded. "And she seems to perceive life as some sort of competition."

"What about Jeff? Do you think he changed his mind about going with me?" Stephanie asked.

"It's hard to tell. Jeff might just want what he can't have," Joelle shrugged and packed up her books. "I think you should forget about it unless something else happens between you two."

That off her mind, Stephanie settled down to do her Curriculum and Ethics essay. She had been doing preliminary work on it for some time, but wanted to finish her first draft. It was on cultural influences and had to be about fifteen-hundred words. The textbook phrases they quoted did not count as part of the word limit, so Stephanie had quite a bit more to write. She went to bed tired that night.

Stephanie had classes throughout the morning and a laboratory session in the afternoon. In the evening there was a knock on her door. It was Phoebe's room-mate Kathy.

"Hi Stephanie, do you feel like taking a break at all tonight?" she said. "I wondered if you would like to come and play a game or two of pool with me."

"Well Kathy, this is a surprise!" Stephanie answered. "I would love to play pool, but I don't really know how."

"It's not that hard - I'll show you," said Kathy.

When they got to the recreation area, it became evident that Kathy, although confident enough to have a go, was not an expert player. Some of the guys stood by watching the two girls attempting to have a game of pool.

Soon two of the boys approached and suggested that they play doubles and they gave the girls some pointers. Kathy, who had a serious boyfriend in her home town, and was comfortable around guys said: "Sure, you can join us".

The guys introduced themselves as Marcus and Lionel. Marcus was a senior English student and Lionel was a second year Science student. They began laughing and talking. Stephanie was surprised that once she was shown how to hold a cue and how to aim, Stephanie could sink the coloured balls AND avoid potting the white ball. By the end of the evening, Lionel was showing her how to "bounce" the ball off the side pad to hit another ball.

Marcus and Lionel invited the girls to play with them again another evening. Kathy and Stephanie both said that they would love to. They didn't set an exact time, it was understood that they would keep an eye out for each other in the recreation area.

Later in the week, Stephanie was going up the stairs from lecture theatre one, where she had Curriculum and Ethics to lecture theatre two, when she ran into Jeff coming down the other way.

Jeff gave her a cute smile, and said "Hello".

Stephanie said "Hello" back, and passed on towards her Education lecture.

When Stephanie got to the landing, she turned and looked back to see where Jeff had gone. He had also stopped and was looking back up at her.

"I'll see you at lunch", Stephanie called. She couldn't say much else down half a flight of stairs.

"Sure," Jeff called back. "I'll probably be with Melanie and

Jonathon."

Stephanie did see Jeff at lunch too. Briefly. He was sitting with Melanie and Jonathon as he had predicted. Stephanie sat down next to Melanie, but the guys were deep in discussion about some mutual acquaintances of Jonathon and Jeff's from Sydney.

It was a while before Jeff noticed that Stephanie had joined them. He looked very pleased Stephanie was present, but all he said was "Hello", once again. Stephanie wondered why he had wanted her to join them.

The Uniting Church organised a special twilight prayer tea for the evening. The name of every student in the university had been written onto a piece of paper, put into a hat and drawn out to form random groups of six. The idea was to break up cliques that had formed, and force them to all talk to someone new. The long trestles had been shifted, and divided up into smaller, more comfortable tables. Deep maroon crepe paper had been laid across the surface, and a plate of nibbles was placed nicely in the centre of each table.

There was a short worship conducted by one of the senior students, and a prayer session designed to mark the setting of the sun. Then they were encouraged to sit and talk to the other people at the table. Getting up and leaving, or swapping tables, was not allowed.

Stephanie found herself seated next to a sincere looking Theology student by the name of Andrew Grosvy. They began talking about the reasons he had chosen to do Theology, and what he hoped to achieve as a minister. They were actually the last people to leave the cafeteria that night. The staff were waiting around and signalling for Stephanie and Andrew to get out so that they could lock up!

After attending the inter-denominational praise service, the next morning, Stephanie began work on her Education essay, and studied very hard. The topic she had chosen was "back to basics", and Stephanie was arguing that it was important to teach spelling and arithmetic in the old fashioned manner. She had borrowed about six texts from the library, and by the end of the day Stephanie had four pages of notes and quotes. Now she just had to conceive of a logical sequence for her argument, and she would be set.

Monday, Stephanie had an "observation" class at the local high school. A group of students from her Practice Teaching tutorial group went out to the school in the university bus. There they sat in the back of the classroom, and took notes. They had a sheet ruled up to fill in the categories of discipline implemented, and a list of questions to ask themselves. Things the students were to observe included: How did the teacher begin the class? What visual aids and equipment did they use? Did they set exercises and activities for the students to complete, and how did they conclude the class?

It proved to be a very interesting exercise. Stephanie was used to looking at the classroom from the point of view of the student, but now she had to learn to think like a teacher. A class didn't just "happen", it had to be designed and planned. It looked like a lot of work.

Tuesday was officially "clash day". All the students tried to dress in as appallingly bad taste as possible. Her wardrobe was filled with neat, well matched things and Stephanie had a bit of trouble putting together a combination that would clash sufficiently. Stephanie finally decided to wear a brown striped skivvy under a green floral tee-shirt, above her navy blue basketball skirt. This didn't seem outrageous enough on its own, so Stephanie wore black spotted stockings with pink socks and orange slippers.

Lunch time they all congregated in the cafeteria to have their outfits judged. The people wearing the most outrageous outfits were asked to stand upon a stage set up along the back wall. There were prizes for the craziest looking girl, the craziest looking guy, and even the craziest looking lecturer! Only two male lecturers had dared to dress up. These were the Biology Master and the Physical Science Doctor. They were both awarded prizes and voted to be good sports for participating. A couple of the female staff had chosen to wear bright scarves. They were complimented for trying.

Stephanie didn't win a prize, but her costume did get a reaction from several people. The Biology Master exclaimed half way through class when she stood up. Until that point he had thought she was dressed pretty normally! Stephanie also caught Andrew Grosvy staring at her legs lunch time. She generally took it as a compliment when a guy looked at her, as long as he doesn't whistle or say anything rude.

After lunch most people changed into casual clothes and the excitement died down. Everyone went to their separate classes, student jobs or home study.

Stephanie was standing in line at the cafeteria waiting to be served lunch time the next day, when Andrew Grosvy came in wearing a shirt and tie. Stephanie was a bit surprised to see him looking so formal, but the Theology students tended to dress up in preparation for their jobs as ministers.

Arthur, who was a couple of steps ahead of her, began to laugh and point: "Clash day was yesterday!" he said.

Andrew looked puzzled.

Stephanie saw what Arthur meant. Andrew had done what a lot of guys do, and tried to make a green tie go with a blue shirt. Her Dad used to do that all the time - sometimes Stephanie suggested he go and change, but other times she let him go about like it. It was no big deal, and she thought it was a bit mean-spirited of Arthur to point it out. But Arthur was a very precise person, and Stephanie knew from personal experience that he could be mean when things weren't exactly the way he believed they should be.

Andrew tried to ignore Arthur, but Arthur had Michael with him, and they both sniggered noticeably. Andrew went red, collected his food and took it to a table as far away from Arthur as possible.

Stephanie discretely spent longer than she needed to pour herself a drink from the dispenser, and then Stephanie followed Andrew to the table he had chosen.

"May I sit here?" Stephanie asked.

Andrew looked up and his face cleared immediately he saw her. "Of course!" he said.

They had a nice little talk. He told her that he was struggling to learn Greek. Stephanie was amazed to learn that a subject so difficult was absolutely compulsory for all Theology students.

The following day was her seventeenth birthday. Stephanie received birthday wishes, cards and little presents from all of her female friends. Stephanie was glad that they weren't into "chaffing" which was a type of birthday teasing a little too extreme to be funny in her opinion.

Work and classes go on, even on a birthday. Stephanie had a Life Science laboratory all afternoon, and they were due to vivisect a frog each. Once Stephanie had steeled herself to make the first cut, the task became quite interesting. Stephanie eventually had the dead frog's skin pinned down to the wax tray and its various systems exposed. By this time it had begun to resemble a plastic model, and was far less reminiscent of the living animal. Luckily there was very little blood. Part of the task involved drawing detailed charts of the digestive system and the reproductive system, and a stylised chart of the circulatory system. They had to work with care throughout the afternoon and consequently ran very late.

The Biology Master phoned the cafeteria to tell the staff that there would be an entire class arriving well after the normal tea time, and asked "Would they please keep some food for them?" Brenda and Cara told the others that it was her birthday, so the guys teased her gently. Dylan and Garry said Stephanie was "Sweet seventeen and never been kissed". It was the standard sort of thing said on someone's birthday, but Stephanie kept quiet, not wanting the boys to guess it was actually true in her case.

CHAPTER THREE: A PUZZLE

Stephanie finished cleaning the women's assembly hall and went to tea early. Jonathon and Jeff were sitting alone at a table near the centre of the cafeteria. She was planning to sit with Debbie, but Jonathon gestured to the empty seat next to Jeff and said: "Why don't you sit with us Stephanie?"

Stephanie sat down feeling a bit nervous. "How are you guys today?" She asked politely.

"I'm pretty good," Jonathon said in his genial way, "Aren't you Jeff?"

"Yes," Jeff said stolidly, "Everything is going great."

"How are your studies Jeff?" Stephanie asked.

"Good," Jeff said, and then added: "I don't enjoy the heavy subjects Stephanie. I just do what I must to get my grades."

"You get the distinctions though - I quite envy you Jeff," Jonathon commented before turning back to her. "Do you enjoy your study Stephanie?"

"Oh! Stephanie's altogether the academic," Jeff answered in her place.

Stephanie stared at Jeff for a moment wondering why he was presuming to speak for her. It seemed to be a natural feature of his interaction with Jonathon, but then the boys had known each other for years.

Stephanie then turned to answer Jonathon herself, "I have found it necessary to study pretty hard since I got here", she said diplomatically. "Some of the subjects are tough, while others are quite interesting. I also like to take a few study breaks."

"Have you found your way to the table tennis area and pool tables yet?" Jonathon asked.

"Of course she has - Melanie has been showing her around," Jeff answered for her once again.

"I do have my own tongue," Stephanie said firmly but gently to the side of Jeff's head. "I can answer Jonathon myself."

Jeff laughed. "But you have already told me," he said amiably.

"It is nice that you remember," Stephanie said, and gave up any idea of correcting Jeff. His new manner was rather cute, and the possessiveness involved was very flattering. It seemed to indicate a significant degree of interest on his part.

Her Life Science field trip write-up was due in a couple of days' time, and Stephanie was still having difficulty. The material was exceedingly unfamiliar to her, and Stephanie was finding it quite daunting.

Brenda told Stephanie that she remembered there were a couple of chapters on ecology and marine systems in their year twelve text book, *The Web of Life*. Stephanie thought it would help if she could find this book, so Stephanie went to the library to look for it, but could not locate a copy. There were several chapters on ecology in their new text, *Biological Science*, and she tried reading them.

In the end, however, Stephanie had to resolve to answer the

questions to the best of her current understanding. It would be very disappointing to start the semester with a low mark, but Stephanie didn't see anything else she could do. Stephanie was sure that the Lecturer would explain the whole assignment after it was marked, and figured mistakes were all part of the learning process.

In the evening Stephanie decided to go and watch television. She knew that a lot of the students watched a show called *Happy Days* and another called *Magnum PI* in the evenings.

Stephanie went across to the recreation area, and peeked into one of the two television rooms. It was very dark and she could not identify anyone, so Stephanie moved on to the other TV room. When she looked in through the door, Stephanie could just see Melanie. Stephanie slipped quietly into the room, and looked for a place to sit. Somebody moved over to make space for her, and Stephanie gratefully sat down.

During the next advertisement, which was brighter and hence gave off more light than the detective show itself, Stephanie peeked to see who was next to her. It was Jeff.

Seeing her move, Jeff stretched out his leg and placed his foot against hers. Stephanie froze. Jeff had long legs and could have just needed the space; on the other hand, he could have been 'playing footsies' with her.

Stephanie sat still as long as she could, and then she felt cramped. Stephanie had to move, and Jeff's foot seemed to follow hers to its new position. That clinched it - he was playing footsies!

Stephanie patted his foot with hers, and Jeff stretched his left leg over her right ankle.

It was warm and very cosy in the television room. Stephanie settled down a bit more comfortably in the seat, and Jeff and Stephanie remained like that until the show finished. Stephanie had hoped that they would talk afterwards, but Jonathon asked Jeff to go back to boys' dormitory with him. Stephanie felt strangely disappointed, like what had happened should have been clarified with words, but she reasoned that would come later.

The Inter-denominational praise service was very good, and Stephanie sat with Phoebe and Brenda. After praise time Phoebe suggested that having attended a service already, they did not need to go to the Reformed Church. Brenda proposed that they go for a walk instead.

The group went through the bush, out across the track known as "girls' way" because it was on their side of campus, and found a road that ran between several farms. They followed this road for a little way before realising that they would miss lunch if they did not turn back.

They arrived at the cafe about a quarter to two. Most of the other students had finished eating. Luckily, the weekend lunch was legendary for running late, and there was still a little hot food left.

A wave of excitement swept through the group. David had asked Debbie to the Champagne Breakfast, and she had accepted!

David was looking proud enough to burst, and Debbie was looking unusually bashful.

"Debbie was pretty hard to persuade," David said. "But I wasn't going to let her get away another time. I actually went down to the Silver Springs Newsagent to buy some flowers. Then I went across to women's hall, and got Debbie called over the public address system."

"Don't read too much into it girls," Debbie said blushing. "David and I are still just friends...good friends."

That started the rest of the girls talking. None of the other guys were as prone to nice gestures as David, so they didn't expect their invitations to be as dramatic, but they did wonder who would ask them.

Stephanie suspected that this time it would work out for her with Jeff. Their acquaintance had been developing, and he had been making discreet moves towards her. Surely even a quiet guy would declare himself in time.

The class had a fascinating discussion in English Literature that morning. The Professor provided them with some background information about classic texts, and read select portions aloud in a dramatic voice. Some people found this a bit 'over the top', but Stephanie really enjoyed it.

At the end of the class Milton approached her, and asked if Stephanie would work on some poetry with him.

"Why sure," Stephanie answered, "I've got about an hour now if you like."

"That would be great," he exclaimed. "Let's find a cubicle in the library".

They settled down and read a couple of Wordsworth's "Lucy" poems, which were predominantly sad and sweet. They made some notes in the margins of their texts, and discussed the questions set for the next tutorial.

The hour was nearly finished when Stephanie said: "Milton - I am going to have to leave soon. Was there anything else you wanted to talk to me about?"

"Why, yes there was Stephanie!" Milton said, going red and fiddling with his pen. "You know your room-mate Joelle, do you think she would go to the Champagne Breakfast with me if I asked her?"

"I don't know for sure," Stephanie answered, "But I think that she would. You will have to ask her yourself and find out."

"I would like to ask her," Milton said, "But I find that sort of thing very difficult."

"You have always talked to Phoebe and me," Stephanie said some-what surprised. "We think of you as a good friend."

"Yes, but you're class-mates of mine, and I have something to talk to you about. Joelle is different...she plays the piano and everything...and she never gives the impression that she is looking for a boyfriend," Milton finished lamely.

"She's not looking for a boy-friend, but she might change her mind if she got to know you," Stephanie said. "Do you want me to ask her for you?"

"No..." Milton said thoughtfully, "I'd better do it myself".

"Well, I'll wish you luck then," Stephanie said, "I'm sure it will work out."

Stephanie had been sent some money for her birthday the previous week. The Dean knew about this, and also that Stephanie hadn't had an opportunity to go shopping since she had come to the university.

"I'll take you to the next town past Silver Springs", she said, "I have some errands to run there. You won't even have to sign a leave form because you are with me!"

So Stephanie packed up and went AWOL. It felt good to be out and about. Marketown was a country town with a traditional main street lined with shops. The streets were lined with magnificent Morton bay fig trees and a farmer's market was held there on selected weekends. Stephanie looked in the designer store first, finding a dress she liked because it was black and had unusual sleeves.

Stephanie showed the Dean, but the woman said: "It's a bit dark for you."

"How old is she?" asked the Sales Assistant.

"Just turned seventeen", said the Dean.

The Sales Assistant disappeared and then reappeared carrying a two piece cotton outfit in pale green. It was very nice except for the colour, as Stephanie never wore anything she considered 'washed out'.

They thanked the Sales Assistant and left the store. Across the road Stephanie found a store called "Trends" which seemed to specialise in youthful clothing.

"I'll leave you here for a while," said the Dean, "Then you can try things on to your heart's content".

By the time the Dean returned, Stephanie had the selection narrowed down to two items. One was a serviceable blue pinafore with a pleated skirt and bib style bodice that would go well with a sweater; and the other was a ballerina style evening frock in a burgundy and gold striped fabric. An extra flounce dropped down from the waist of the burgundy dress to just below the hips, and the skirt finished two inches below the knee. It was very up-to-date and very eighties.

Stephanie didn't know which to choose! One would be useful every day, and the other was absolutely perfect for the Champagne Breakfast, which would be a formal occasion.

The Dean said she didn't know what to advise her. "The evening dress is lovely, but it definitely is a 'one-off'. Once people have seen you in it, they will remember it," she said.

Stephanie was inclined to agree with the Dean, but at the last minute she decided to get the party dress. She had never had anything like it before, and the Champagne Breakfast might also prove to be a 'one-off' event.

As they were driving home, the Dean asked Stephanie how she was settling in, and which girls were becoming her friends.

"I'm glad to hear you are finding your feet", she said. "Is there any boy in particular that you are hoping will ask you to the

Champagne Breakfast?"

"Well", Stephanie answered, "I've gotten to know quite a few boys, but there is one who stands out from the crowd".

"I hope you are being careful," the Dean said, "Sometimes I worry about you girls dating."

"I would never do anything wrong!" Stephanie protested indignantly, assuming the Dean was talking about her moral behaviour.

"That's not what I meant dear," The Dean said carefully. "It's just that you have to watch the boys sometimes. Some of them are more reliable than others."

"I'm sure Jeff is a good Christian person," Stephanie said, "He always attends the Reformed Church service".

The Dean dropped the subject and they continued on the way back to campus.

Lunch time Jeff reminded her that he played basketball on Thursdays. Stephanie had watched several matches recently, but not one in which he was playing. Stephanie promised him that she would try to finish her Life Science lab early, and come along to cheer for him.

Stephanie didn't dare submit shoddy work to the Biology Master, so there was nothing for it but to concentrate very hard and move purposefully around the work-stations in the lab session. By using the text book as a reference Stephanie was able to answer the questions quicker than usual, and found herself finished by 4:30.

Stephanie hurried to the gymnasium. Jeff's game had already started, so she sat down on one of the benches. His team was going well, and were already four points ahead. It wasn't the fiercest game Stephanie had ever seen, but a couple of the guys were almost good enough to make it into the A grade. Those particular guys shot most of the baskets, with the others supporting well.

Jeff appeared to be a relatively competent player. The others relied upon him to be active in defence, and pass the ball to the main point scorers.

The whistle blew for half time, and the players stopped for a drink. Play recommenced after a few minutes with Jeff's team continuing to control the ball. At full time they were eight points ahead. The Referee blew the whistle and declared them to be the victors.

Stephanie walked up to Jeff and congratulated him on winning.

Jeff looked pleased. "It was a good game", he said. "I reckon we'll make it to the finals."

"Yes, you are doing well," Stephanie said. "It was an interesting game, and you worked pretty hard."

"I'm glad you got here in time," Jeff said, "Did you finish your lab okay?"

"It was a bit of a rush," Stephanie said, "I haven't had tea yet".

"Nor have I," Jeff said, "I'd better get changed if I'm going to get anything. I'll catch you up there."

"Sure," Stephanie said. "I'll wait for you in the cafeteria."

Jeff met her at tea, and they ate a quick meal together. The conversation centred on basketball, and it was soon time to return to their separate dormitories and prepare for their dormitory meetings.

Despite Stephanie making an effort to watch his basketball match, Jeff still had not asked her to the Champagne Breakfast. Stephanie was getting a bit worried, so she decided to consult Melanie.

"I am a bit surprised he hasn't already arranged it with you", Melanie said when I told her. "Perhaps he is finding it hard to ask. Jeff hasn't ever socialised much."

"That could be it," Stephanie said thoughtfully. "What do you think I should do?"

"Well...you could drop a hint," Melanie suggested.

"Oh, no!" Stephanie said: "Don't you remember what happened when I asked him to the Reverse Tea? I would far rather wait until he asked me himself."

"Sit tight then," Melanie advised, "You two have been spending a lot of time together lately. You can reasonably expect him to ask you."

"Are you positive?" Stephanie asked anxiously.

"As sure as I can be - Jeff obviously likes you," Melanie concluded. "Don't panic! I think you'll find that a lot of the girls are still waiting to be asked by the guys they like."

The Uniting Church vespers program was conducted by the university choir. The music was classical, and Joelle was busy playing the piano. Stephanie was sitting with Phoebe and Melanie, Jeff and Jonathon.

Stephanie was puzzled to see Milton sitting with Grace a couple of rows ahead of them. Debbie and David were not with them, and Grace was laughing up at Milton the way she always did when she wanted something from a guy.

Stephanie managed to get a quiet moment to speak to Milton after worship. "What is going on with you and Grace?" Stephanie demanded.

Milton looked sheepish, "I am taking her to the Champagne Breakfast!" he said.

"How did that happen?" Stephanie queried.

"She practically asked me herself," Milton answered, "I was just sitting there and she came up, and asked me who I was taking. She made it sound casual, but I knew she was looking for a date."

"Weren't you going to ask Joelle?" Stephanie said, "I thought you told me that is what you wanted."

"I hadn't gotten around to it," Milton said. "I kept wondering whether she would turn me down."

On her way into the meeting hall for the Reformed Church service, Stephanie passed Joelle. Her room-mate was deep in conversation with Jeff. This surprised Stephanie a little, because normally Joelle didn't have a lot of time for Jeff.

Stephanie stopped and waited for them to notice her, and when they did, she thought Joelle gave her an odd look. Then the other girl excused herself and went ahead into the campus meeting hall.

"Hello Stephanie," Jeff said.

"Hi Jeff," Stephanie replied, "How are you this morning?"

"Pretty good Stephanie", he drawled, "How are you?"

"I'm well, thank you Jeff," Stephanie answered, "And I am glad it is weekend. We don't have to study or work today."

"Yes, I like to get some extra sleep in the afternoon," Jeff agreed. "Shall we go and find ourselves seats?"

Jeff and Stephanie sat together towards the back of the meeting hall, and Stephanie forgot what she had seen until after lunch, which was when Joelle delivered the clanger.

Joelle was waiting for Stephanie in their room when she returned to get changed for a walk with Debbie and David, Phoebe and Garry. They were going to go along the river bank on the path known as "men's walk". Garry had just asked Phoebe to go to the Champagne Breakfast with him, but it was on a casual basis, so Stephanie wasn't going to be stuck with two couples.

"Hello, Stephanie," Joelle said when Stephanie entered. "I have to talk to you about something."

"What is it Joelle?" Stephanie asked. She wondered if it might be about Milton, because Joelle and Stephanie rarely had domestic problems.

"Jeffrey asked me to go to the Champagne Breakfast with him," she said.

"He did what?" Stephanie exclaimed. "You must have misheard him."

"I am sure, Stephanie. I think it is a way of getting close to you without actually asking you," she deduced.

"How odd!" Stephanie exclaimed. "Are you sure you did not flirt with him?"

"No, really," Joelle said. "To be honest, I am surprised you are still interested in Jeff. He doesn't seem to be a very straight-forward person to me."

"I don't know what to think", Stephanie cried, all her hopes fading.

"I haven't been asked by anyone else," Joelle said, "So I am thinking about going with Jeff. It might even help you."

"However would it help me?" Stephanie asked.

"I could find out more about him. What he is like, why he did it," she suggested.

"I could find out those things myself, and I would much prefer to get my information directly", Stephanie said indignantly. "Admit it, you are looking for a date for yourself."

"I might be at that, but I still don't think my refusing Jeff would make him ask you. Not if he is determined to operate this way," Joelle concluded.

"Personally I think it is a waste of a date for you to go with Jeff," Stephanie said. "And whoever would I go with?"

"Kathy will probably be going on her own because Owen is not a university guy," Joelle said. "You could ask her to keep you company."

"Nice of you to think of me. Did Jeff suggest it?" Stephanie asked.

"He thought it was a good idea," Joelle agreed.

"Who knows, I might do it," Stephanie said. "I am going for a walk now. I am pretty upset...If you do decide to go out with Jeff I don't want to hear any of the details. There is no need to rub it in."

"I am surprised that Joelle is allowing herself to be put in the middle like this," Kathy said when Stephanie told her. "At some level she must be flattered that your associate has asked her out."

"I know that Joelle does not want a boy-friend at this stage," Stephanie said, "But she does want someone to escort her to each of the functions."

"It is a funny thing for a friend to do," Kathy mused. "If Joelle wasn't in the way, you and the boy might talk this thing through. If he asked a third girl, you would know for sure there was something wrong, and forget him immediately. Are you sure she plans to go with him?"

"Joelle seems pretty determined," Stephanie said. "She has promised not to flirt with him, but that is not the whole point."

"Which guy is it anyway?" Kathy queried.

"Jeffrey Mannington," Stephanie replied.

"Ah! Jeffrey Mannington...personally, I wouldn't have started a thing with him," Kathy said.

"Why not?' Stephanie asked in surprise.

"He is not assertive enough. I much prefer the out-going type," Kathy declared. "Still you must see something in Jeff that the rest of us don't."

"He listens to me," Stephanie explained. "Most of the guys here just talk about themselves."

"I guess you have a point," Kathy admitted. "The other guys do have a lot to say about their own ideas. It doesn't always occur to them that we girls have brains."

"Well, can you keep me company at the Champagne Breakfast?" Stephanie asked.

"I'm sorry, Stephanie, but I have arranged to go with Lionel. We both have off-campus partners. This way, we can have someone to go with, and still be faithful to our partners."

"Oh! I don't know what else to do," Stephanie murmured.

"Normally I would think it great that you are considering going to a function with another girl. There are lots of girls who wouldn't do that!" Kathy said. "But in this case, Jeff has been very cunning in asking your room-mate to go with him. He gets to be close, but not with you, and you can hardly take offence at Joelle. I am worried that you might be doing exactly what he wants in going with another girl."

"What is wrong with doing what Jeff wants?" Stephanie said. "I am hoping he will ask me next time, if I do the right thing this time."

"And he will know it!" Kathy pointed out. "We must not let the guys walk all over us. Moreover, you deserve to enjoy the function just as much as the rest of us."

"What do you suggest then?" Stephanie asked.

"Is there any other boy you have been talking to lately?" Kathy queried.

"Why, yes!" Stephanie answered.

"Do you think he will have asked anyone yet?" Kathy continued.

"I don't know. Probably not. He is the shy type," Stephanie mused.

"Well, go down to the cafeteria and sit with him for lunch or tea. Talk nicely, just the way you have been. Nothing extra, nothing fancy...or you will seem desperate," Kathy advised.

Stephanie got up to go, and then she turned back: "I don't want to give Andrew the wrong idea. I do like Jeff and I'm not looking for another boyfriend."

"You won't give Andrew the wrong idea - not if you are modest. A sensible guy looks at what we are like on more than one occasion," Kathy laughed.

So there Stephanie was, tea time in the cafe, looking discretely around for a particular guy. Stephanie felt mildly apprehensive as she planned to do something quite new to her social experience.

Luckily Andrew smiled when he saw her: "Come and sit down, Stephanie," he said.

"How are you Andrew?" Stephanie said.

"I am well thank you," Andrew said, "and yourself Stephanie?"

"Good thanks," Stephanie blushed. "How is your Greek subject progressing?"

"It's getting better as I work on it," Andrew said. "It will always be hard, but then, I didn't expect being a minister to be easy. There will be other challenges like 'practice-preaching'."

"Practice-preaching! What is that? Is it like practice-teaching?" Stephanie asked.

"We go out to one of the churches for a few weeks during the break, and assist the minister there. We even take meetings!" Andrew explained. "There is a lot of people-work involved."

"That sounds interesting," Stephanie said, "You will soon find out how you go with public speaking."

"That will be tough for someone like me, but I believe it can be learnt," Andrew said. He looked enthusiastic. "I say, Stephanie, it's awfully late notice, but are you already going to the Champagne Breakfast with anyone?"

"As it happens, I am still free..." Stephanie answered.

"Would you like to go with me?" he asked tentatively.

"I would love to Andrew. It sounds like quite a novel occasion," Stephanie replied.

"It is something different!" he said. "I'll pick you up at girls' hall at 6:20 am tomorrow then".

"I'll see you then," Stephanie said. "Thanks for asking me".

Stephanie spent the night in Kathy's room so that they could get dressed together and do each other's hair. Normally Stephanie would have done that with Joelle, but under the circumstances Stephanie felt a bit odd around her.

The alarm went off at five am, and they rushed for the showers along-side a number of other girls who were not usually around at this hour.

Kathy persuaded Stephanie to wear her new dress even though she was not going with Jeff. "Andrew deserves to have you make an effort for him," she said. "He has asked you very nicely. Besides, you will feel much better about yourself in a nice outfit!"

About twenty-past six they heard their names called over the public address system. "Kathy Shipton and Stephanie Lowood to the foyer," the Dean on duty announced. The girls hurried up the stairs from Kathy's basement room, and greeted Lionel and Andrew, who were waiting for them together.

The Champagne Breakfast was a cooked meal, complete with a number of courses. There was no real champagne of course, but bottles of non-alcoholic sparkling grape juice were placed on each table. The food was served fairly quickly, so that those students who had seven-thirty classes could still make it on time.

Stephanie had thought she couldn't enjoy going with anyone other than Jeff, but she found myself happily talking to Andrew. He was very practical, and he was willing to make an effort to learn new things. He must have liked talking to her too, because at the end of the breakfast he asked: "What are you doing next Saturday night?"

"I don't know," Stephanie said, "That is in the holidays...none of us will be here!"

"Of course we won't!" Andrew looked slightly disappointed. "I'll be seeing you around then."

After that, the whole day seemed backwards. Stephanie was almost surprised that the cafe did not serve them cereal for their tea!

Stephanie was frolicking around in the gymnasium when Jeff came in to the playing area. Stephanie was fond of badminton, and had persuaded Cara to join her for a game. The only problem was that they had to wait for a time when there was no basketball being played to put the nets up.

Jeff saw her, walked over and said: "Hey Stephanie, are you looking for me?"

"No, Jeff," Stephanie said semi-humorously, "I'm looking for that shuttle Cara is about to serve to me. If you don't get off the court, you will be hit."

Jeff wandered off, and began practicing baskets on the half-court at the other end of the gym. A few guys came up and joined him.

"He doesn't believe you!" Cara commented, "I think he is convinced that you are here for him."

"Let Jeff flatter himself!" Stephanie said, successfully returning her serve. "I like badminton. My brother and I used to play all the time. We didn't have our own net, but we put a rope up between two convenient trees."

Cara and Stephanie continued to play for some time, counting the number of returns they could make without dropping the feathered shuttle. Then Cara, who wasn't as keen as Stephanie was, decided to pack up and go to tea.

"Jeffrey is still waiting," Cara said teasingly, "He has had so much basketball practice they had better transfer him to the A grade."

"I guess I ought to talk to him," Stephanie said, and sat down on the bench.

Jeff shot a couple of more baskets, checking all the while that Stephanie was watching, and then he came and sat down beside her. "How are you Stephanie?" he said.

"I am well Jeff," Stephanie answered.

"Did you have a good time at the Champagne Breakfast yesterday?" Jeff asked.

"Oh, yes! I went with Andrew Grosvy," Stephanie replied.

"I thought you would go with Kathy, or one of the girls," Jeff said.

"Is that somehow significant to you?" Stephanie asked.

"Umm, I just didn't expect you to do that. I thought maybe...you might join..." He let his sentence trail off.

"You thought I would come along with you and Joelle?" Stephanie asked incredulously, "But that was not how the invitation to Joelle was worded".

Jeff seemed to be trying to offer her an explanation. Stephanie thought that he must have cared to do that!

"I don't know...possibly," he said.

"Did Joelle get things wrong?" Stephanie asked furrowing her brow in perplexity.

"Oh no!" Jeff said. "I did ask her to go with me."

"Then I am confused," Stephanie said. "Perhaps you would like to interpret things for me."

"I just asked Joelle to be friendly," Jeff said. "I like having you around Stephanie."

Stephanie smiled. It sounded as though Jeff's heart had been in the right place, even if his actions had been misguided. "The Champagne Breakfast is not the only function we will have the opportunity to attend," Stephanie said generously, "Let's see what happens another time."

"Yes - we'll see", Jeff said becoming suddenly cheerful. "It is almost time for worship now, are you coming?"

Stephanie forgave Jeff easily and went with him to the women's assembly area. That is what her heart told her to do at the time. Stephanie had a generous nature which inclined her to almost always see the best in people. There was only a small voice in the back of her mind which continued to ask why, if Jeff wanted to be with her, he had chosen such a round-about method of achieving his goal.

Thursday was the last day of classes before the break. The students were all called to a special campus assembly which commenced with singing "Advance Australia Fair" which was to officially become the National Anthem. Despite being selected some years ago, it had remained the National Song for some years, with "God save the Queen" functioning as the actual Anthem.

At lunch Stephanie said goodbye to all the first year crowd (who were also off for their very first vacation from university) and talked for a while to Melanie, Jonathon and Jeff.

Melanie pulled her aside for a moment: "You and Jeff sure have made up quickly after the Champagne Breakfast," she said. "I don't know quite what happened there, but it definitely is good to see my friends all getting along together!"

"Thank you Melanie," Stephanie said, "It does seem to be sorted out now".

After lunch Stephanie grabbed her bags and caught the university car into Northcoast. The car was a few minutes late, so Stephanie missed the first train, but caught the second and arrived in Brisbane finally.

Stephanie made a superhuman effort to carry her cases down the steps herself, and onto an airport bus. Then at the airport Stephanie learnt how to "check in". It was her very first flight on an aeroplane rather than the bus or train, and she enjoyed it immensely. She arrived in Adelaide late that evening.

CHAPTER FOUR: PAIRING UP

Stephanie had arranged to meet Mandy at Adelaide Airport, so that they could fly back to Queensland together. They both believed it would be much more fun to have company than travel back to the university alone. The plane was due to leave at 3:25 pm. Mandy was a bit late and Stephanie began to worry, but the girl arrived just in time to register her baggage.

Mandy had three bags and Stephanie only had one, so Mandy checked one of her bags under Stephanie's luggage allowance. Their bags were extremely heavy because they were full of jumpers and jackets to keep the girls warm through the cooler winter months.

Once Mandy and Stephanie were on board the plane, they settled down to gossip. They had both gone to their home churches during the holidays, and caught up with old friends. Mandy had a large family who had all gone camping over Easter. It sounded invigorating.

Stephanie had gone shopping and bought some black boots, and her Aunt Moira had given her a plain grey woollen suit to wear to the various church services around Silver Springs University. In her free time, Stephanie had listened to the top forty on the radio, with some of the most popular hits being by Phil Collins, Billy Joel, and Bruce Springsteen. Stephanie's favourite pop-group was Bananarama, although she didn't mind a bit of country music with Kenny Rogers occasionally.

Stephanie had also sewn a bias cut plaid woollen skirt to team with her jumpers on cold mornings and compiled comprehensive notes from a week's classroom observation completed at a local high school.

Arriving in Brisbane at five-thirty-five, the girls collected their baggage and caught a taxi to the train station; from there they booked their luggage onto the train and caught the service to the country.

Stephanie found that she was looking forward to arriving back at Silver Springs University. She had been home and found that her family and friends were still there, and this alleviated her homesickness. South Australia also seemed nearer than it did before, being a mere three hour plane trip away.

The Deans met Mandy and Stephanie at Northcoast station, and drove them back to campus. Joelle had already arrived, so Stephanie said "Hello" to her. They unpacked their bags and talked to other girls late into the night.

Stephanie spent the first day after the holidays getting back into her university routine. There were classes to attend and a few more clothes to unpack. She drew up a study plan to help her complete her remaining assignments on schedule.

Stephanie's friends were all in the cafeteria and she stopped to talk to them over tea. They all planned to study very hard this half of the semester, because assignments were due and exams coming up soon. Few of them had made as determined a start upon their essays as Stephanie had, and some of them were worried about falling behind.

Melanie and Jonathon were in the cafeteria and Stephanie said "Hi" to them. However, Stephanie noticed that Jeff was not with them. Jonathon said that Jeff had been sick during the holidays, so after tea Stephanie went across to men's hall and had him called down to the foyer.

Jeff seemed pleased to see her. He explained that he had not gone home during the Easter break. Instead he had stayed at the university and worked as a caretaker. Then he had come down with a bad cold. He was beginning to feel better, but believed he might still be a bit off-colour.

Stephanie asked him why he hadn't gone home even once, and he said that he needed to earn the money to pay his fees because he did not receive a student allowance like she did, due to his course not qualifying for priority funding. Stephanie was impressed by the boy's seriousness and determination to earn his way through university. She also suspected there might be more to the story, possibly some family problem that he was not yet ready to confide. Stephanie went back to girls' dorm deep in thought.

Stephanie was studying in her room when Melanie knocked on her door. A little surprised, Stephanie invited the older girl to enter. Melanie sat down and began to talk to her about university life in general. It was a pleasant enough conversation, but Stephanie kept wondering why her friend had really come to visit. Melanie was a busy girl, always popular, frequently in demand, and not prone to idle gossip.

"That was a nice thing you did yesterday, going to visit Jeff like that," Melanie said finally. "I believe he was quite touched."

"I like talking to Jeff," Stephanie said. "Sometimes it's a bit difficult to get a conversation started, but he seems pretty deep."

"He probably is," Melanie said. "I have known Jeff for three years and I'm sure there is a lot I don't know about him."

"Jeff is somewhat different than most of the students," Stephanie said thoughtfully. "He has made the campus his permanent home. There is nothing of the fish-out-of-water about him around here. He is really settled. It's quite attractive in its way."

"Yes," Melanie agreed somewhat vaguely. "What I was meant to tell you, was that I have it from a reliable source that Jeff would really like to go out with you, if you are able to manage the emotional side of the friendship for the both of you."

"Would this reliable source be Jeff himself?" Stephanie asked sharply.

"Maybe...I am not allowed to say," Melanie hedged.

"I don't listen to hear-say Melanie," Stephanie said quite firmly. "Are you carrying a message from Jeff himself?"

"Possibly. I assure you it is true whoever sent the message," Melanie said.

"Well, tell Jeff that I will think about it," Stephanie said. "But I won't even consider trying to take on all the emotional work in the friendship. Jeff is not stupid academically, and there is no way I will help him play dumb emotionally."

"Most guys are better at their careers than their friendships," Melanie said defensively.

"But they can learn, given time can't they?" Stephanie said, "Jonathon learnt as your friendship progressed, didn't he?"

"Yes...but he started off more out-going and sociable than Jeff," Melanie reasoned. "You might need to be particularly understanding towards a quiet guy."

"Once again, I will think about it," Stephanie said. "That is all Jeff can really expect after sending the message through any number of third parties."

Stephanie saw Jeff briefly during convocation that morning, and said: "Hi". She had not actually had time to think about the message Melanie delivered, because she had been occupied with her study. She didn't know what more she could do about it anyway. According to her understanding, a romantic friendship had to grow through consistent interaction over a period of time. It couldn't be hurried or pushed, and it shouldn't involve an uneven amount of effort between the parties. Still, it was exciting to know that there was something going on - maybe even the seed of something bigger and better to come.

Stephanie had an Education tutorial to take on the morrow, even though it was their first week back after Easter. Stephanie had completed the essay before Easter, but she needed to brush up on the material and prepare a speech. A printed handout was not essential, but might be worth more marks as part of the presentation, so Stephanie had decided to prepare one.

Phoebe and Milton were doing the same topic, so they planned to meet later that afternoon to discuss how they were going to divide the presentation into three even sections.

The tutorial went well, and the team got eight out of ten. They had decided to commence with Stephanie presenting an introduction to the topic, and handing out a fact sheet. Then Milton divided the members of the tutorial group into two teams, and conducted an impromptu debate on the teaching of basic maths and spelling. Phoebe judged the debate, and wrote a list of conclusions on the white board. Stephanie believe that it was one of the most active and innovative tutorials that had been conducted that year.

Phoebe, Milton and Stephanie were all very pleased that the tutorial had been successfully executed, and decided to celebrate at tea. They toasted each other with orange juice, and made a fuss over their savouries. The Lecturer had discovered one spelling error in the handout Stephanie had prepared, and Milton teased her unmercifully.

Stephanie had invited Joelle to join them, and she noticed that Milton was beginning to lose his inhibitions and talk to her room-mate. This was a good sign, presuming he still liked Joelle.

In the evening the university administration screened the film *The Bounty,* which had been released on May 4 in the cinema. The film was being projected on campus in the gymnasium. Milton asked Joelle and Stephanie to go with him as a threesome. Stephanie had hoped to locate Jeff, but as the other two seemed more comfortable in a group than on their own, she agreed to accompany them.

Stephanie made sure that Joelle sat between Milton and her, and encouraged them to talk about their History class, which Stephanie knew they both enjoyed. They seemed to be doing very well together.

The Bounty was one of those great Hollywood productions with a stellar cast and costumes. It ran pretty late, and the door to girls' dorm had to be held open past the usual electronic lock-down time to allow the residents to retire for the night. Everyone raved about the dramatic scenes, but Stephanie was secretly disappointed that it did not emphasise the conversion of the crew to Christianity, one of the most romantic parts of the story in her eyes.

When Stephanie arrived at the cafeteria the next day, Jeff was already seated at one of the tables. He made deliberate eye contact with her, and indicated towards the empty chair beside him, so Stephanie carried her tray across and sat down.

They talked for a while. Jeff said that he was feeling better, but that his essays would be heavy for the rest of the semester. Stephanie sympathised because her study load was looking tough too.

Jeff described his study method, and Stephanie was amazed at his ability to complete essays at the last minute, and still get a great mark. Stephanie knew that he wasn't the only student who worked this way, but it usually cost the others a percent or two!

"I could never leave it that late myself," Stephanie said. "Slow and steady with lots of research is the only way for me. If I tried to write it all the last evening I would probably get sick instead of producing an essay!"

Jeff laughed, "I'm a bit of a procrastinator," he said, "It's my biggest fault".

"It's not much of a fault if you get things done anyway", Stephanie said. "Besides, you seem to be able to prioritise things, so that you only do the most necessary stuff. To someone like me - who does everything the hard way - that seems pretty smart."

Jeff looked pleased and hinted that if Stephanie located him at the United Church vespers, she would be welcome to sit with him again. The implication was that Stephanie was one of the exceptional things for which he would find the time; making Stephanie feel very special and important.

Stephanie did as Jeff suggested and located him in the women's assembly hall that evening. It was pretty crowded in their pew, and Stephanie found herself pushed up against Jeff. Their arms were touching from shoulder to elbow, and neither of them made any effort to move away. It felt warm and exciting, especially to a girl who wasn't used to getting that close to boys.

The next morning, Joelle had a break from playing the piano for the Reform Church, and so was able to be persuaded to visit the Uniting Church situated in the local township. The off-campus Uniting Church service was attended by some of the staff, local residents and married students.

The girls attended the Inter-denominational praise service in the women's assembly hall and then located Debbie and David, who had become surprisingly exclusive of late. The couple agreed to go with them, and David went off to invite Milton and Garry. When the guys returned, the group walked down University Drive, past the trees, the gardens and the staff houses into the township of Silver Springs.

Their party arrived just in time for the beginning of the main service and climbed up the back staircase into the balcony from where they could view the entire congregation. The service at the off-campus Uniting Church proved to be more traditional than any of the services available on campus and the bulletin contained a number of local news items they usually missed at university, because the campus seemed to be on a timeline entirely of its own.

The students all agreed that the atmosphere was a lot more homely than that of the university. In some ways it was like making a tiny visit to their home churches. However, the program also ran quite late, and they had to march back at top speed to get to the cafeteria before the end of lunch.

Stephanie spent the next morning cleaning the women's assembly area. When Stephanie was finished she went across to the cafeteria for lunch. Jeff was sitting with a group of his mates, and there were no empty seats near him, so Stephanie went to pass them and sit further down the table.

It was a bit of a surprise when Roger spoke and asked whether he had taken her place. "I can shift if you like", he offered.

"Oh! Don't worry," Stephanie replied, never one to be pushy. "I can sit by Melanie and Jonathon."

Jeff however said: "Go on, shift and give Stephanie her place next to me."

Roger shifted further down the table, and Stephanie sat next to Jeff. Stephanie was secretly very pleased that Jeff had identified that chair as hers in front of all his mates.

It was one of the first times that Stephanie found herself the centre of attention in a predominantly male circle, for she usually stuck to the girls or joined evenly mixed groups. Stephanie felt self-conscious, but asked the guys whether they had enjoyed the film Friday night before. Most of them had, but a few said that they had seen an earlier version on television. Some made wisecracks and other blokey comments about the romance themes in the movie. Stephanie tried to look unconcerned, but she felt herself going red.

Later that week, Stephanie had a Practice Teaching presentation to give. It involved designing a lesson plan, and presenting a story telling segment to her tutorial group. Stephanie was told to learn to speak louder, otherwise she did very well. She was awarded 7/10.

Stephanie had been working very hard on her English Literature essay. She'd written three thousand words, which was actually over the word limit. Hence, Stephanie needed to go through it minutely, check the grammar and cut any unnecessary material out. She believed that a few extra words would prove better than too few, but even so, she had been advised to stick to within ten percent of the word limit.

Stephanie saw Jeff in convocation and said "Hi", but she couldn't go and join him because she was sitting with Phoebe and Cara, with whom she had some study to discuss. Jeff looked a bit disappointed, but Stephanie decided to let it go, and catch up with him at lunch.

Stephanie spent the afternoon writing out the good copy of her English Literature essay. It was now ready to be handed in, but Stephanie read it through and checked everything carefully.

Although Stephanie was confident about her academic ability in general, she was nervous about this essay. Drama was her chosen major and hence English Literature was her most important subject. Stephanie would have liked to get particularly good marks in the subject. It was also a subject which couldn't be approached quantitatively and objectively. Part of her did prefer to work with the practical and the tangible, like Life Science.

Unfortunately the Life Science practical took all afternoon, and made her late for tea. Stephanie regularly worked with Cara now, because Brenda had dropped out of their class just before Easter. She had been particularly discouraged by the results of their first field trip write-up, and found the lab work confusing and demanding throughout.

Jeff and Roger were still at tea when Stephanie arrived. She got the impression from Jeff's manner that they had been waiting for her to arrive. (Jeff had become thoroughly familiar with her routine by now, and knew when to expect her.)

Stephanie sat down beside Jeff, and they talked about basketball for a bit. Then the guys began to talk about the Rugby League, and asked her whether Stephanie followed the footy at all.

Stephanie said, "I barracked for Port Adelaide for several years and followed their progress up the premier table".

Roger, who was sitting on her other side, laughed and said: "Wrong type of football."

Stephanie felt a bit put-out, and looked to Jeff to defend her. He smiled to take the sting out of Roger's comment and said: "That's Aussie Rules, and we follow the Rugby League here".

After they had finished eating Jeff asked Stephanie, on the grounds that he had work to do in the dormitory, whether she would walk him back to men's hall. Stephanie thought it was a bit topsy-turvey, and that a gentleman would be offering to walk her across to girls' dorm instead, but she complied because she wanted a few more minutes of Jeff's company.

Jeff's team played a basketball match at four-thirty on Friday. Stephanie was pleased to be able to watch the match from the beginning this time. The season finals were due to be played in a couple of weeks, and Stephanie had been told that Jeff's team, if they continued to perform well, would be amongst the finalists. It was getting quite exciting.

The whistle blew and the Captain of Jeff's team managed to

knock the ball towards their side of the court. Another strong player caught the ball on the first bounce, and passed it to Jeff. Jeff passed it back to the Captain, who was well positioned to shoot a goal.

Stephanie couldn't help clapping lightly. Stephanie wasn't the only one on the benches, and she certainly hadn't been the only one to cheer, but Jeff looked directly across at her.

Stephanie quietened down because she didn't want to distract Jeff from the game, nevertheless, he glanced over at her whenever he had done something especially noticeable with the ball. The game continued with Jeff playing the ball in an increasingly reckless manner.

Despite Jeff's show-off tactics, his team established a strong lead by half-time. They played dynamically throughout the second half of the game, and doubled their lead by full time.

Jeff stood around talking to the guys after the match. They slapped him on the back and congratulated him on having kept on the ball so well.

"A bit of male chest beating," exclaimed the Captain's Girlfriend, who was sitting next to her. "Jeff is not usually such an aggressive player. He was obviously trying to impress you. You should be flattered."

"Yes I am," Stephanie said. "Or I will be when he deigns to talk to her. These macho displays do nothing for communication."

Gloria looked amused: "You are supposed to faint and swoon until he is ready for you," she said. "Come on, I'll take you over there!"

They walked across the gymnasium, and Gloria put her arm around the Captain, sweaty though he was. "All hail the conquering heroes!" she said.

Warren turned to Gloria, and Jeff turned to her. "You played very well," Stephanie said. "You are sure to make it to the finals."

"Yes, we should," Jeff said. "And whoever the other team is, we will give them a run for their money."

"I am sure you will!" Stephanie said, and repeated her praise for his tactics. She felt a bit fulsome, but Jeff seemed exceedingly satisfied, and suggested that Stephanie meet him at vespers Friday evening.

Stephanie awoke at five-thirty am, because the fire alarm was ringing throughout Girls dorm. The Dean's voice sounded over the public address system, telling them not to panic because this was a fire drill.

They were to evacuate the dorm through the nearest exit or fire escape, and form their designated groups on the lawn outside. It was essential, the Dean stressed, that they take this exercise seriously. They were being trained and timed for their own safety.

Stephanie grabbed her dressing gown, and shook Joelle.

"What is it?" Joelle said, starting up in fright.

"Fire drill," Stephanie said, "Come with me".

They hurried outside, and stood on the lawn. Girls slouched everywhere in diverse stages of undress and disarray, but luckily the boys were not up and about to see them.

The Student Dean from each floor counted her charges. One girl remained unaccounted for, and someone ran inside to get her.

"She would have died!" Phoebe exclaimed.

When the girls were all assembled, the Deans thanked them for their co-operation, and reminded them of the importance of the procedure they had just followed, should there be a real fire. The girls had all exited the dorms within ten minutes, the Deans said, but the next time the Deans wanted them to do it within seven.

It wasn't worth going back to bed after that, so Stephanie had a shower and went for a quick walk before breakfast. Consequently she was a bit tired all day.

Stephanie made a lot of notes for her Practice Teaching write-up. It was very important because there was no exam for the subject, only practical exercises, observations and assignments.

Stephanie also had to study for a Life Science test. They had been having them throughout the semester, just like school. Stephanie had begun to do better in Life Science as the semester progressed and she gained an understanding of the material.

Stephanie talked to Jeff at tea. He said that he had been working hard at his paid work, not study. Stephanie admired his dedication and stamina, but sometimes he seemed unusually tired and run down.

Stephanie mentioned her concern to Jeff, and he shrugged.

"I have to work," Jeff said. Stephanie wondered exactly what he meant, because she knew that he was ahead on paying his fees.

Periodically Jeff appeared to have no appetite, and made

elaborate patterns with his food on his plate. Stephanie hadn't seen anyone do that since she was about six, but all his mates made a joke of it. Stephanie learnt to joke about it along with the others, but she couldn't always look, because the end result was pretty disgusting. Luckily, it was only one of Jeff's little habits, and most of the others were endearing, if she looked at them the right way.

Stephanie attended the Inter-denominational praise service and Reform Church on the weekend as usual, and as was their habit nowadays, Jeff and Stephanie sat together in the Reform Church. There was going to be a baptism at the beach in the afternoon, and it sounded quite exciting. Stephanie asked Jeff whether he was going, but he said that he was going to be in charge of the reception desk at men's hall all afternoon.

Stephanie said that she would miss him, but was independent enough to be happy on her own.

Several busses arrived to take them to the beach. Stephanie joined Debbie and David, Cara and Phoebe, and Garry. Milton seemed to have disappeared, and Joelle was playing the piano in one of the lounge rooms. Stephanie wondered briefly if there was any connection!

At the beach, the Chaplain conducted a short service, and then four students were baptised in the ocean. A shelter had been erected for them to get changed so that they did not have to spend the evening wet, and when they were dressed, they joined the other students for a walk along the rocks.

It was hard to keep up with her group, and Stephanie quickly found herself on her own, dodging amongst the rocks and pools.

Someone called, "Hey Stephanie," from just behind her and Stephanie turned to see Jonathon.

"Hello, Jonathon," Stephanie replied. "Where is Melanie?"

"She's walking with some girls," Jonathon said, "Stephanie I wanted to speak to you about something".

"Go ahead Jonathon," Stephanie said curiously.

"You and Jeff are connecting pretty well nowadays aren't you?" he said.

"Most of the time..." Stephanie replied.

"I know he really likes you," Jonathon said.

"People keep telling me that," Stephanie said, "And I suspect Jeff has asked some of them to do so". Stephanie knew that she was blushing as she continued: "But the guy himself is not the most demonstrative."

"Give Jeff some time," Jonathon said. "I'm his best friend, and it took him a while to open up to me."

Stephanie shrugged, "I sometimes feel there is a gap of age and sophistication between us. Jeff is a serious guy, he is graduating and has his career practically sorted out. I am going to be studying for years, if not here, somewhere else. I wonder how long he will stay interested under those circumstances."

"Isn't it worth finding out?" Jonathon suggested. "You might be able to keep in touch later on."

"Perhaps," Stephanie said. "We have been spending some time together anyway."

Stephanie was studying in her room after lunch, when she heard Joelle and her names called over the public address system. Stephanie went down to the foyer to find out what it was all about, and found Milton waiting there.

"Hello Milton", Stephanie said.

"Hi, Stephanie," Milton said, and then went red. "Isn't Joelle with you?"

"It's really Joelle you want isn't it?" Stephanie suggested. "She is down in women's assembly practicing the piano. Go on down there, you don't need me!"

Milton looked uncertain.

"Time to be brave," Stephanie added, "Faint heart never won no fair lady."

Milton laughed nervously and went on his way. Because he wasn't allowed to go through the corridor in girls' dorm, he went out around the courtyard.

Stephanie crossed her fingers for the two of them.

Joelle appeared back in their room in about half an hour's time, looking flustered. "Milton just asked me to the Mexican Night," she said.

"About time!" Stephanie said, "He has liked you for ages - even before the Champagne Breakfast!"

"That long?" Joelle queried. "And you knew?"

"Yes, but I had promised not to tell," Stephanie answered.

"Well, I said that I would go with him," Joelle said. "I quite like Milton. I just hope that he understands I am not looking for a boyfriend at this stage."

"I think Milton is perfectly sensible of that - and I believe it is one reason why it has taken him so long to ask you out!" Stephanie assured her. "He is also a very mature guy and wants to concentrate on his own studies."

"You make it sound like Milton and I are perfectly suited!" Joelle laughed.

"I think that you could be!" Stephanie asserted. "But of course, that is up to you two to work out...."

"There is a lot to find out actually," Joelle said seriously. "Milton has an interesting character. Did you know that he is twenty-five? And that he worked in a variety of jobs before he decided to get a degree."

"No, I didn't," Stephanie said. "Does the age gap worry you at all?"

"Not really", Joelle said. "It just means that we will have a lot to talk about before we get romantic."

At the combined assembly in the evening, Stephanie stopped and talked to Andrew Grosvy for a while. He was a gentle guy, and seemed mildly intimidated by her friendship with Jeff. Stephanie wanted to make it clear to him that she had no intention of dropping old friends simply because she had found someone special.

Andrew had been to Northcoast that day for an appointment and had returned with one of the new one-dollar coins the Australian government was bringing out. He pulled it out of his pocket and showed it to Stephanie, who exclaimed how small it seemed. The one-dollar note had traditionally signalled the change between low value currency and significant money. However, due to the high inflation rate, it seemed that one-dollar was now worth so little it had become a coin.

As Stephanie talked to Andrew she became aware of Jeff looking at her intently. It appeared that he might not like her talking to another guy after all. Jeff's gaze made her increasingly uncomfortable, and Stephanie eventually abandoned any intention of sitting with Andrew.

Stephanie went across to join Jeff. He made room for her next to him, but continued to look sullen.

"How are you Jeff?" Stephanie inquired.

"Good Stephanie," Jeff answered, but that was all he would say.

Stephanie leant against Jeff, and stroked his arm. He didn't push her off, and by the end of the evening he was talking to her again. Stephanie congratulated herself upon having appeased him so quickly.

"At least Jeff didn't indulge in a long sulk", Stephanie thought. "If he had, I might have to get worried about his temperament. I don't want to go out with a cantankerous guy."

In the afternoon Stephanie went to the gymnasium to watch

Jeff's team play basketball. There was a degree of excitement in the air, because this was one of the semi-finals. The team that won this match would play the winner of the other semi-final next week, and the team that lost the semi-final would be eliminated from the competition.

Stephanie sat down beside the captain's girlfriend, Gloria. She moved along to give her some more room on the bench. "Are you here as Jeff's personal cheering squad?" Gloria asked.

Stephanie laughed, "I'm sure Jeff sees it that way, but actually I've watched some of the A grade boys', and even a few of the girls' matches."

"Have you ever thought of joining a team?" Gloria queried.

"Yes! Actually it was an ambition of mine," Stephanie said. "But when I tried out, I found that it was much tougher than high school basketball."

"You need to practice," Gloria said. "Don't let anyone put you off, even by laughing at your style. They all learnt somehow."

"I think I'm a bit too far behind," Stephanie observed wryly.

The whistle blew, and Gloria and Stephanie turned their attention to the game. The players had been divided into "huddles" to discuss team strategy, now they approached the court with serious faces and awaited the initial toss of the ball.

"There is none of the usual comradery," Stephanie remarked, observing the players' attitudes.

"This is not one of their muck-around games," Gloria explained, "The guys take this one pretty seriously. They all want to make it into the final. Even if they don't win the game after that, they will have played a good season."

"I guess both teams are pretty good to have made it this far. The competition will be tough," Stephanie said.

"Yes", Gloria said. "The team they are playing now is the most forceful of the B grade teams. It is bad luck that they drew them as opponents in the semi-final."

"Oh!" Stephanie said, "Well, let's hope our guys can prevail."

The two teams appeared to be evenly matched, both having good offensive players, and the ability to shoot baskets. The number of points on the score board grew steadily, with first one team, and then the other in the lead. At half time the score was even, and it looked as though the match could go either way.

The guys sat down on the benches panting heavily. Most of them had brought bottles of water from which they drank thirstily. Warren passed his bottle to Gloria, and called his team to attention, admonishing them to increase their defensive play and prevent the other team from shooting baskets.

The match resumed, and the players from both sides appeared to be concentrating on preventing the other team from shooting. It was almost full time, with the score still even when the Referee called a foul against the opposing team, and awarded Warren a free shot.

Everyone on the benches called out "Go Warren", as he stood on the edge of the key aiming. The ball went up into the air and settled neatly into the basket. There was a collective sigh, and the Referee blew the whistle for full-time.

"That was a great match. I haven't seen anything quite so exciting in university basketball before," Stephanie exclaimed, running up to Jeff.

"It was very close", Jeff said, "I wouldn't want to have to play that one again!"

"At least you got through to the finals!" Stephanie said.

"Yes," Jeff said. "It is hot in here, do you want to go outside and get some fresh air?"

They went outside, and Jeff stood on the cement for a few minutes cooling off.

"Let's sit down," Stephanie said, linking her arm in Jeff's and leading him to a park bench. "Who do you think you will be playing in the finals next week?"

"Depends who wins the other semi-final", Jeff said. "I reckon it will be Tony's team. That will give us a sporting chance in the final."

"Will you go and watch to see who wins?" Stephanie asked.

"I wouldn't miss it for the world!" Jeff said. "You've got that lab thing haven't you?"

"Yes, it could go pretty late. You will have to tell me all about it," Stephanie suggested.

"Sure, I can do that," Jeff replied. "Just catch up with me soon after it."

"Listen Jeff," Stephanie said. "You know that Mexican Night on Sunday - it sounds like fun, how about we go together?"

"I guess we've got to get tea somehow," Jeff said lightly. "Will you meet me across there? I don't go for the picking the girl up bit."

The Life Science lab for the afternoon proved to consist of a hike into the mountains, to observe undergrowth in a semi-tropical rainforest habitat. The Biology Master parked his Land Rover beside the mountain track, and led them along a series of foot trails.

Stephanie looked around and enjoyed the scenery, despite the disorienting effect of the forest and the detailed commentary the Biology Master expected them to understand. The rain forest habitat was new to most of the first year students, who came from Victoria, Southern New South Wales, and South Australia, where the vegetation was far less tropical.

After about an hour, Garry started stamping and looking down at his foot. "I think I have a leech!" he exclaimed. He rolled down his sock to reveal several thick blood suckers attached to his ankle.

Stephanie looked down, there were some black worm-like things on the outside of her shoes. Stephanie kicked them off, and prayed that none had gotten inside.

Cara screamed, and Dylan bent to pull a black slug off her leg.

"Lunch!" he said teasingly, and Cara squealed again, this time in disgust. She skipped off to walk with Garry, who told her he had heard leeches avoided soap, and she would be safe if she rubbed some on her socks before they came out another time.

They walked fast and kept to the middle of the path after that. The Biology Master looked at them in amusement, for he had worked so long with creepy crawlies that he had developed an amazing tolerance for them.

"I am glad that Milton asked you out," Stephanie said to Joelle as they were getting ready to go to bed. "I was beginning to think he would never be gallant enough."

"Not like Jeffrey Mannington," Joelle began. "That guy is going to railroad you, without a single word that you can pin him down on. It is positively irresponsible."

"Don't talk like that about Jeff," Stephanie said hotly. "You wanted to go to the Champagne Breakfast with him, and I am still a bit mad at you for choosing to do so, even after I told you how I felt."

"I am sorry I did that," Joelle admitted. "I was never the focus of his attention - I should have left the two of you alone to work things out."

"Yes, you should have!" Stephanie said firmly, "I believe things would be a lot clearer now if you had. As it is, I have to wonder why he did that. We ought to have been at a more significant point in our friendship by now."

"I am sorry," Joelle repeated. She hesitated for a moment: "Just be careful, you seem to be in pretty deep water with Jeff."

"I appreciate the thought, if it really is me you are thinking about this time," Stephanie said. "But I have to follow my heart."

"You have a good head too," Joelle said. "You used it with Arthur."

"I've considered that," Stephanie protested, "But there is no similarity. Jeff is much more sensitive than Arthur."

"Perhaps that is the way Jeff wants you to see him," Joelle suggested. "I think that he is a cunning guy."

Before Stephanie could respond to this, there was a knock at their door, and Kathy appeared looking very excited.

"Guess what girls!" Kathy exclaimed, "I've persuaded Owen to come down for the weekend, and take me to the Mexican Night. He is going to be staying with Lionel."

"That's great!" Stephanie said, "I am dying to see what Owen looks like."

"He is very good looking," Kathy said crossing her arms over her chest in a hugging gesture. "And you will meet him at worship in about ten minute's time!"

"I am so glad Owen could visit," Joelle remarked. "You two can't see a lot of each other."

"I know!" Kathy exclaimed. "It's terrible. We were beginning to have problems...little tiny ones."

"Well, this weekend should fix them up," Stephanie declared staunchly. "I'll make sure I talk to Owen at vespers if I don't get a chance before."

Owen turned out to be a brown-haired young man of average height, and slim build. His most attractive feature was the warm smile with which he greeted all Kathy's friends.

Joelle and Stephanie sat just behind the pair during the services, and she was able to observe the relaxed way Owen put his arm around Kathy. It was very sweet, and all in all, they made a cute couple.

After lunch on the weekend, Kathy was granted special permission to bring Owen into girls' dorm for the space of half-an-hour. The Deans figured that being the afternoon, everybody could reasonably be expected to be fully dressed and well behaved. Owen was ushered in with much giggling, and an announcement over the public address system warning the girls that there was a "Man in the dorm".

Another announcement was made when it was time for Owen to be ushered outside. Kathy and he disappeared down one of the bush walks to spend some time alone, and Phoebe accompanied Joelle and her back to their room.

"How are you Phoebe?" Stephanie said, settling down comfortably on her bed.

"I'm fine," Phoebe said, "I even have a date for tonight."

"Oh - who asked you?" Joelle queried.

"Some guy I hardly know asked me last night. He seemed nice enough, so I said yes," Phoebe said. "I thought it couldn't hurt anything."

"He has probably been admiring you from a distance for weeks. You will find out all about it tonight," Stephanie teased. "Actually, I am surprised that you are not going with Garry again."

"Garry asked Cara last Thursday night, right after your Life Science excursion," Phoebe explained.

"Oh...", Stephanie said, "Now I think about it, I did see something working up there!"

"What about you two?" Phoebe queried.

"Milton asked me," Joelle said. "And Stephanie has a sort of regular arrangement with Jeff," she added diplomatically.

"Doing good girls!" Phoebe said jokingly, "Not a wallflower amongst us. I'll tell you who doesn't have a date yet though...Grace!"

"You're kidding!" Stephanie said, sitting bold upright. "Grace really hasn't been asked?"

"No - despite that low necked dress she has been wearing the last couple of days," Phoebe said.

"I liked the dress," Stephanie said, "It had an unusual tie at the front. I think she must have got it at Katie's."

"It's not the dress," Joelle remarked, "It's the way she was wearing it. Leaning forward to give the guys a good view of her cleavage as she talked to them."

"Why didn't they ask her?" Stephanie was puzzled. "I thought guys liked that sort of thing!"

"Most of the guys here are looking for serious girlfriends," Phoebe explained. "And none of them want to be part of a stampede."

"Grace really doesn't have a date?" Stephanie mused, "I cannot believe it! She is sure to do something about that before tomorrow evening comes."

The Mexican Night was designed to be a merry occasion, with the correct attire being costume rather than formal. Stephanie wore a peasant style blouse that she had bought during the Easter holidays, and the red and black checked taffeta skirt she had made herself.

The blouse had an elasticated neckline that could be worn either on, or off the shoulder. Stephanie pulled it off the shoulder for this occasion, and positioned it carefully. Stephanie was never quite comfortable in strapless outfits, and worried about the top falling down. However, this felt quite secure, and showed a tendency to tighten and move up into a more modest position as Stephanie moved.

Jeff was waiting for her near the entrance to the cafeteria. His idea of western style outfit was a white tee-shirt with blue jeans, and a RM Williams leather belt. He looked very handsome nevertheless.

They collected their trays, and went across to the table upon which all the ingredients for making their own tacos (or haystacks as some people called them) was assembled. Stephanie followed the others example, and created a pile of corn-chips and beans, topped with cheese and salad.

Stephanie didn't recognise the homemade chilli sauce, so she put took a scoop and put it on left of her plate. She tried a spoonful of it on its own, and just managed to avoid pulling an inelegant face! The others were joking about how hot the sauce was, and pouring themselves drinks of water. Luckily they hadn't noticed her mistake.

Sitting down, Jeff and Stephanie admired the decor. Red and white checked paper was spread across the tables, and the serviettes were all red. Several large straw hats were attached to the walls to provide atmosphere. Stephanie remarked to Jeff that it was "Pretty cool".

Off-beat Latin music was provided by a group of university students who had been enterprising enough to form a band. The lead singer operated as the Master of Ceremonies for the evening, announcing different songs including fifties rock-and-roll pieces, and some of his own compositions.

Stephanie admired the original tunes very much and commented to Jeff. Jeff wasn't quite so keen, so she decided not to push her point.

There were tubs of ice-cream set aside for desert, with a choice of flavours and toppings. Stephanie served herself several times and generally made a glutton of herself.

Jeff also took too much ice-cream, and finding himself unable to eat his last bowl, he did his funny ritual with it, swirling the confection around in the plate. At the last minute, he decided that was not messy enough, and added a generous squirt of tomato sauce to the concoction.

They all talked late into the evening. Stephanie got tired and ended up leaning her cheek against Jeff's shoulder, while he chatted to his mates.

Jeff got enough into the spirit of things to walk her back to girls' dorm at the end of the function. Stephanie finished the day perfectly happy, and wished Jeff could be that gentlemanly all the time.

CHAPTER FIVE: BASKETBALL

Stephanie saw Kathy in Ethics, where the friendly girl told her that Owen had taken a couple of days off work, and would not be going home until Tuesday.

"Owen is your boyfriend, isn't he?" piped up Grace from the row in front of them. (Their Ethics class was very large, because it was a house requirement for all first year students, regardless of the course they were doing.)

"Yes," Kathy replied, "He has come all the way up from Armidale to see me."

"He is pretty cute", Grace said.

"I wouldn't have put it that way," Kathy said, "But I do think Owen is handsome."

"I am glad he could stay a while," Stephanie said, returning to her original conversation with Kathy. "It gives you two more of a chance to spend time together."

"Yes", Kathy agreed. "It's great! But he is going to have to amuse himself while I am in class this morning."

"It is a pity you have classes all morning", Grace chipped in with a theatrical air of sympathy.

Kathy gave her a cautionary look. "It is really none of your concern," she said. "Please don't interfere."

"What do you think Owen will do?" Stephanie asked.

"Watch television or go for a walk I guess," Kathy said. "He can explore the campus on his own, or with Lionel."

When lunch time came, Kathy and Stephanie hurried across to the cafeteria, where Kathy fully expected to find Owen waiting for her. However, he wasn't anywhere to be seen.

Puzzled, Kathy used the internal phone to call men's hall, the library, and even reception at Girls dorm, to see if Owen was in any of those places.

"I have a bad feeling about this," Stephanie said. "Owen wouldn't just forget he was meeting you."

"He has lost track of the time," Kathy said. "That's all there is to it. It has to be."

"It is getting late Kathy," Stephanie said. "You had better have some lunch. They will find Owen afterwards, wherever he has gone to."

After a quick lunch Stephanie suggested that they try the recreation area: "That is somewhere we haven't looked, and Owen could easily be there."

But he wasn't.

Kathy was frantic with disappointment by now, and Stephanie could empathise with her. She and Owen had so little time together, it was tragic to lose even half an hour of it.

Kathy and Stephanie exited the recreation area, and walked across to girls' dorm. Stephanie was just going to suggest that they use the phone once again to try and locate him, when Kathy pointed to a couple walking up University Drive.

"There he is - with Grace hanging onto him as bold as brass!" Kathy cried.

"Careful Kathy," Stephanie said, "You don't know how this came about."

"I can hazard a guess!" Kathy said wryly.

When Owen and Grace saw Kathy, they turned and came towards where she was standing along-side of her. Kathy had herself under control by now, and was smiling.

"Owen," Kathy said, "You know those photos you wanted to show me? I think this would be a good time to look at them. Why don't you go across to men's hall and get the album?"

Owen said, "Sure", and stepped away from Grace. "Thank you for keeping me company this morning," he said politely. "However, I really did come down here to spend time with Kathy."

He hurried off towards boys' dorm and Stephanie got the impression that he was relieved to be spared the upcoming confrontation between the girls.

Kathy approached Grace, and placed her mouth close to the other girl's ear. "Thou shalt not covert, and thou shalt not steal," she whispered.

Grace bridled. "I wasn't doing anything!" she professed. "Owen can hang out with me if he wants!"

Kathy sighed. "I am only going to explain this to you once Grace," she said, "And then I am going to expect you to understand it for all time. Owen and I have agreed to what is known as an 'exclusive' arrangement. Our friendship is unique and special, belonging to him and me alone."

Grace simpered, "Owen is so lonely with you away at university. I was just providing him with a little companionship."

"I go home as often as I can," Kathy said. "Are you prepared to go to Armidale and keep Owen company all the time?"

"No...", Grace faltered.

"Well then you had better leave him to me!" Kathy concluded.

Owen returned just then and he and Kathy went into the reception lounge. Grace and Stephanie made their way upstairs.

The basketball final on Tuesday attracted attention, even amongst the students who didn't normally follow sport. Stephanie arrived at the gymnasium in the afternoon to find rows of seats placed all around the outside of the courts, and people sitting there already.

Stephanie picked her way through the spectators, and sat down with Gloria and the other players' girlfriends. They had choice positions near the bench.

The players entered from the side of the gym and jogged around the court several times to warm up, while the spectators cheered, and called out the names of the captains. There was a chorus of "Go Tony's" and "Go Warren's", from all sides.

The referee blew the whistle, and the teams took their positions. Jeff's team took control of the ball early in the game, and shot several baskets. They played assertively throughout the first half, and it looked as though they were going to win easily.

Half-time was quiet and tense. Jeff's team looked depleted, and Tony's team looked worried. The teams huddled together for a strategy session.

In the second half Tony's team appeared determined to make a comeback. They pursued the ball aggressively, and managed to contain the play in their half of the court. A series of well shot baskets brought their score to just below that of Jeff's team by full-time. A final basket shot the second before the whistle brought the two scores level, and the referee declared that the game would go into overtime, with five minutes play in either direction.

Warren called his team together for a brief strategy session. "Don't let the other team near the ball," he said. "Jeff, you are to pass the ball to me or Harry, whenever you get it."

Play resumed with both teams attempting an onslaught on the ball. Jeff caught the ball, and passed it to Warren, who shot a basket. The ball was returned to the centre, and Warren made every effort to direct it back to Jeff, who passed it to Harry. Harry missed the basket and the ball bounced out. It was returned from the side. Jeff defended and passed the ball back to Warren. Warren shot another basket and the whistle blew to declare the game complete.

"What an exciting finish," Stephanie said to Jeff, when Stephanie could get to him through the crowd of on-lookers.

Warren slapped Jeff on the shoulder. "Thanks man," he said, "Those last two goals were as much yours as mine!"

Then Warren turned to Tony and shook him by the hand: "Great game mate, you almost beat us!"

Gloria came up and added her congratulations, and the girlfriends proceeded to escort their conquering heroes to tea.

The next day, Stephanie's English Literature group was divided into teams, and given the task of dramatising a fable and producing a film segment. This would be worth about ten percent of their mark for the semester. The assignment was designed to give them an understanding of modern dramatic media from the inside.

Team one consisted of Phoebe, Milton, Bradley, Anita, Tom, Elisabet and Stephanie. Anita and Tom were assigned responsibility for preparing the script. Stephanie was privately disappointed because she loved to write, but she was promised a dramatic part. That was okay, Stephanie also loved to act. The group met on their own time after lunch to plan the drama, and after much discussion, they agreed that they would do a modern rendition of the fable of the "Tortoise and the Hare".

On Thursday the Biology Master relented, and allowed the class to begin the afternoon lab an hour early, so as to finish in time for the Basketball Tea.

Dylan and Garry were both keen basketball players and wanted to attend the trophy presentation. Dylan was a C grade player, and Garry was a substitute for one of the B grade teams.

The class worked steadily throughout the afternoon to finish about four pm; then taking their folders with them, the students hurried to the crowded cafeteria. The players were seated in their teams, so Stephanie collected her food, and picked her way through the assembly to take her place next to Jeff.

A small platform had been set up along the cafeteria wall. Jonathon, who was one of the Referees, climbed onto it and blew his whistle. Everyone quietened down.

Jonathon made a short speech about the skill and teamwork required to play basketball, and said that he was very proud of all those who had been involved throughout the university season. Then he called upon a couple of the other Referees to help him present trophies to the winning teams in each category.

The A grade trophies were presented first. The A grade boys' final had been a fiercely fought contest, and Jonathon spent a few moments describing the match to those who had been so remiss as to miss it.

The A grade girls' competition, as described by Melanie, had involved more strategic play than force, but had also been a fascinating match.

Jeff's team was called up to receive the trophy for winning the B grade boys' competition. It was handed to Warren, as the captain, and he made a short speech of thanks. Before they were allowed to sit down again, several players were presented with individual trophies. Warren received 'best and fairest' and Jeff was given 'most improved'.

Then the C grade winners were called up to join the guys and girls by the platform. There was less general interest in the C grade series. Some of the players were quite good, but most of them were average players who just enjoyed playing a game.

When the guys came back to their seats, they passed the trophies around the table for everyone to look at. After his trophy had done the rounds, Jeff gave it to Stephanie to hold. It was a small wooden block upon which a brass figure stood holding a ball. "Jeffrey Mannington" and "most improved" was etched onto the brass plaque.

The guys were laughing and joking about all the games of the season. When they had exhausted that topic, they turned to Jeff and Stephanie, and began to tease them about having become an item recently.

Stephanie found the teasing a bit embarrassing, and looked at Jeff to see how he was taking it. He was smiling, so Stephanie tried to relax. They were all Jeff's mates, and she assumed they would not say anything he did not want to hear.

As Stephanie was returning from breakfast, she met Melanie coming out of her room. The older girl was looking very sleepy-eyed. She smiled, however, and Stephanie stopped to talk to her.

"That was a lovely ceremony yesterday evening", Stephanie said.

"Oh yes!" she agreed. "Jonathon has enjoyed organising basketball this year, and I have enjoyed helping him."

"It must be great doing something like that together," Stephanie exclaimed.

"It does help bring a couple closer together," Melanie commented, and then she lowered her voice: "Actually, I have a secret to tell you, as long as you don't tell anyone before this evening."

"Oh what is it?" Stephanie asked puzzled.

"Jonathon and I have decided to get engaged," Melanie whispered. "We are going up to Northcoast this afternoon to choose a ring."

"How exciting!" Stephanie whispered back. "When are you planning to get married?"

"If Jonathon gets work at the end of the year, we will get married in February," Melanie replied.

"And if he doesn't?" Stephanie queried.

"Then it will be a slightly longer engagement. We should know by about October, which is when the graduate placements start coming out," Melanie said.

"I wish you all the best!" Stephanie said. "It will be so exciting having a friend getting married. I'll come to the wedding if it is not too far away."

"Do remember to keep it quiet until tonight," Melanie admonished her, "I want to have a ring to show everyone when we make the announcement."

"I think I can keep it quiet for that long," Stephanie said, "But not too much longer, so I hope you find that ring!"

When Stephanie saw Melanie that evening, she and Jonathon were surrounded by a group of well-wishers. The news was obviously out! Stephanie pushed her way into the group, and gleefully added her congratulations to all the rest.

"Where is the ring?" Stephanie said.

Melanie extended her hand to display a sapphire solitaire, with two shoulder diamonds. Sapphires had been immensely popular ever since Prince Charles gave a massive oval one to Lady Diana a few years previously.

"It's beautiful!" Stephanie exclaimed.

"I didn't dare look at the nice ones at first, because Jonathon is just a poor student," Melanie said. "But Jon insisted. He said he had been saving for weeks."

"I wanted to get Melanie something she really liked," Jonathon explained. "It is a symbol of what I intend for her in the future, and she will be wearing it all the time."

"It didn't cost an outrageous amount though," Melanie said. "We have other things to save for...like a whole future together."

"You are a lucky girl," Stephanie said hugging Melanie, "And I don't just mean because of the ring. Jonathon is a very responsible and generous guy."

Stephanie turned to Jonathon: "And you are a lucky guy too," She said. Stephanie had never hugged a guy in public before, but she squeezed his shoulder, "Melanie is the sweetest, most thoughtful girl I know."

Saturday was the day Stephanie's English Literature group were supposed to shoot their film assignment. They were using a super-eight movie camera which belonged to the Education department. The camera could not be removed from within the Education building, but they were allowed to utilise one of the classrooms as a studio.

They all grabbed an early breakfast, and arrived at the location around eight o'clock. Some of them were brighter than others at that hour!

Milton, whom they had elected as director studied the room, wondering how to create a convincing 'set'. Stephanie's experience with school theatrics came into its own here, and she stepped into the breach, suggesting that they film the race on location along a strip of men's walk. The fable only had two main characters, but their script required other contestants, spectators and race officials to make it realistic. Milton was relieved, and despatched the girls to collect a few props from their rooms, and the boys to locate cords and lamps from the Education department cupboards.

When they had set up the race area out-doors, it looked quite convincing. It was now ten-thirty am. Milton frowned and said that they were behind the schedule he had designed for them, and needed to get straight into the filming.

Stephanie's part in the play was to observe the race as a well-dressed spectator on the arm of her handsome escort, fellow English student Bradley. They were also the spectators who finally discovered "the hare" napping under a tree instead of finishing the race.

Milton proved to be a very demanding director, and Bradley and Stephanie spent the rest of the morning marching up and down being filmed from different angles, until Milton had the shots he wanted. Brad was quite sweet, and made a joke about them being required to link arms for the purpose of the play.

Milton, who had come out of his shell and become completely business-like, decided that there was not enough time for a lunch break, so a couple of the girls were sent up to the cafeteria to collect trays of food for the group. Stephanie escaped this task because she was still being filmed.

At last Brad and Stephanie were allowed to sit down, and the camera was turned upon the students acting as the hare and the other tortoise. After the drama was completed, Bradley and Stephanie were required to re-appear, and read some statements explaining the connection between the story they had acted and the original tale.

Milton finally declared himself satisfied that they would get a good mark after the film was processed, edited and spliced. He shut down the camera, and ordered everyone to help take the equipment back to the Education department. When they emerged from the building, they noticed that it was getting dark.

"Quick", Brad said, "If we run we can still get some tea." He took her by the arm, as he had been doing all day in the play, and propelled her towards the cafeteria.

Bradley and Stephanie arrived at the cafeteria, and grabbed some trays and plates of food.

Jeff was still sitting in the cafeteria with some of his mates. He gave Bradley a pointed stare, and the younger boy visibly tensed.

Jeff then turned to her: "Where have you been all day?" he

demanded.

"I've been making a film", Stephanie said sitting down beside Jeff. "Did you miss me?"

"I think I'll leave this to you," Brad said, making a discrete exit.

Stephanie regaled Jeff with the story of their video assignment and day's work, making it clear how she came to be arriving with Brad. He looked amused and said that he might see the film sometime. Stephanie relaxed as it became evident Jeff understood what she was trying to tell him.

The next day, Stephanie wore the grey suit she had acquired during the holidays, and the other girls said that she looked very refined and exceedingly smart. Jeff appeared to like the neat look too, for he smiled when he saw her.

After sitting together in the Reformed Church, Jeff and Stephanie walked across to the cafeteria for lunch. Jeff led her through the queue, and sat them down amongst his third and fourth year friends. Stephanie hadn't been formally introduced to all of these people, so she felt a bit lost as she attempted to participate in the conversation.

Stephanie nodded in agreement when someone said something she understood, and smiled at what were obviously 'in-jokes' for the group.

Whenever Jeff sensed that Stephanie had been particularly left out, he turned to her to explain a point especially. Stephanie appreciated him doing this, and it made her feel like she was important to him, if not to the rest of the group.

Most of Jeff's friends shared classes, and the talk turned to their lecturers and assignments. This was their second-to-last semester, and they were taking their results seriously.

As Stephanie couldn't share this specific experience, she found herself going quiet and put her hand down on Jeff's knee to remind him that she was there.

After the others had finished their meal, they packed up and left. Jeff and Stephanie remained in the cafeteria, talking most of the afternoon. They shared their thoughts on study and careers, and moved onto travel, which turned out to be an interest for both of them.

The week commenced with classes all morning, and lunch with Jeff. He told her about a major assignment he had due that very afternoon. He had only just begun work on it, and was counting on putting in an intense effort during the day.

Stephanie walked across to men's hall with him, and wished him luck with his assignment. Jeff thanked her, and said that he would try to have some time free to spend with her after tea.

Stephanie returned to her room to concentrate on her own study. Tea time Stephanie re-joined Jeff in the cafeteria, and he said that his assignment hadn't gone very well during the afternoon, and he was looking at sitting up all night writing. Jeff hoped that if he managed to complete the assignment before seven-thirty the next morning and slide it under the Lecturer's door before classes commenced, it would be counted as being handed in on time.

Stephanie sympathised, and said that she understood the importance of the assignment. Her assignments had all been completed a long before time, and Stephanie once again expressed her surprise that he could survive the pressure of completing the entire task at the last minute. If Jeff was used to working that way, however, Stephanie said that she was confident that he would do well on this assignment.

Jeff said that the pressure provided him with his inspiration, and that he would come up with the required material if he kept working on it. Then he went back to the men's dormitory.

When Stephanie saw Jeff in the morning, he told her that he had successfully completed his assignment, and put it under the Lecturer's door as planned.

"That's excellent!" Stephanie exclaimed. "I knew you could do it!"

They hurried off to their respective classes.

Lunch time, Jeff and Stephanie were sitting in the cafeteria with Jonathon and Melanie. They began to talk about their hopes for the future, and the work placements they were applying for after graduation.

Jonathon hoped to get work in one of the capital cities, either Sydney or Melbourne. Melanie had applied to be sent to the same places, but she was prepared to give up work altogether, if she was not offered something compatible with Jonathon's placement.

Jeff said that he had stipulated "Brisbane and Brisbane only", on his application.

Stephanie was thrilled to hear this, because Brisbane was not far away from the university. (In fact, it was only a little under an hour's drive.) Stephanie asked Jeff whether he thought he would really be given a job in the Brisbane area.

Jeff said he believed there would be a large number of private sector jobs available in Brisbane the next year, and that there was a good probability of his getting exactly what he wanted. Moreover, he declared that he would get a job with another employer, if he could not get a job with a Christian employer.

For the first time, it looked as if Jeff had a plan to ensure their friendship lasted beyond the end of the year. It was unlikely that Stephanie would be able to go to Brisbane very often to visit him, but he would be able to come up to the university on weekends and special occasions.

The three seniors made an effort to include her in the conversation, and asked Stephanie what she thought she would do after her own graduation.

Although this would be some years away for her, Stephanie answered that she would be prepared to be flexible, and take whatever further training required to help her get work in the geographical area her significant other, whoever they turned out to be, chose to live.

Jeff looked exceedingly pleased when he heard her say that.

Stephanie began revising her subjects and organising her notes. There was only a little over a week to go before exams commenced. The task looked huge, and Stephanie became a little panicky.

Stephanie saw Jeff during convocation and at lunch, and he was very reassuring. He gave her some study hints, and suggested Stephanie consult the files of previous exam papers kept in the library. This would give her a fair idea of the questions that were likely to be in the exam, Jeff explained.

Stephanie thought that this was a good idea and followed it up, as well as planning her own revision, and writing a study timetable.

Thursday morning was occupied by classes, and the afternoon by her Life Science lab, so Jeff suggested that they go to the gymnasium after tea to play basketball together.

Stephanie warned Jeff that she was out of practice, and had never developed the level of skill displayed by the members of his team, but he said that he didn't mind just mucking around for a while.

Jeff and Stephanie met in the cafeteria and ate a leisurely tea. Then they sat talking until they felt that their food had been digested enough to allow them to exercise. At that point they walked across to the gymnasium, and Jeff requisitioned a ball.

They selected one of the practice rings hanging on the side of the gym, and begun to bounce the ball around, passing it between them. They took turns aiming at the basket. Jeff sunk a couple of baskets, and Stephanie managed to bounce the ball off the edge of the ring several times.

"You are getting there", Jeff said. "Just don't flinch when I pass you the ball on a full toss."

"It looks like it is coming straight at my face," Stephanie said, "That was my main problem playing netball."

"The ball won't hit you if you catch it first," Jeff said.

"I know that," Stephanie said, "It's just a reflex thing."

"Were you any good at netball?" Jeff asked.

"I was keen, if not good," Stephanie answered. "It is a very social game, based on passing the ball efficiently, and requires a great deal of team spirit. I enjoyed the interaction immensely."

They moved on to practice dribbling the ball. Jeff could bounce it while running along, but the ball kept spinning away from her when Stephanie tried.

"It isn't as easy as it looks," Stephanie said. "I can see why your team won the final."

On Friday, classes finished around lunch time, and the study-vacation officially commenced. Stephanie retreated to her room, and put in a solid four hours study before tea. Stephanie was re-reading her notes and text books, especially the ones for Life Science.

Stephanie only stopped for brief meal breaks, subsequently seeing very little of Jeff. Stephanie wasn't quite sure he would understand, but figured that he had his own study to do. Besides, they had been spending a lot of time together lately, practically breakfast, dinner and tea, with recreation and assembly as well!

At this point in time, Stephanie felt that she really needed to concentrate upon her studies and not her friendships, precious to her though they were. Therefore, she settled down to study all day. Not counting study breaks, she managed to fit in about eight hour's revision. This allowed her to form a good overview of all her subjects, and to list topics that needed further consideration.

Stephanie had a quick tea, saying "Hi" to Jeff only briefly, and rushed down to women's assembly area to put the finishing touches on it before the Uniting Church vespers commenced.

Back in her room, Stephanie had just finished changing into her grey suit for vespers, when she heard herself paged over the public address system. Descending to the foyer, Stephanie was delighted to see Jeff waiting there for her.

"Hi," Stephanie said greeting him, "I am surprised to see you here!"

"I thought I would pick you up for vespers", Jeff said. "I haven't seen much of you today."

"It's a lovely thought," Stephanie said. "I am ready if you want to go to women's assembly hall now."

Stephanie linked her arm through Jeff's, and they went out the steps and around the courtyard to one of the side doors of the women's assembly hall. It felt great to be entering on her escort's arm, rather than arriving alone and scanning the crowd for him.

Jeff chose a seat for them and led her to it. "You are quite the gentleman tonight," Stephanie said, squeezing his arm. "I really appreciate it."

Stephanie had never dared to insist Jeff adopt more gentlemanly manners towards her, because he was so set in his ways. He had specific patterns and routines that he seemed compelled to keep following, come what may. Overlooking ungentlemanly behaviour was a compromise that Stephanie had been prepared to make because she had fallen in love with this particular guy; but deep in her heart, she had always hoped Jeff would learn to behave in a more chivalrous fashion. Tonight her dream seemed to be coming true.

Stephanie woke up the next morning feeling pretty tired, because they had sat in the assembly hall talking for several hours about religion after vespers finished. Jeff, like Joelle, was solidly committed to the Reform Church and only visited the other services out of the occasional sense of religious curiosity. Stephanie's background was mainstream Anglican and she was most comfortable with the Uniting Church or Inter-denominational services. However, Stephanie appreciated some of the events organised by the Reformed Church on campus.

Stephanie only just managed to get dressed and breakfasted in time for the Reform Church service. She couldn't find Jeff amongst the crowd, and when Debbie and David suggested that Stephanie join them (along with Phoebe, Cara, Garry and Bradley) for a walk to the swinging bridge instead of the church service, she happily agreed.

A couple of the girls went back to their rooms, and collected lightweight blankets to sit upon. They sat down by the suspension-bridge, and David conducted an impromptu worship service.

It was nice to take a break, and do their own thing instead of having it all regimented and prepared for them. David's public speaking ability had developed considerably in the time that they had known him, and he had the makings of an excellent evangelist. He also allowed them to enter into discussion as it progressed, making the proceeding much more sociable than the typical sermon.

Stephanie arrived at the cafeteria in high spirits, and seeing that Jeff had saved her a space, she slipped into it. He was looking a little perplexed.

"Where did you go?" Jeff queried. "I saw you outside the campus meeting hall, and then I couldn't find you anywhere."

"A group of us went and had our own worship down by the suspension bridge," Stephanie said.

"I was ordained as a deacon during the Reform Church service," Jeff said.

"Oh!" Stephanie murmured. "I would have loved to have seen you ordained. I am disappointed I missed it."

"It was an important day for me", Jeff said accusingly, "You really ought to have been there".

"I am truly sorry Jeff," I said. "You should have told me that it was going to happen."

"I was tense, and I expected you to be around," Jeff muttered.

"I appreciate that," Stephanie said, "But if you had told me beforehand, I would not have accidentally accepted another invitation".

"You usually find me - or at least wait for me", Jeff grumbled.

"Yes, I do. And that works most of the time. But if a matter is especially significant, you do need to tell me about it beforehand," Stephanie said.

"I don't know, Stephanie," Jeff said. "Maybe you should learn not to wander off."

Stephanie fawned upon Jeff all afternoon, but this time, he could not be coaxed out of his position. According to him, if Stephanie left his side and missed something important, she would be the one to blame. They parted on a slightly strained note.

Stephanie was surprised when Bradley had her called over the public address system and down to the foyer, around mid-morning. He had searched through the pile of marked Education essays for her paper when he collected his, and brought it across to girls' dorm.

"Why - thanks Bradley," Stephanie exclaimed. "I was planning to go across to the Ed building, and check for my essay later."

"Well, now you don't have to," Brad said. "You did very well too. I couldn't help noticing."

"Yes," Stephanie said, "That gives me an average of thirty out of forty for Education. If I do well in the exam I could get a credit or distinction. I would like that. How did you go?"

"My mark was fairly good. I am confident I will get a credit, but I don't know about a distinction like you," Bradley replied.

"You are a bright guy, Brad," Stephanie said, "You are sure to do well in the exams. You just don't take your studies quite as seriously as I do. When you begin to, you will absolutely shine!"

"I hope so. Do you want to come across to the cafeteria for lunch now?" Bradley asked. "I know it's a bit early, but they should be beginning to serve something."

"I suppose I could. I usually meet Jeff there though," Stephanie mused.

"Jeff knows I am one of your classmates," Brad shrugged. "You explained about the film didn't you? He should be okay with it."

"Alright," Stephanie said. "It would be nice to talk about our subjects. I might have to move when Jeff comes though. He doesn't usually join my friends - I have to join his. I sometimes wish it wasn't that way."

"From what I've seen, most couples have one partner who calls the shots," Brad observed. "Unless they are lucky enough to have all the same friends and interests."

"It always seems to always be the guy who makes the rules", Stephanie grizzled lightly.

"I don't know about that!" Brad said. "Some girls are pretty bossy. Quite frankly, that type of thing spooks me, whether it is amongst guys or girls."

"Do you think that men and women should be equal?" Stephanie queried.

"I don't know," Bradley said, "I haven't thought it through enough. I simply think that everybody should be allowed to be themselves."

"I agree!" Stephanie felt a momentary glow spread across her face as she recognised a kindred spirit in her fellow classmate.

"You are pretty when you smile," Bradley said impulsively. "Did you know that?"

Stephanie sighed, "I wish Jeff thought so," she said.

"Who cares what Jeffrey Mannington thinks?" Bradley exclaimed. Then he looked contrite. "I'm sorry Stephanie, I know you care."

Stephanie got four and a half hours study done between breakfast and lunch. After having a quick meal with Jeff, Stephanie returned to her room and did three more hours study.

Stephanie was tired of reading and simple revision at that point, and decided to go to the library for a change of scene. When Stephanie arrived there, she saw Jeff standing amongst the main stacks.

Stephanie went up and said, "Hi".

"Oh, hello, Stephanie, you have come across here too," Jeff said. "I thought you were going to be buried in your room all day."

"Not quite," Stephanie replied, "I thought I would try a different approach this afternoon."

"I can't ever seem to concentrate in the library," Jeff said, "I just came across to photocopy some articles." He indicated the sheaf of foolscap paper in his hand.

"I see," Stephanie said. "Well that will keep you busy. Good luck with it."

"Thanks. I'm going back to my room now," Jeff said, "I'll see you at tea."

Jeff left, and Stephanie selected a cubicle and settled down to write some sample poetry analysis. One of her worst nightmares was approaching an English exam, sitting down, and suddenly having a bad case of writers' block. Stephanie hoped to guard against this by practice and preparation.

In the morning Stephanie sat her Standard English Language exam. Stephanie had stressed about it beforehand, but it turned out to be a glorified test. There were grammatical passages to correct, parts of speech to identify, and paragraphs to punctuate.

Stephanie treated herself to a long lunch hour, sat talking with Jeff for a while; and then after he left, chatted with her other friends.

Stephanie returned to her room to spend the afternoon preparing for her Life Science practical exam.

The Life Science practical exam was in the afternoon. Stephanie found that this gave her the entire morning to worry about it. Her experience in the weekly labs had shown her that the practical side of Life Science was exceedingly intricate and challenging.

To control her stress level, Stephanie spent the extra time attempting to memorise the names of the main animal families, and other highlights of the taxonomic charts. By the time the exam arrived, Stephanie believed that she would do well.

Once in the laboratory, Stephanie was faced with a number of microscopes, and other pieces of equipment spread around the room. Stephanie was required to approach each one, follow the instructions appended to the bench top, and answer the question written there.

One microscope was focussed on an epidermal cell. It was fairly easy to sketch, and with a bit of squinting, Stephanie located some specks analogous to its internal structure, marked them in, and labelled them. That was worth twenty marks.

There was a preserved crustacean on a tray at the next work-station. Stephanie sketched it and described its family tree as far as she could remember. That was another twenty marks.

There was a mystery slide under the next microscope. Stephanie looked at it in horror, guessed it to be part of some internal organ like a kidney, and passed on. That was ten marks Stephanie would never get in a million years!

There were some ferns to sketch and identify the basic leaf structure on the next desk. That was worth ten marks. Finally, there was a bone to sketch and identify. It appeared to be the leg of a small animal. Stephanie couldn't quite fix on what type of animal, so she wrote down "rabbit". That was worth ten marks - if she was right.

There was a sheet of various questions about laboratory procedures, and the expected results of various tests. A piece of litmus paper was provided, and they were required to test the contents of a beaker and describe the result as either positive or negative, giving their reasoning. That was worth the remaining number of marks.

The whole class staggered out of the laboratory at 4:30,

completely exhausted. They began to compare notes immediately. Absolutely no one had managed to identify the mystery slide. The Biology Master was appealed to and told them that it had actually been the cochlea, a part of the inner ear.

Garry thought he had passed. Dylan said that he didn't care. Cara was really upset because she thought she might have failed, and Stephanie comforted herself with the thought that she could make a few marks up in the theory section.

Stephanie's Education exam went well the following morning. It consisted of a hundred multiple choice questions, and four short essay questions. Stephanie always performed competently on both. She found that multiple choice questions assist her recall, and essay questions usually provided her with the inspiration to write a page or two.

Stephanie had a quick lunch with Jeff, and spent the afternoon cleaning women's assembly area, and generally preparing for weekend. Stephanie meant to take a real break from study on the morrow, and encourage Jeff, who also appeared quite stressed from study and exams, to do likewise.

CHAPTER SIX: MID-YEAR

When Stephanie arrived at the cafeteria for breakfast, Roger waved at her. Stephanie looked, and Jeff was sitting next to him. This was something of a surprise, because Jeff was a late riser and rarely beat her to the cafeteria.

Stephanie carried her tray across to them and sat down. "How are you boys this morning?" Stephanie asked.

"We are both well," Roger answered. "Jeff has some news too."

"I am going to be on duty in the Reformed Church service tomorrow," Jeff announced with pride.

Stephanie was impressed. The role of deacon carried some responsibility and implied a certain amount of moral authority.

"That is great," Stephanie gushed. "Are you taking up the offering?"

"Yes - I will have to make sure I sit on the end of one of the benches, so I can get in and out easily," Jeff said. "I will save a seat, if you would like to join me."

"I would like that," Stephanie replied.

"Okay then," Jeff said, "I will see you there." He stood up to leave the cafeteria. "I guess I have to hit the books for once. It's pretty close to exams."

"Yes," Stephanie said. "Well, good luck and all that!"

The weekend dawned sunny even though it was winter, and

seemed just right for wearing her maroon crochet dress. The dress was princess-line in style and had to be worn over a pink chemise. Aunt Moira had made it for her and it was quite special.

Stephanie arrived at the campus meeting hall, and slid into the vacant seat beside Jeff. He gave her dress an inquiring look, and Stephanie suddenly became aware that the lacy weave might be considered revealing by a male.

"Jeff thinks that I am trying to be provocative", ran through her mind, and Stephanie squirmed, feeling half naked, even though she had worn this outfit to church hundreds of times at home and it had a matching under-dress.

Jeff put his hand down on her buttock, and touched the chemise through one of the spaces in the lace. Stephanie tried to give him her hand to hold instead, but he pushed it away. She tensed up and stared straight ahead.

Jeff frowned. "I have to talk to you after the service," he muttered ominously.

After the service they went outside, and sat down on a bench near the entrance to the cafeteria. There was no one else in sight and Stephanie was beginning to shake apprehensively.

"I don't know where to start," Jeff said.

Stephanie stayed silent. Her intentions in dressing had been innocent, and Stephanie felt it was Jeff who owed her an explanation.

"There is something I have been wanting to talk to you about," Jeff said. "I tried to wait until after the end of the semester, this being your first lot of exams and everything..."

"That was very considerate of you", Stephanie said. "But you had better go ahead now. You have me seriously worried."

"I've been thinking a lot about us," Jeff said. "You've been my friend for some time now, and..."

"And what Jeff?" Stephanie asked.

"I don't know whether we should start a liaison or not," Jeff said. "Because my parents are divorced, I don't believe in marriage – if that is what you are looking for."

Stephanie was shocked. She had never discussed this particular subject with a male of her own age before, and she felt like she was drowning. Stephanie was afraid of losing Jeff if she complained, but she sensed something very worrisome, a distinct lack of moral certainty in his statement.

"If you don't believe in marriage – what else is there?" Stephanie stammered. She knew some couples just lived together; the term "de-facto" had recently come into use on forms for live-in-relationships of more than two years in duration, and there was an act due to go through parliament describing such relationships. However, she had always assumed she would eventually be offered marriage by her boy-friend.

Moving exclusively in Christian circles, Stephanie presumed that she and Jeff had both been brought up to keep the Ten Commandments, which her family had interpreted as setting limits on pre-marital sex. Stephanie had expected such limits to be automatically understood by other religious youth. Apparently it wasn't that simple.

Stephanie had absolutely no idea what Jeff meant by the word "liaison", but the way he said it sounded very dirty. His use of the term was utterly unlike the manner in which the other couples referred to themselves as 'going out' or 'dating steadily'. He seemed to be referring to something more than age-appropriate holding hands, hugging and kissing. It sounded degrading and unromantic to her.

"What gave you the impression I would agree to anything like that?" Stephanie asked.

"It's where things have been heading", Jeff said.

"I see," Stephanie said, "Let me get this straight. You know that I want something we have certainly never discussed?"

"Yes," Jeff said. "That's about right. I believe I do know you pretty well."

"Oh! Were you going to consult me at all before moving our friendship through into this next stage?" Stephanie queried.

"No", Jeff said. "I want to be fair to you, but I think that it should definitely be my decision."

"Oh really," Stephanie said feeling completely lost. "Isn't that taking male privilege a bit too far?"

"I don't know about that," Jeff said. "I have my reasons. I don't want to hurt you, but I have some personal problems to worry about as well."

"This is way too heavy for me Jeff," Stephanie said. "You can think and make your decisions. Just don't expect me to fall in line with any I find inappropriate. I wasn't ready for this topic to even be brought up between us."

"Wait a minute, Stephanie," Jeff said. "I hope that I have not offended you".

Jeff had SERIOUSLY offended her, but Stephanie didn't have the courage to tell him so. Instead she stood up. "It is almost time for lunch, and I am going to get something to eat. Are you coming?"

"No, I don't feel like anything," Jeff said.

Stephanie bravely went into the cafeteria, but she was struggling to deal with the shock and hold back the tears. Roger stared at Stephanie when she entered alone, and she felt embarrassed. She suddenly wished that she had gone back to her room to unload her emotions instead of braving the lunch hour crowd.

Stephanie made a valiant effort to study, but she found that she kept getting distracted by concerns arising from the conversation she had with Jeff. After a while, Stephanie crept across the hall to Melanie's room, to ask her advice.

"Are you all right Stephanie?" Melanie said as soon as she saw her face.

"No," Stephanie said breaking down and crying. "I think I have had a fight with Jeff."

"You only think you had a fight?" Melanie queried.

"Yes! Sometimes it is hard to tell," Stephanie sobbed. "The outcome wasn't very clear."

"Tell me exactly what happened," Melanie instructed, putting an arm around her.

"Jeff said that he had to talk to me - and it was about something heavy. It was so confusing. I didn't even know what he meant," Stephanie confided.

"Ah! Your first deep and meaningful," Melanie said. "Your friendship is progressing."

"I could do without this type of progress," Stephanie gulped.

"I think I know what you mean!" Melanie said. "You should tell Jeff how you feel."

"Should I?" Stephanie said. "I don't think he would understand."

"Of course he would," Melanie said, "If you were clear enough in your explanation."

"No really," Stephanie said. "In the past few months I have had to be more understanding towards Jeff, than he has been towards me. He is quite inflexible."

"Guys and girls do think differently," Melanie reasoned. "That is all the more reason for making an effort to communicate."

"I am still worried," Stephanie remarked. "Jeff said that he had other problems - ones that I don't comprehend. I need to know what they are, before I tell him all my confidences."

"Then this is an opportunity to get to know Jeff better," Melanie said. "You must sit him down and ask him what these other problems are. Don't stress - I am sure that he likes you and it will turn out all-right."

"I will think about it," Stephanie promised. "Thank you Melanie."

Stephanie returned to her studies with a slightly clearer head, and began to re-read some of the relevant chapters in their Life Science textbook. Stephanie managed to fit four hours study in before tea.

At tea Stephanie saw Jeff. He said "Hi", and Stephanie said "Hello". They sat together pretending that there was nothing wrong between them. Then both of them returned to their respective dormitories to study.

Stephanie successfully put Jeff out of her mind, and settled down to study. Her Standard English Language exam was coming up the next day, so she had a lot of notes on poetic figures of speech, tenses and styles of narration, to get clear in her mind.

Stephanie also borrowed a book of short stories by Guy de Maupassant from the library to read and analyse. Stephanie had been told by the lecturer that one of the stories would be re-printed in the exam. As there were no classes to attend, Stephanie managed to do about ten hours study.

Long distance phone calls were cheaper in the evening, so Stephanie waited till then to ring home. Mum and Dad asked her about her study, and the exams she had so far. Stephanie was pleased to be able to tell them that she had been doing well. They wished her luck, and told her that they were praying for her. Stephanie felt strengthened and comforted by that.

After Stephanie had talked to Mum and Dad for a while, Stephanie rang Aunt Moira. Aunt Moira asked Stephanie about her studies too, and then sensing that there was something else bothering her, asked her how things were with "that boy you like".

"Well, Aunt Moira," Stephanie said. "I don't quite know what to do about Jeff. I have talked to Melanie, but I could do with a second opinion, and I always value your advice."

"What is it dear?" Aunt Moira asked.

"Jeff said some funny things the other day," I answered. "I am not sure what he meant."

"I think that you need to be very careful with this boy Stephanie," Aunt Moira warned. "Especially if he is beginning to say funny things."

"I sort of agree with you Aunt Moira, and I have always been careful around Jeff," Stephanie said. "But could you tell me exactly why you are saying that? You don't even know him."

"I do know that Jeff is considerably older than you, dear. He could have expectations that you are not ready to fulfil," Aunt Moira explained.

"What sort of expectations?" Stephanie wondered.

"Well, he is graduating isn't he?" Aunt Moira continued. "And his friends are getting married aren't they? He may want to rush you into the same sort of thing, with or without a marriage ceremony."

"Oh no, Aunt Moira, surely not!" Stephanie exclaimed.

"It is all part of having a romantic friendship with a boy," Aunt Moira said. "You know what is right for you. Make sure that you stick to it. A nice boy would wait till you were ready."

"And what if Jeff won't wait?" Stephanie asked shakily.

"If he doesn't want to wait, you may decide that you are better off with a boy at your own stage of life," Aunt Moira said firmly. "A boy who would be more likely to want the same things you want, than this Jeff does."

"So I have some decisions to make for myself," Stephanie reflected.

"Yes, you do dear," Aunt Moira agreed.

"Melanie thought I could just tell Jeff how I felt, and that it would be all right," Stephanie said.

"Sometimes Melanie sounds like she is too nice for her own good!" Aunt Moira commented. "She is very lucky that she is going out with an honourable boy like Jonathon. I would advise you to talk to Jeff, but take care what you say in case he misinterprets it."

The morning of her Standard English Language exam dawned cold and clear. Stephanie browsed through the summary sheets once again, and then put them away because she liked to take a few minutes to calm down before an exam. Stephanie believed that her primary learning had been completed in the days and months previous to this anyway.

Down at the examination hall, other students were stressing about their lack of English subject background knowledge. Standard English Language was compulsory as an introduction to written communication skills, for the Business and Theology students as well as all teachers.

David and Andrew, who both found English studies quite alien to their interest in Theology, looked particularly worried. Stephanie tried to reassure them without picking up any of their distress.

The doors to the examination hall opened, and they all filed inside. Stephanie looked around for a table that appeared quiet and comfortable. Settling herself down, Stephanie looked steadily at the back of the exam papers on her desk.

The exam commenced. Stephanie found that the Maupassant story they were to assess had not been amongst the ones in the volume she had read, but the extra familiarity with his style helped her draft a competent analysis.

There were several other passages of non-fiction and news reports for them to analyse and comment on the style, grammar and word choice. Stephanie completely filled the blank pad provided and felt that she had done a good job.

The next day Stephanie had her film analysis exam for English Literature. The whole class went down to one of the tutorial rooms in the Education department, and watched a movie created by an Australian director. They were asked to describe the visual effects and comment upon them.

Stephanie know that she lost marks in this section. The segment of film passed by her eyes as a series of disconnected and segregated images, and she had difficulty following the story-line. All the male characters in particular, appeared indistinguishable in their plain suits; while the somewhat poor lighting and indistinct focus made the plot difficult to follow.

Stephanie discussed the exam with Milton and Phoebe at lunch, and felt even more discouraged. Phoebe appeared to have managed to follow the characterisation, and Milton had some clever comments to make about the artistic effect of the camera angles and directorial 'cuts'. Bradley was a bit more sympathetic about her confusion.

Friday morning Stephanie had her English Literature text exam. She had spent a fair few hours reading and re-reading the novels, to develop the degree of familiarity required to locate a series of passages relevant to any question that could be set. In addition to this, Stephanie had made notes on the major themes, series of images, and twists of plot found in the texts; in the hopes that these would be universally applicable.

During the exam, Stephanie found that the information returned to her head, and the ideas flowed fluently. Stephanie used the question sheet as a piece of spare paper, and jotted down a rough point-form essay outline.

As Stephanie wrote each section, her argument developed in her mind complete with quotes, and she turned to the novels she had been allowed to bring with her to locate the relevant page numbers. Stephanie left the exam satisfied that she had done very well.

Stephanie saw Jeff in the cafeteria lunch time, and asked him how he was going. He said that he was doing as well as he could, given that he had some heavy exams. Stephanie wished him luck, and he said that he was in a hurry and would see her at tea.

Stephanie sat her Life Science exam in the afternoon. In addition to being her last exam, this was probably the hardest. Stephanie took the precaution of requesting extra writing paper before the exam commenced, so that she had two entire booklets at her disposal.

There were about a hundred multiple choice questions to answer, then some short 'paragraph' answer questions (like in the average test), and finally there were four essay questions to answer. The essays required were not going to be marked on structure and composition like the English ones, but nonetheless, Stephanie tried to design them well, using good grammar as well as lots of information. Stephanie was still writing and adding extra touches when the exam was called to a halt.

Stephanie and her classmates staggered up to the cafeteria together, reporting a mutual level of exhaustion from the effort required by the exam. Dylan and Garry asked Stephanie how she thought she went, and she said she was confident of a pass. They stuck together tea time, comparing their reactions to the questions, and generally commiserating with each other.

After tea, the guys walked Cara and Stephanie back to girls' dorm. Garry asked them if they would like to go for a walk tomorrow afternoon. Cara said that she would love to go, and Stephanie said that she would think about it, but she might have something else to do.

Stephanie was resolved that Saturday would be the day that she talked things through with Jeff. The problem had been at the back of her mind all week, causing her extra stress and tension, although Stephanie had not indulged herself by thinking much about it.

Jeff came to breakfast early, and seemed very pleased to find her there. After they had eaten, Stephanie told Jeff that she felt they needed to have a serious discussion. Jeff said she should go for a little walk with him, and led her half way back to men's hall, to a seat set amongst some flower beds. They sat down.

"What is it, Stephanie?" Jeff asked, although he must have had a fair idea what was bothering her.

"Well Jeff," Stephanie said, "Last week you wanted to have a talk with me. A talk that was obviously very important in your eyes, but I found fairly hard to understand."

"What didn't you understand?" Jeff muttered.

"Well, were you saying that you liked me?" Stephanie inquired. "The strange way you put things, I couldn't even be sure of that!"

"I do like you Stephanie," Jeff said. "You can rest assured of that fact".

"What was it that you had to think so much about?" Stephanie asked. "Was it about us going steady? Or possibly getting even more involved than that?"

"Getting even more involved...", Jeff answered.

Stephanie took a deep breathe, and proceeded to make the scariest speech she had ever made in her life.

"Jeff, I like you too. I really do. But I do not want to get involved in anything heavy this year. Is that clear?"

"I don't know," Jeff said. He sounded displeased. "I don't know if that is what I want either."

"I think the best thing for us to do, would be to remain good friends throughout this year," Stephanie said. "We don't know what will happen next year. You will be graduated and all that, won't you?"

"Yes," Jeff agreed.

"There will be a lot of changes for both of us over the next few years", Stephanie continued. "If our friendship is strong enough, it should be able to change with us. It can't be allowed to restrict us and tie us down. Not if it is going to last, and have any chance of working out."

"You have really thought this through, haven't you?" Jeff remarked somewhat snidely.

"I had to. Especially after what you said!" Stephanie answered. Stephanie wasn't following anyone's advice exactly, she thought that she had found her own solution, one that took into account exactly who Jeff was too. "I'm sorry if something about your experience has put you off marriage, but you don't know what would happen in the future, especially if you find the right girl."

"It is a nice picture, and I will have to think it," Jeff said. "After all, I am the one that will be facing most of the changes. Beginning at the end of this year."

"I understand that Jeff," Stephanie said. "You also said that there were other problems. What were they?"

"They were family matters," Jeff muttered. "I never really fitted in at my parents' house."

"Is that why you don't go home for the holidays?" Stephanie queried.

"Yes!" Jeff said, "My mother has a new husband and I am really not comfortable there."

"I am sorry," Stephanie murmured. "Is it hard for you to conceive of making a happy home with anyone in the future?"

"Yes - pretty hard," Jeff admitted. "I need a lot of space, and a fair bit of independence."

"I had noticed!" Stephanie said wryly, "I have to work around your needs all the time. Still, the future doesn't have to be like the past. We are on the threshold of our lives, and with God's help can make better families for ourselves than perhaps your parents did. I don't know exactly what went wrong, so I don't want to say too much. What do you see happening with me?"

"I like you Stephanie, I really do," Jeff replied, "But I still don't know what I see in the future for us."

"I can't fix your problems for you Jeff, if that is what you are hoping," Stephanie said. "I'll tell you what I'll do though. I will pray all throughout the holidays, and trust that God sends us some guidance. Is that okay by you?"

"It sounds good Stephanie," Jeff replied.

"Do you want to try praying too?" I suggested.

"Yes," Jeff said. "It might do some good."

Stephanie wore her grey suit to church because it was quite formal and Jeff always seemed to like her dressed that way. When she went to sit with him in the Inter-denominational praise service, Jeff smiled and made room for her, and after the service, they went across to the cafeteria to have lunch together. They talked for a while, and exchanged holiday details. Stephanie was going home to stay with her parents, but Jeff was going to be working around the university throughout the entire mid-year break.

"It will get very cold", Jeff said, "Because they turn the boiler off while the students are away."

It sounded like a dreary and lonesome life to her, but Jeff assured her he knew how to look after himself, and there would be one or two others around for part or all of the break.

They said "Goodbye", and Jeff wished her a safe journey home, warning her to bring some warm jumpers back to university because August could still be cold.

On Monday, before she left, Stephanie went down to the classrooms to check for any marked assignments put out on the return piles. As she was walking down the main concourse in front of the main building, she bumped into the Biology Master.

The Biology Master stopped to talk to her. "You write excellent essays in exams Stephanie," He exclaimed, "I was really surprised."

"Why, thank you!" Stephanie said, and went on her way greatly cheered. While her practical exam marks might drag her down a little, it was evident that Stephanie would get a comfortable mark for the subject, maybe even a credit.

Stephanie packed her bags, and then visited her friends to say goodbye to them. Kathy was looking forward to spending the entire six weeks of the holidays with Owen - for them, she explained, it would be a welcome break from long distance communication.

Melanie was excited because she was taking Jonathon home to

Melbourne to meet her parents. Stephanie was a bit surprised that they had not done this earlier in their relationship, but Melanie said that this was one of the drawbacks of getting to know someone at Silver Springs University. One could became very intimate with the person from living right alongside them, but did not get to do normal 'family stuff' with them. Stephanie hugged Melanie, and wished her all the best for the holidays.

Then Stephanie hurried off to get a lift in the university car to the closest train station, which was Northcoast. It turned out that Brenda and Cara were also catching the train to Brisbane, and would be taking similar flights. The girls decided to share a taxi to the airport.

During the mid-year break, time seemed to pass slowly. The magic had somehow gone missing from her poetry writing and sewing, and even the radio seemed full of mournful songs. British duo Wham had recently brought out a catchy tune, *Wake me up before you go-go*, and while its connotations were a bit sexy, Stephanie felt that the singer described her need not to be left in uncertainty very well.

Stephanie also found she missed the excitement of university social life, and even the routine of classes. Stephanie threw herself into all the activities of the local church, contacted old friends, and ran as many errands as she could for her Mum and Dad.

Stephanie often found herself thinking about Jeff alone in the dorms, and wrote to him once, keeping her tone as light as possible.

Stephanie longed to be back at the university, sorting things out with him, but something also told her to take things slowly, and not to allow the older boy to touch her any more intimately than he had up until now. At least, not until he had sorted out whatever conflicts he had over his family life.

Even if Stephanie had not had strong moral beliefs about pre-marital sex, her instincts would have told her this. There was something threatening in the way Jeff hovered over her when he ought to be standing next to her, and something fierce about his eyes when he looked into hers. These things made her uncomfortable.

Stephanie found her subconscious repulsion difficult to reconcile with the fact that she did honestly have warm feelings for Jeff, and had no idea what it meant. Stephanie speculated that it might be her age, that she was too young for anything more than linking arms. On the other hand, in the light of some of the things that Jeff had told her, Stephanie found herself worrying about his emotional health. Stephanie didn't dare discuss the problem with anyone - it was somehow way too shocking.

Stephanie went shopping several times during the holidays. She located some white sandals at a factory direct store that had just opened. Mum took her to Elizabeth shopping centre one day, and Stephanie found a long-sleeved white silk dress with a ruffled front like a formal shirt. That would be perfect for church during spring.

In a little boutique, Stephanie located a black taffeta cocktail style dress, with a sweetheart neckline and shoe string straps. The neck and hem were edged with a thin pleated strip of black and white chiffon. Stephanie thought that it would be perfect for the next formal function. Being conscious of her student budget, Stephanie had not spent a lot of money, but she was excited by her purchases. Stephanie couldn't wait to show them to the other girls at the university.

Stephanie arrived back at Silver Springs University tired from the plane and train travel. She took an hour to unpack and showered to freshen herself up, before going across to men's hall to tell Jeff that she was back.

Stephanie found him working on the reception desk over there. (Apparently that was one of the jobs that he had done during the holidays.) It was a little while before he could swap with someone and talk to her, so Stephanie sat down and waited.

When Jeff had arranged for someone else to take over the phones, he invited Stephanie to go for a short walk. They went outside and strolled along the main path, towards the Meeting hall and recreation area.

Jeff said that he had received her letter. "It sounded like you had a busy holiday," he said.

"That's right," Stephanie agreed, knowing that she had emphasised all the activities she had been involved in at church and tried to make her home life sound interesting. "It is always great to catch up with people in Adelaide."

"It was pretty bleak here," Jeff said, "But I got by."

"Why didn't you write to me?" Stephanie asked.

"You hadn't put your address on the postcard," Jeff answered.

"I am sure I did," Stephanie said. "But it might have been a bit hard to find. I always seem to run out of space on postcards." They fell silent. Stephanie wasn't sure whether to believe Jeff about the letter or not. In her experience, men were reluctant letter writers. He wouldn't be the first male making nice sounding excuses for not having written.

"I should have written to you," Jeff said at last. "There was something I wanted to say."

"What was that Jeff?" Stephanie asked.

"Stephanie", Jeff began, "I regret telling you that I liked you."

"Why would you regret having told the truth?" Stephanie asked, even though she had a fair idea where he was leading.

"It probably made you think we had a future together," Jeff said. "But I didn't mean to make any promises. I hope you haven't built up any hopes."

This was portentous. There was probably a lot in it to cry about later, but Stephanie had her own bit to say. Jeff's speech had just proved her instincts right.

"Actually, Jeff," Stephanie said, "When I was praying and thinking over the holidays, I came to the conclusion that we should keep things, what is that word? - Innocent, between us. You know, no confusion about the physical."

"I still want us to be good friends", Jeff said somewhat anxiously.

"I want to be friends too," Stephanie said.

"That's good", Jeff said, "I don't want to lose you."

"So what do we do now?" Stephanie asked. "Do we spend our time together as usual?"

"Of course!" Jeff said dully. "I will always be pleased to see you."

Stephanie took this to mean that they had an understanding. However, like so many of the things that had happened between Jeff and herself, there was no clear etiquette that Stephanie could draw upon, and she remained somewhat uncertain as to exactly how she should behave in the future.

CHAPTER SEVEN: STUDY

Stephanie didn't have time to worry any more about her uncertain relationship with Jeff, because she found herself immensely busy with new subjects, new classes and new assignments. The settling-in process was similar to that Stephanie had under-gone at the beginning of the year, except she adjusted far more quickly second time around.

Her timetable had changed considerably. English Literature was in a similar time-slot to the previous semester, as was Life Science, but many other subjects were different. Child Development replaced the previous Education subject, and sounded absolutely fascinating. It covered human physical, mental and social development - from the formation of the foetus until adulthood; and fitted in beautifully with her interest in Psychology.

Fundamentals of Computing replaced Ethics as a 'house requirement'. Stephanie felt that she had a head start on this subject as she had been one of the very few girls who had signed up for computing as an elective at high school. The Dick Smith System 80, Commodore 64 and Apple II were all very difficult to program, but Stephanie was assured that the IBM Personal Computers they were using at university would be more technologically advanced. The university was also expecting an order of the new Apple Macintosh which was predicted to have an exciting new multi-media capability and user friendly interface.

Practice Teaching sounded similar to its first semester complement, but had been re-scheduled, and required a week's classroom experience to be completed during the September break, (which was cleverly scheduled never to coincide with the school holidays).

Standard English Language had sub-sections covering "the Bible as a form of literature", "communication skills" and "modern journalism". It sounded quite adventurous for a first year subject!

Stephanie saw Jeff at lunch. He was surrounded by a group of his friends, and had not saved her a seat. Stephanie tried to catch his eye, but he did not look up. He was either highly pre-occupied, or attempting to discourage her from joining him.

"Well", Stephanie thought, "We did say that we would move backwards in our friendship. This hurts a bit, but I guess it is the way things are going to be. I must accept it."

Stephanie went and sat with Debbie and David. "How are you guys?" she said.

"We are great, aren't we Deb?" David said. "But how come you are alone Steph?"

"Jeff's busy," Stephanie shrugged, "And not all couples are as inseparable as you two."

"She's right Dave," Debbie said, "It takes all types. I admire your independence Stephanie."

"You were pretty independent at the beginning of the year!" Stephanie exclaimed in surprise.

"And look how long that lasted," Debbie said. "I wouldn't know myself without David now."

"But that's sweet," Stephanie said.

"It is good most of the time," Debbie said. "However, sometimes I miss the girl talks we used to have."

"I don't stop you seeing the girls," David said indignantly.

"No," Debbie said, "You just call me at the dorms morning, noon and night."

"I can stop doing that if you like!" David retorted jovially.

"Don't stop anything," Debbie said, "I like it."

"Then how are you going to see more of the girls?" David demanded.

"Think creatively I guess," Debbie said with a smile. "Maybe Stephanie has some ideas."

"How about you come to my room after curfew, Debbie?" Stephanie suggested. "That is not David time and we can have a great chat, as long as we don't go past eleven, I have a seven-thirty lecture in the morning."

"That sounds good," Debbie said. "I will be able to tell you all about the shopping trip I went on in the holidays. David didn't want to hear much about that."

Convocation Wednesday was rowdy and cheerful as it was taken by the "year-book team". The *Year Book* was put together by the students, and contained photos, poems and personal stories. They all received one copy free, but additional copies could be sold to their families and members of the public as a fundraising exercise.

Stephanie had come to convocation directly from class, and was consequently sitting with Phoebe, Joelle, Milton and Bradley. They were just a couple of rows back from Jeff and his mates. When the meeting had finished, Jeff turned and saw her. He looked slightly surprised, and began walking towards her.

"Hello Stephanie," Jeff said when he was close enough.

"Hello Jeff," Stephanie replied. "How are you today?"

"I am good," Jeff said. "I am going across to the student union. If you are going that way at all, I can walk you."

"Thanks," Stephanie said, "I am going to lecture theatre one."

They waited for the crowd to thin a bit, and then walked down the stairs and across the concourse.

"I have been wondering a bit what has become of you lately," Jeff said as they walked.

"I have been around Jeff," Stephanie said. "I had a lot of classes and everything."

"I have classes too," Jeff said. "I can't go chasing after you all the time Stephanie."

"I understand that," Stephanie murmured. "Well, we are here".

"I will see you at lunch then?" Jeff said, stopping in the middle of the corridor.

"Sure", Stephanie said.

Jeff went into the library, and Stephanie stepped into the lecture theatre. They met for lunch an hour later, and enjoyed a great deal of jovial banter with Jeff's mates. It was almost like old times.

Thursday afternoon, the Life Science class drove some distance out and up into the mountains, and hiked to a significant point near the source of a stream. The Biology Master set a brisk pace, and Stephanie got quite puffed, but she tried valiantly not to show it.

When they had located the stream, they discussed the vegetation and the rocks they could see. The Biology Master informed them that if they journeyed down-stream, the channel would widen, and a number of other ecological changes would be noticeable. Eventually, the rocks would give way to soil, and the stream would be joined by a number of other waterways on their way to the ocean.

They collected some water samples to take back to the laboratory, and returned to where the Land Rover was parked. The Biology Master strode ahead, telling them to hurry if they wanted to get back to the university in time for tea. Dylan and Cara were joking around together, and Stephanie found herself walking with Garry.

"Did you have a nice holiday, Stephanie?" Garry asked.

"Pretty good," Stephanie said, "Although home is quiet after university."

"I know what you mean", Garry said, "There is nothing like living with a couple of hundred other people to keep you busy."

"Do you like Silver Springs University Garry?" Stephanie asked.

"Mostly," Garry said, "It is a good place to get an education. If your degree is in the Sciences, you have a good chance of being employed by industry. That is what I am hoping for in the long run."

"How interesting," Stephanie said, "So you are not going to join the throng of teachers and church workers being transferred to another area every few years?"

"No. That doesn't really appeal to me," Garry answered, "I want something more permanent, and a project to get my teeth into."

"I like the way you think!" Stephanie remarked. "It is realistic and opens up options I had not considered."

They were interrupted by Cara squealing. Dylan had almost tripped her up, and she was hopping around on one leg.

"Come and join us", Garry called. "You will be safer!"

"Thanks!" Cara said, "Dylan is such a tease."

"He likes you," Garry remarked.

"I wish he would figure out a different way of showing it," Cara said. "That was pretty immature."

"Well, I'm not on the receiving end," Stephanie remarked, "But it looks like fun at times."

"It is until Dylan goes too far," Cara said. "Garry is much more of a gentleman."

"I can be a bit of a tease too," Garry said, and winked at her.

The room at the end of their corridor had been vacated by Mandy and Lisa, who had now moved on to the hospital to do the practical part of their Nursing course. Stephanie was curious to meet the new occupants, who would be from the second intake of students.

Seeing the door ajar sometime after tea, Stephanie knocked and introduced herself.

"Hello, my name is Stephanie. I live in number 12."

The occupants looked like a nice pair of girls. The girl closest to the door held out her hand.

"Hello," she said, "I am Bethany. Have you been here long?"

"About six months," Stephanie said, "I am a first year Education student."

"That's great," Bethany said. "We are both Nurses." She appeared to be a bright outgoing person, with a knack for stating the obvious. Stephanie thought that she would be an amusing addition to her regular group of friends. She would also be popular with the boys.

The other girl was slower to speak, but Stephanie found herself liking the quiet girl instinctively. "What is your name?" Stephanie asked.

"I am May," she replied. May was very neat and self-possessed. She was of Chinese heritage, and looked like she would take a practical approach to life.

"What do you think of the university?" Stephanie asked.

"It is all very new to me", May replied. "I am just beginning to find out about things."

"It was like that for me last semester too," Stephanie said.

"Did it take very long for you to settle in?" May asked.

"No," Stephanie said, "I soon learnt the ropes. It's not the same as home though."

"We didn't expect it to be," Bethany said brightly. "I for one, could do with a change. May, I think, only wants to study."

"Don't listen to her!" May said. "I would like to go for some nice walks and meet some nice people too."

"You can do that here," Stephanie said. "Did you girls know each other before you came here?"

"No," Bethany said. "We have just met. But being thrown together like this, we are getting to know each other quickly. We have also got the same classes."

"Perhaps I could introduce you around at the Uniting Church vespers tomorrow night," Stephanie suggested. "Then you will meet a lot more people."

"I would like that," Bethany said. "The boys join us on Friday nights don't they?"

"Ah yes," Stephanie said. "You appear to know the essentials already!"

Stephanie was determined to get a head start on her studies for second semester, so she sat down to read *The Hobbit*, by J.R.R. Tolkien which she had been pleased to find on their syllabus. Most of the texts for this semester were modern, and quite daring for a traditional English Literature course.

Stephanie made herself comfortable down in the communal lounge in women's hall. There were only one or two other girls studying down there, and the chairs were nicely padded.

Stephanie had a pad of foolscap paper positioned conveniently next to her, and made extensive notes as she read. Stephanie had decided to do her English Literature essay for this semester on the use of landscape and imagery in the novel. *The Hobbit* was a large book, and reading it took her the entire day, with brief breaks for meals, and an hour off cleaning the women's assembly area.

After Stephanie had finished her studies, she knocked upon the door of the room belonging to May and Bethany, and they went down to the vespers program together.

On Sunday, Stephanie wore a pale grey dress, with gathered bows on the shoulders and a cross over bodice. It was necessary to prevent the neck from popping too far open, so she pinned it shut with an antique broach Aunt Moira had given her last Christmas.

The seniors at Silver Springs religious high school, together with the school band, were taking the Reformed Church service. It seemed as though most of the school had come with them, and the meeting hall was quite crowded.

Stephanie just managed to locate Jeff amongst the crush, and made her way towards him. He had an empty seat next to him, so it looked like he wanted her to sit with him.

Jeff said "Hello" when Stephanie sat down, but remained pretty quiet throughout the service. Stephanie concluded that he was tired, knowing that he sometimes wore himself out with extra hours of cleaning work during the week.

"The band music is really lively," Stephanie remarked half way through the program. "I always enjoy marches and African American Spirituals".

Jeff shrugged. "It's a bit noisy for my taste", he said.

"Do you prefer the classics?" Stephanie asked.

"Yes," Jeff said, "That is, when I listen to music at all."

"I like songs and ballads," Stephanie said. "Things that match the poetry I study."

Jeff grunted non-committedly, but Stephanie could tell he did not agree.

After the service Stephanie went to say "Hello" to several of the high school students she had gotten to know socially. Stephanie was always happy to meet people who lived in the local area, and tried not to confine herself to the university social circle.

Jeff, who was not much of a mixer, declined the invitation to be introduced to the schoolies. He elected instead to go ahead to the cafeteria, and get himself lunch. Stephanie noticed immediately she arrived at the cafe that he had not saved her a seat.

"It's probably Jeff's way of punishing me for having disagreed with him earlier over not one, but two things", Stephanie thought wryly.

Stephanie sat with Phoebe and Kathy and tried not to worry about Jeff, but out of the corner of her eye she could see him deliberately turning his back towards her.

Phoebe noticed Jeff's manner too, and remarked: "What an eloquent back Jeffrey Mannington has - his shoulders can almost talk! Whatever have you done to cop all this from him, Stephanie?"

"I haven't done anything, except not do things his way today", Stephanie said.

Kathy gave her a sympathetic look and said, "Don't let him rule you, girl."

"I try not to," Stephanie said, "But I can't always fathom him."

"Is it worth trying?" Phoebe asked.

"Let's not get into that," Stephanie said. "I once thought so, and I can't change my feelings over-night."

"It might be an idea," Kathy murmured.

"Jeff is still nice to me sometimes," Stephanie said uncomfortably. "And besides, we are living on the same campus. I couldn't get very far away from him even if I wanted."

"Yes", Phoebe said. "I can see why you would want to avoid a messy break-up, especially if you still care for him."

After classes finished on Monday, Stephanie worked on an analysis to present at a poetry tutorial for English Literature on Wednesday that week. Stephanie wanted to get her paper out of the way, and had been assured that the Professor would make sure she was not disadvantaged by going first.

Stephanie had to analyse some pieces by T.S. Elliot. She concentrated on identifying and describing the patterns, poetic effects, and diction used in the poem. Stephanie was bothered somewhat by the lack of narrative clarity in the Modernist style, but attempted to enter into the spirit of the piece and described it as an integral part of the poetic message. She did a bit of reading from books of literary criticism found in the library to back her argument.

Stephanie saw Jeff at tea and was uncertain whether she should approach, even though there was an empty seat beside him. Jeff, however, waved and invited her to sit down.

"Are you sure?" Stephanie queried, looking him straight in the eye.

"You are welcome," Jeff said. "Melanie, Jonathon and I were just talking about basketball."

"Yes", Jonathon said. "The competition re-commences this week."

"Jeff has joined us on the administrative team," Melanie informed her. "He will be acting as a referee this semester."

"That is great", Stephanie exclaimed.

"I am also coaching one of the C grade teams," Jeff said. "I could find something for you to do Stephanie, if you want to come along at times."

"I would like that", Stephanie replied, "But remember that I have that late class on Thursdays."

"We will work around that," Jeff said. "Actually, I believe one of your classmates is in my C grade team."

"Dylan plays C grade", Stephanie said.

"Well, I'm his boss now," Jeff said.

"Try telling the Biology Master that!" Stephanie said.

"Only if it becomes necessary," Jeff said whimsically.
Stephanie laughed.

Lunch time Tuesday, Jeff told Stephanie that the team he was coaching would play a match in the afternoon, and invited her to attend. Stephanie arrived at the gymnasium in good time for play to commence.

Jeff was there already, putting the boys through their paces. He waved when he saw Stephanie, and handed her his jacket and a clip-board to hold. (Apparently that was what he meant by giving her something to do.)

"Sit over there," Jeff said, indicating a position along the side of the court.

Stephanie sat down and watched Jeff as he gave the guys a few last pointers, reminding one to "Concentrate on defence", another to "Remember to pass", and several to "Stay with the ball".

When play commenced, Jeff came and sat down beside Stephanie. They concentrated on the game, watching the players, and noting their individual strengths and weaknesses. Several times Jeff asked her to jot down an idea. It was the beginning of the season, and he hoped to encourage the players to improve their skills.

It was an energetic, but slow scoring game, with both teams pursuing the ball from one end of the court to the other. Whenever it looked like someone was going to throw a basket, they were blocked, and the ball was headed down in the opposite direction. Occasionally a strong player managed to get through and sink a basket.

"The defence is adequate," Jeff commented, "But they need to work on their offence and shooting."

"They do seem to lack focus", Stephanie observed, trying to sound knowledgeable.

"The captain is new, but he will get the hang of it. It is a matter of learning to lead from within," Jeff remarked. "Maybe I should make Dylan the vice-captain, he is good."

"They are working very hard," Stephanie said, "But it would be nice to have more baskets to show for it."

"That it would!" Jeff said. "I will speak to them at half-time."

Half-time came and Jeff got up to have a word to the players, outlining a strategy for outwitting the other's defence and concentrating on throwing baskets.

"Get the ball up our end," Jeff urged them, "And don't let them take it back. I don't want to see it cross the half-way mark until you have sunk a basket. Pass the ball to another player when you think you are going to be tackled."

Jeff sat down next to Stephanie again, and the second half of the match got underway. He remained intent on the whereabouts of the ball, and called out "Go, go now", to several players. Thus encouraged, the team lifted their offence and ended the match a number of points ahead.

Jeff was pleased that his team had won, and walked onto the court to congratulate and mentor them. Stephanie was left holding his belongings, and feeling a bit superfluous. Eventually Jeff came back to Stephanie, and suggested that they go to the cafeteria and get some tea.

Stephanie presented her analysis of T.S. Elliot in the English Literature tutorial time Wednesday. Stephanie concentrated on style and ambiguity, and the possibility of multiple meanings. It went down quite well and generated a great deal of discussion. Stephanie got eight out of ten for the paper.

Milton, who had also chosen to do T.S. Elliot, was far more outspoken in his extrapolation of the meaning of the poems than Stephanie was prepared to be. He sounded pretty well read, and just a bit more 'worldly-wise' than her. She heard he got nine out of ten for his effort.

Thursday Stephanie saw Jeff at lunch, where he was sitting with Roger and Tony. There appeared to be a space next to him, so she went to join them. Almost immediately, Jeff stood up and prepared to leave.

"I have to go now," he said.

"Oh no Jeff," Stephanie said, "That is a bit abrupt!"

"I really am busy", Jeff replied. "I have something to do this afternoon".

"I don't mean to doubt your word," Stephanie said, "But are you sure you can't stay for a minute?"

"I'm sure!" Jeff said, "I have to get to work." He walked off and left her alone with the other guys.

"You have chased Jeff off," Roger said mockingly. "I think he is getting tired of you."

"Ha, ha, funny joke", Stephanie said. "I hope it is not really like that."

"That shouldn't be the problem," Tony said. "We have been sitting here for a while. I am nearly ready to leave myself."

"The seed of worry has been planted now," Stephanie gave

Roger a wry look. "I am going to fret throughout Life Science."

Their Life Science lab was mostly theoretical for a change. They discussed the observations made during last week's hike, and worked through some formulae based upon the results of the water PH and phosphate tests.

They had caught a jar full of swimming creepy-crawlies, and the Biology Master explained that a special statistical computation could be used to calculate the population density of the species in that particular section of the stream. Then they were given some time to write their results up. They got out about half-past four.

Friday Stephanie had a busy morning with classes, and spent the afternoon cleaning the women's assembly area and preparing it to be used by groups of visitors over the weekend. This particular weekend comprised a type of reunion for Silver Springs University graduates, and was known as the "Alumni Festival". Hence a number of additional meetings had been scheduled for the former students benefit.

To her surprise, Stephanie ran into Jeff at the university post office on her way back to girls' dorm. Stephanie was uncertain of his mood, so she did not approach him.

Jeff saw her, however, and said "Hello".

"Hi Jeff," Stephanie said. "So you are talking to me now!"

"Sure," Jeff answered. "Why wouldn't I be?"

"You were pretty brusque yesterday afternoon," Stephanie

explained. "The guys commented after you left."

"Don't worry about them, Stephanie," Jeff said.

"I'm not worried about them, at least not very much," Stephanie said. "I would like some consistency from you though."

"That might be asking a bit much, Stephanie," Jeff said, "I have to do things my own way. Forget it, and come up to tea with me."

"But Jeff...", Stephanie began.

"Don't you want to come to tea with me?" Jeff asked manipulatively.

"Of course I do!" Stephanie said. "I missed having lunch with you."

"Well, come along then," Jeff said.

They went up to tea and had a pleasant enough time. Jeff made an effort to entertain her by telling amusing stories about incidents that had occurred around the university during the two years prior to her arrival.

Friday Stephanie saw Jeff at tea, and he said that he would meet her by the far-left door to the women's assembly area, so that they could sit together during Uniting Church vespers.

"Are you sure?" Stephanie said. "There will be a fair crowd."

"Yes," Jeff said, "I will be there, and we can go together."

Stephanie was thrilled and took care dressing. She decided that she would wear a soft jumper and matching woven cotton skirt, because it was a cool evening. The jumper was made of cream wool with pink and gold threads passing through it. Jeff had seen her in this outfit, and always seemed to like it.

Stephanie arrived at the women's assembly hall a few minutes early, and positioned herself where she would be sure to be seen. Joelle and Milton passed by and invited her to join them, but Stephanie said that she was waiting for Jeff.

Time passed, and Stephanie got tired of standing alone as the hall filled. She began to worry that she had misheard Jeff and was standing by the wrong door, but Stephanie did not dare leave in case he arrived and she missed him.

The meeting started, and Stephanie waited a few more minutes in case Jeff showed up tardily. When Stephanie was sure that he was not coming to that particular door, she allowed herself to move, and went around to check the other doors.

Stephanie stepped into the back of women's assembly area and scanned the crowd for Jeff's shaggy head. She could not see him, but she could see Melanie and Jonathon sitting towards the back. Stephanie slipped into the pew beside them, asking in a whisper whether they had seen Jeff. They said they had not.

"I don't think that Jeff is coming," Jonathon said. "He doesn't really like Alumni Festival, it is too crowded."

"How could Jeff not be coming?" Stephanie said. "He said that he would meet me by the door."

"Well, if Jeff said he would be here, he will be," Melanie said. "Can you see Roger anywhere?"

"Roger is near the front," Stephanie said, "And Jeff is definitely not with him."

"Well, why don't you check where he said he would meet you again?" Jonathon suggested. "Jeff may be very late, that would be like him."

Stephanie followed Jonathon's suggestion, and slipped out of the women's assembly hall to stand waiting by the door for a few more minutes. Stephanie finally had to conclude that Jeff was not going to be there.

Thinking that if he had missed her, Jeff may have gone to the girls' dormitory to get her called, Stephanie went into the foyer of women's hall. Gloria was there taking care of reception and the phones. As it was Friday night and he had no other task, Warren was keeping her company.

Stephanie went up to Gloria and said: "Have you seen Jeffrey Mannington? He might have been looking for me."

"No," Gloria said. "Are you absolutely certain he was coming over here tonight?"

"Yes," Stephanie assured her. "He promised he would meet me at a certain place."

"Well, you might have missed him, or you might have been stood up," Gloria said.

"Steady on!" Warren broke in, "Jeff wouldn't do a thing like that!"

"Wouldn't he?" Gloria said. "I have seen him be careless of Stephanie's feelings before."

"I can hardly believe that of a mate," Warren said. "I am sorry Stephanie."

"Do you want me to try boys' dorm for you?" Gloria asked me. Stephanie nodded.

Gloria picked up the internal phone, and dialled through to men's hall. "Can I speak to Jeffrey Mannington please?" She covered the mouth piece and spoke to her, "I think he is there. They are paging him."

A minute later Gloria spoke again. "Yes, Jeffrey is that you? I have Stephanie Lowood here. She has been waiting for you for some time." There was a pause while Gloria listened to Jeff on the other end.

"You are not coming?" she echoed. "You want me to tell Stephanie that you are sorry, but you are tired?" Gloria's voice rose sharply. "You should have called her yourself to tell her that. The poor girl was quite worried...I am glad that you know you should have! Goodbye, Jeffrey."

Gloria hung the phone up abruptly, and turned to the younger girl. Stephanie couldn't help it, she started to cry right there in the foyer.

"Jeff is scoundrel sometimes," Gloria said putting an arm around her.

"I must admit, he has been very thoughtless," Warren agreed.

"It is too embarrassing for words," Stephanie said. "Please don't tell anyone."

Stephanie had drawn 'weekend duty' for Alumni Sunday. This meant that she had to perform one day's voluntary work in the cafeteria (or on the reception desk, or somewhere else that was too essential to be completely neglected) because it was weekend. This system had been instituted so that the majority of the students got their weekends free most of the time.

Stephanie reported to the cafeteria about six am, and elected to go on dish-wash. This meant that Stephanie had time for a quick breakfast, and then she had to begin work.

The dish-wash was a medium sized room situated between the servery and the dining area of the cafeteria. It was lined with sinks, taps, and a mechanical garbage disposal unit along one wall. Plates and cups were rinsed at the sinks, and stacked onto large flat trays, which were then placed upon a conveyor belt and passed through the industrial dish-washing machine built into the other wall.

Dylan and Garry, by some coincidence, had also drawn weekend duty and joined her in the dish-wash. They soon had an effective production line arranged, and were putting the plates through as fast as they were sent to them.

Breakfast wasn't too bad, but lunch was busy and tiring, and because of all the extra people, took an hour longer than usual. Tea was quieter and slower once again, as people lingered over their food. The guys working with her were very cheerful, and listening to them joke around kept her from becoming bored by the repetitious task.

On Monday, Stephanie began work on her essay for Standard English Language. She had chosen to do it on the Psalms, and to describe and analyse the Hebrew method of writing poetry. Stephanie found the topic particularly interesting, and spent most of the day closeted with her Bible and a pen.

Tea was an outdoor barbecue, with tables set up down the orchard side of the cafeteria. Stephanie joined the students lined up to collect long oval buns, then crossed to the griddle to have the bun filled with a pink sausage and fried onion rings.

When Stephanie had collected her food, she looked around for somewhere to sit. Luke and Tess were sitting with Phoebe and Bradley, so Stephanie went to join them.

"Hi guys," Stephanie said, and they moved over to make room for her.

"Hello Stephanie," Luke greeted her, "Long time no see."

"It has been a while," Stephanie said. "How are you two?"

"We are doing pretty well," Tess replied. "Aren't we Luke?"

Luke nodded in agreement. He had his mouth full.

"What is it like being one of the oldest new couples on campus?" Stephanie asked.

"Comfortable," Tess said. "We seem to have escaped the dramas you other girls have been having."

"You don't miss having looked around a bit more?" Stephanie queried.

"No," Tess said. "I knew just what I wanted in a guy, and when Luke seemed to like me too, I knew that he was it."

"That is amazing," Stephanie said. "So it just happens that way for some people? I can't imagine it happening for me."

"Maybe that is the problem," Tess said. "You don't have a clear enough vision of what you want."

"I hate to spoil your fun Stephanie," Bradley broke in from behind her, "But Jeffrey Mannington is staring at you."

"Jeff wouldn't be looking for me," Stephanie said. "Not after the way he has been behaving lately."

"He is holding two bowls of ice-cream," Phoebe pointed out, "And I don't think that he is planning to eat both of them himself."

"Typical!" Stephanie said, "Just when I get settled with my friends. It is like he has something against that."

Stephanie took a couple more minutes to say goodbye to her friends, and then she crossed over to where Jeff was standing. He brightened when she arrived.

"Hello Stephanie," Jeff said. "I got you some desert."

"Thanks," Stephanie said taking the bowl, "Chocolate and vanilla with a little bit of strawberry, fantastic!"

"I remembered exactly what you like," Jeff said, looking pleased with himself.

"Yes you did," Stephanie said, "But there was no need to bribe me."

"It's not a bribe Stephanie," Jeff said. "You are always wishing I was more like the other boyfriends, and I am obliging."

"I like you the way you are Jeff," Stephanie said. "You could just be a bit more attentive sometimes."

"I am attentive this afternoon," Jeff said. "Shall I get you a drink now?"

"Only if you want one too," Stephanie said somewhat bemused.

The team that Jeff was coaching was due to play another match Tuesday, and Jeff asked Stephanie to come along and observe. When she arrived, play had already commenced, and Jeff was perched on the edge of the stage.

He indicated that Stephanie should sit next to him there.

"How do I get up?" Stephanie asked.

Jeff extended his hand to help her jump up, but it was still too steep for someone her size.

"I'm sorry," Stephanie said disengaging her hand from his, "I'll have to go around by the steps."

Jeff retracted his hand and looked annoyed, "What is the use of reaching out to you Stephanie?" he said.

"Oh come on Jeff", Stephanie said. "I appreciate the gesture, it's just that I don't have big long legs like yours."

Jeff looked slightly appeased, and when Stephanie arrived at his side, he gave her the stop-watch to hold.

"The team is improving", Stephanie observed after a few minutes. "You have got a couple of players shooting quite neat baskets."

"Yes," Jeff agreed, "I've been drilling them all week."

"Oops," Stephanie said, "That was out".

"It happens sometimes, even with the best players," Jeff said. "And these have a bit to go to get their act together."

"Still," Stephanie commented, "They are pulling steadily ahead of the other team. You can be very proud of them."

"Yes," Jeff said, "They may win the C grade series if I keep working with them."

The team in question won that match by a comfortable number of points, and Jeff was very pleased. He jumped down from the stage, and joined the players on the court, chatting and congratulating them.

Jeff had left without collecting the stop-watch from her, so Stephanie went up to him to return it. She tried twice to speak to him, and finally had to tug gently on his arm.

Jeff looked at her in surprise. "What do you want Stephanie?" he said.

"Just to give you this," Stephanie said meekly.

"Oh," Jeff said and took the stop-watch from her. "That could have waited."

"Sorry Jeff," Stephanie said. "Will you be coming to tea soon?"

"No," Jeff said, "I have to speak to the guys."

"I will wait for you then," Stephanie said. "I am prepared to be patient."

"No, you go ahead Stephanie," Jeff ordered. "You will be in the way here anyway."

Stephanie left feeling snubbed and humiliated. Jeff may have had his reasons, but there was no need for him to have spoken to her in that manner. He did it in front of the other guys too - they must have wondered what was going on, and possibly thought the worst! Stephanie choked back the tears, and carried on bravely towards the cafeteria.

Stephanie was sitting in their room doing the weekly reading report for Child Development, when she looked up to catch Joelle gazing at her.

"What is the matter?" Stephanie asked.

"There is nothing wrong with me," Joelle said. "It's just that you didn't look too good last night Stephanie."

"I wasn't feeling the best," Stephanie admitted.

"You can talk to me, you know," Joelle said. "I would hate for what happened earlier this year to come between us permanently."

"Thank you," Stephanie said, "But I don't really enjoy talking about the problems I am having with Jeff. People come down so hard on him...and then I feel stupid for still liking him."

"We can't always choose who we like," Joelle said. "Things don't go smoothly for me and Milton all the time, either."

"I wouldn't have guessed," Stephanie said. "Milton seems like such an earnest guy. And he really likes you."

"Most of the time he is great!" Joelle said. "But we do have occasional disagreements - mostly because he has not been part of the Reformed Church all his life. He has done a few things I wouldn't have done, and we see things differently."

"I am sorry," Stephanie said. "I hope that it is something you can sort out."

"It most likely is," Joelle said. "What about you and Jeff. Where do you stand?"

"Well, we got really close for a while," Stephanie said. "Then Jeff got weird. Friendly one moment, and stand-offish the next. And just when I am convinced that it is over, he acts as sweet as pie."

"Sounds like the hot and cold treatment," Joelle said. "Jeff obviously means to keep you worried and insecure."

"Well he is succeeding!" Stephanie exclaimed. "And the funny thing is, I feel more intensely about him now, than I ever did before."

"He is laying siege to your self-respect," Joelle said. "Have you ever refused him anything he wanted? That gets guys worked up."

"Hard to tell," Stephanie mused. "Jeff always has to be the boss."

"I'll bet you have denied him something, somewhere along the line," Joelle said. "He wants it, and is reeling you in like a fish."

"What would you do if you were me?" Stephanie asked. "Do you think I should try to find out what I did wrong?"

"No I don't think so," Joelle mused. "I would stand firm, concentrate on my study and try not to let him get me down."

"Does that work with Milton?" Stephanie said.

"Mostly," Joelle said, "But then, Milton is not as peculiar as Jeff."

CHAPTER EIGHT: A SOCIAL LIFE

Stephanie had classes in the morning, and a long Life Science laboratory in the afternoon. Some of the questions were tricky, and she took her time getting all of the sketches right. Stephanie was the last to leave the science building. She was tired, and had to admit that she was missing spending time with Jeff.

The cafeteria was almost deserted and Stephanie grabbed the last of the hot food. She ate in silence, and then remembering that the gymnasium was a hive of activity at this hour, Stephanie decided to drop by there.

Jeff was sitting on a bench watching an A grade match. By some coincidence, it was the team that Bradley played for, so Stephanie sat down to watch too. It was some time before Jeff spoke to her, and when he did, he was rather gruff. "How are you today Stephanie?" he said.

"I am okay Jeff," Stephanie answered.

"What do you think of this match?" Jeff asked.

"The players are pretty smooth," Stephanie said. "I can see why they are in A grade." (Actually, Bradley was a better player than Jeff, light on his feet and well-coordinated, but Stephanie judged it was not politic to say as much.)

"Yes, they are pretty good," Jeff said, "But you are late, the match is almost over."

"You know my Life Science lab almost always runs late,"

Stephanie said despondently.

"You don't sound very happy," Jeff said.

"I am confused," Stephanie said. "I thought we had agreed on a certain style of friendship a while back, but sometimes you don't act like we are friends at all."

"I am still thinking about that," Jeff said.

"Can't you make up your mind?" Stephanie said. "You can't like me at breakfast, not like me at lunch and then like me at tea again. It's wearing me out."

"Sometimes that is exactly how I feel," Jeff said.

"Do you have any idea what is setting it off?" Stephanie asked.

"You don't fit into my routine," Jeff said. "I have a lot to do."

"I have been trying," Stephanie said.

"That has been good," Jeff said, "But it hasn't been enough. I still feel pressured. I don't know what would fix it."

"Nor do I," Stephanie said.

"Try to forget it," Jeff said. "I just don't like knowing that things are expected of me. It's too much pressure."

The next day, Stephanie devoted the free period between assembly and lunch to her "Bible as literature" essay, bringing the rough draft almost to completion. After lunch Stephanie spent an hour cleaning the women's assembly area, and then Stephanie went across to the library to find some commentaries in the hopes of locating some authoritative quotes to back up her own conclusions.

Stephanie collected several large volumes from the reference section, and made her way towards the religion section. Andrew Grosvy was there, carefully scrutinising the titles.

"Hello, Andrew", Stephanie said.

"Oh, hi Stephanie," Andrew said, looking surprised to see her.

"How are you doing with your Standard English Language essay?" Stephanie asked.

"Great!" Andrew said, beginning to look enthusiastic. "It is much better than what we had to do last semester."

"Yes, it is more relevant to you Theology guys," Stephanie agreed. "Do you know which of these books has a good section on the Psalms?"

"There are a couple here that are just on the Psalms," Andrew said, "Let me see if I can find them".

"Thanks," Stephanie said, "I have a couple of Dewey numbers here too."

"I don't use the Dewey system so much as browse," Andrew said. "Here are two good books. Would you like to study together for a while?"

"That would be nice," Stephanie answered. They chose one of the larger tables and shared it quietly, occasionally drawing one another's attention to an especially interesting section in their respective books. It was nice to have some neutral, non-demanding male company for a change.

When Stephanie arrived at the Uniting Church vespers, Jeff was in a pensive mood. He had saved her a seat, but merely sighed when

Stephanie arrived and sat in it.

"How has your day been?" Stephanie asked.

"I have been on the computer all day." Jeff said. "I have been writing a program in Pascal."

"How is it going?" Stephanie asked.

"Okay I guess", Jeff answered, "There is a lot of typing, and I am finding a lot of errors whenever I try to run the program."

"No wonder you look tired," Stephanie said.

"Listen Stephanie," Jeff said suddenly, "I am sick of sitting still, let's get out of here and go for a walk."

"Sure," Stephanie said, "But we had better move quickly, the song service is about to begin."

Jeff took her by the arm and led her outside, across the campus, and towards the area behind the workshops. Stephanie started getting a bit nervous, because it was her understanding that this area was out of bounds after dark, but she continued to follow him.

"Are we meant to go down there?" Stephanie inquired anxiously.

"I don't care," Jeff said. "I want to be alone with you."

"Oh," Stephanie said, "I don't want to get into any trouble."

"You won't", Jeff said, "Trust me."

Jeff stopped suddenly on a pathway in a shadowy area and turned her around to face him. Stephanie gazed up at him breathlessly.

"I am sorry I have been taking things out on you lately," Jeff burst out. "I did mean it when I said that I liked you, and wanted us to stay friends."

Jeff was leaning over her, and it would have been easy to touch him, but Stephanie held back. Even if he had brought her down here to get physical, Stephanie was determined to stick to her resolution to avoid imprudence. Anyway, there were things they needed to sort out first.

"I get the impression that you only like me when I stay in the little box you have designed for me," Stephanie said.

"That's exactly right!" Jeff said. "I couldn't have put it better myself."

"I am sorry Jeff," Stephanie said. "It isn't humanly possible for me to live like that."

"You may be right," Jeff said. "Sometimes I wonder whether we ought to forget our friendship. Hurting you was the last thing I wanted to do."

"No Jeff," Stephanie cried. "I have become very fond of you while we have been together."

"Me too," Jeff said, "That is what makes it so difficult."

"Tell me what it is that I could do to make you like me all the time," Stephanie begged.

"I don't know," Jeff said, "There's nothing, nothing specific."

"Please Jeff," Stephanie sobbed. "Tell me just one little thing I can do to fix things."

Jeff was silent for a long minute. He continued to lean over her, and Stephanie could feel the heat radiating from his body in the cold night air. Stephanie stepped closer to shelter from the wind, because he had dragged her out here without a jacket. Jeff seemed to relax a bit as she moved towards him.

"Talk more when you come up to me at mealtime," Jeff said at last. "I like girls who sound bright and cheerful."

"I'll try, Jeff," Stephanie said. "Can we go inside now? It is really cold out here."

"Yes," Jeff said, "It is probably time."

Sunday, after the Reformed Church service, May asked Stephanie if she would like to go for a walk. They had a quick lunch, and then set out down boys' walk and along the creek towards the plantations. When they reached the end of the track, they decided to retrace their steps back to campus, and ended up walking across the oval behind the campus.

It was a pleasant sunny day, not too warm, and yet not too cold if one was wearing a jacket. As the grass was dry to touch, Stephanie suggested that they sit down to do some winter sun-baking.

The girls sat and talked about simple things like their mutual love of the countryside, and finally fell to searching amongst the grass for clumps of clover. Stephanie was surprised to find not one, but two four leaf clovers, which she took back to her room and placed between the pages of her *Good News Bible*. Now she was assured of luck!

By this time, the sun was setting, and it was almost time for tea. Stephanie and May went across to the cafeteria, and waited on the side veranda for it to open. When it did, they were the first through the door, and had their pick of the food and places to sit.

Their other first-year friends trickled slowly in to join them, and even Jeff, who rarely joined her peers, came across to sit with her. He seemed amused, and remarked that Stephanie appeared very relaxed.

When they had eaten, Stephanie turned to May and said: "Thank you for the pleasant afternoon."

"You are welcome," May said. "I enjoyed it too."

"We will have to do it again sometime," Stephanie said, "Especially in spring when the wild flowers come out."

"I would like that!" May said. Soon after that, she excused herself and went back to the dormitory to do a bit of study.

Jeff asked Stephanie whether she would like to go to the recreation area and watch some sport on the television, as the New South Wales Rugby League season was in full swing, and the rest of the evening passed very pleasantly.

Stephanie spent her free time Monday working on her database for Fundamentals of Computing. She had already completed the compulsory word processing exercises, and the addresses from the database were to be merged into the printout. Stephanie continued work on the computer into the afternoon, typing as accurately as she could.

In the evening when Stephanie was all computer-screened out, she decided to visit May in the other room.

"Hi," Stephanie said. "I am just taking a break."

"So am I," May said pushing aside her books, "Would you like to play a game of scrabble?"

"Did you bring a board from home?" Stephanie exclaimed.

"Yes," May said, "I like the game a lot."

"I would enjoy a game then," Stephanie said.

They set up the board for a lengthy tournament. Stephanie was used to winning quite easily, and was surprised to find that May outclassed her severely. May always seemed to manage to place the consonants on double and triple word score squares, and clocked up absolutely enormous scores.

After a while, her attention wandered and Stephanie began to eavesdrop on the conversation between Bethany and Grace, who was also visiting in the room. It concerned her somewhat that the straight-forward Bethany had taken to hanging around with the more devious Grace.

"We don't have to worry about dates for the up-coming tea," Grace was saying, "The computer will match us with partners."

"I wonder how it will do that?" Bethany mused.

"It will look for things people have in common, I guess," Grace said. "It would be funny if it split all the established couples up because they didn't suit!"

"What a mess that would make," Bethany said. "But it is not very likely, the people who are together must suit, or they wouldn't be together."

"I don't know," Grace said. "It would give us a go at the cute guys the other girls are hogging."

"You know Bethany," Stephanie broke in, "It might be better not to take all your relationship advice from Grace."

"Don't get your advice from Stephanie either," Grace retorted. "She overlooks perfectly nice guys, and lets herself be treated like a doormat by a creep like Jeffrey Mannington."

"That's a bit strong Grace," Stephanie said.

"The truth hurts does it, Stephanie?" Grace said. "If I were going out with Jeffrey, I wouldn't let him treat ME the way he does you."

"However would you stop Jeff behaving the way he does to me?" Stephanie said asked.

"That's easy", Grace smiled fatuously, "I know exactly what guys want."

May and Bethany were both listening to this exchange with bated breath. Stephanie looked to them for support, but obviously neither knew what to say.

"If it were as simple as turning on the feminine wiles, I would have Jeff eating out of my hand already," Stephanie said.

"I am prettier than you", Grace said. "I could take him off of you any time I liked. Lucky for you, I am not interested at the moment."

"If you think that Jeff is a creep, why would you want to go out with him?" Stephanie queried.

"He is a man," Grace said fluttering her eyelashes, "And he will probably make a lot of money after he graduates."

"That is disgusting", Stephanie said, "You are talking like a hustler."

"Now you are being catty!" Grace said.

"Don't argue girls," Bethany said peaceably. "I don't think you would be half so mercenary if you found true love Grace."

"As long as it came with all the trimmings," Grace said.

"We all want security," May said diplomatically. "And we all want an attractive partner. You two need to find some middle ground."

Tuesday, Stephanie was back in their room after class, doing more Education reading, when Joelle came in carrying some sheets of coloured paper.

"Hi, Stephanie," she said, "I have got the forms for the Computer Tea."

"Let me see," Stephanie said.

"Sure," Joelle said, "I got a spare one for you."

"And one for Milton too, I see." I said.

"Yes," Joelle said. "They say that if a guy and a girl give exactly the same answers to each of the questions, they are sure to be matched together by the computer."

"So you and Milton are thinking of rigging it," Stephanie said. "I knew there must be a way for couples to stay together!"

"It's not entirely fool-proof," Joelle said, "But they say it works nine times out of ten."

"That's great," Stephanie said. "I wonder if Jeff would like to do that."

"You could ask him," Joelle suggested.

"I think I will," Stephanie said. "There are only about ten questions here. Sex, height, weight, age, favourite lecturer, various interests. It's not very discerning."

"It's only a game really," Joelle said. "Computers can't literally match people up."

"It might be fun," Stephanie said. "Grace is looking forward to a blind date."

"All of Grace's dates are blind," Joelle commented wryly. "She puts that little intelligent thought into them!"

"Her main criterion seems to be that the guy is going out with someone else," Stephanie complained. "She was threatening to steal Jeff yesterday."

"It's the extra sense of challenge," Joelle explained, "Together with the feeling that she is winning over another girl."

"Did you feel like that when you went out with Jeff?" Stephanie asked, giving her room-mate a long stare. It was still a sore topic.

"Only the tiniest bit," Joelle said. "It seemed fair enough for me to accept the date. I was being naive, and I am not proud of myself."

"You are okay with Milton now, aren't you?" Stephanie asked anxiously. Stephanie had never thought of Joelle as 'naïve' or even particularly vulnerable before, she seemed so self-contained.

"Yes," Joelle said, "We are on a good streak."

Wednesday, Stephanie had a busy day with classes and study, and did not get to speak to Jeff about the Computer Tea until after worship that evening. To her surprise, he did not like the idea.

"I don't want to be matched up with anyone by a computer," Jeff said. "I won't be going. I never have before."

"Would it be so bad to be matched with me?" Stephanie asked.

"Probably not," Jeff admitted, "But what about the outside chance that we don't get put together? I don't want to get stuck with someone else."

"You would live you know!" Stephanie teased gently.

"I can do without the agro," Jeff grouched. "It is a silly function."

"Come on honey," Stephanie said, putting on her best "bright" manner, the one that Jeff said he liked. "How else will you get tea?"

"I will go to Sydney for the weekend," Jeff said looking stubborn. "Then you can't make me go to anything I don't want to."

"Sorry Jeff," Stephanie said. "I wasn't trying to make you do anything against your will, I just wanted your company at a special evening."

"No," Jeff said frowning, "I am going to fly down to Sydney, and it is too long since I have been."

"I thought you weren't happy there," Stephanie said.

"Some things you can't get away from," Jeff said.

"Will you stay with your family?" Stephanie queried.

"Nowhere else to go," Jeff grumbled.

"It isn't just the Computer Tea is it?" Stephanie said with sudden insight.

"No, they have been putting the pressure on for some time," Jeff reported.

"They still care about you then," Stephanie said.

"Only enough to be demanding," Jeff concluded, "Not enough to be supportive."

"And would you have liked them to be supportive?" Stephanie asked.

"Of course," Jeff said. "Things have been hay-wire for me for a few years, and all they have done is criticise me."

"What is it this weekend?" Stephanie queried.

"My Sister's nineteenth birthday." Jeff answered.

"You could send a card, or get flowers delivered," Stephanie suggested.

"I would never hear the last of it," Jeff said. "Get off my back, Stephanie."

"I didn't know there was that much contact between you and them," Stephanie said. "You haven't mentioned any before."

"There isn't usually," Jeff said. "I've managed to have a quiet life here, but sometimes they call."

"Well, good luck with the visit then," Stephanie said.

"Thank you," Jeff said. "I'm going to need it."

Thursday, the Life Science lab dragged on well into the afternoon, prompting the class to gossip as they sketched specimens and answered questions. Dylan began talking to the plastic skeleton in a doleful voice, and asked it what it did at night when the lab was closed. Stephanie began to giggle helplessly, and Cara told him to be quiet.

At last they were all finished, and on their way up to the cafeteria for tea. Stephanie went to put her books down outside the cafe foyer, and her half filled out form for the Computer Tea fell out.

Dylan pounced on it, and asked Stephanie whether she thought that the computer would match her with the guy of her dreams. "What are you looking for?" he said. "Someone tall dark and handsome?"

"Obviously someone nothing like you," Cara retorted.

"I am heartbroken," Dylan wailed. "How can you talk like that Cara? I love you so."

"Actually," Stephanie said, "I had forgotten that was there. I am not planning to go. Jeff will be away that weekend, and I can't really attend it alone."

"Oh no," Cara cried. "You must put your form in! If you do, the computer will assign you a partner."

"I'm not so keen on that," I said, "Not when I am otherwise connected."

"Since when did you become a snob, Stephanie?" Dylan asked. "You used to join in with everybody."

"Here, give that to me," Garry said. "I am going to make sure that you put it in." Taking the form from Dylan he quickly ticked all the remaining boxes.

"Not fair," Stephanie said, trying to snatch it back. "You have filled in my height, and weight, and everything. You can't possibly know those."

"I'm a good guesser," Garry said holding the form above her head, "Aren't I Dylan?"

"Right every time!" Dylan said and laughed. "That's why he does so well in Life Science."

Garry folded her form over twice, and strode over to the cardboard post box in the foyer. He dropped it through the slit in the top, and they all heard it fall with a plop onto the pile of other forms in there.

Just then, the Director of Student Services arrived to empty the box for the day, and Stephanie watched in consternation as it was carried away.

"Now you have to go Stephanie, or you will be leaving some poor guy all alone," Dylan crowed.

"You guys are awful," Stephanie said.

Cara took her by the shoulders, and propelled her into the cafeteria. "Normally I would agree with you, Steph," she said, "But this time they are right."

Stephanie looked around for Jeff at breakfast and lunch on Friday. He was no-where to be seen, so she concluded that he had already left for his weekend in Sydney. Stephanie said a couple of prayers that God would be with him, and then turned her attention to her own weekend.

Kathy had invited Stephanie to go shopping with her. They met at the back of women's hall at one-thirty, to catch the university car on one of its regular trips to Northcoast train station.

Luke was now one of the regular drivers, and he dropped them off at the station, telling them that he would see them at 2:30, 3:30 or 4:30, depending which service they wanted to take back to university.

Kathy's first port of call was the Westpac Bank, where she

withdrew some money, and used their travel service to book herself a ticket to Armadale for the September break.

"Home to see Owen?" Stephanie said.

"Yes, Kathy said, "At least for the first week."

"That will be nice," Stephanie said. "I honestly don't know how you two manage so far apart."

"It is a strong friendship," Kathy said. "We have known each other since we were kids, in fact we have been going out since I was fifteen, and Owen was sixteen."

"How did you get together?" Stephanie asked.

"Local Evangelical Church activities," Kathy said. "Owen was always very active, and that caught my eye."

"And when did you decide to come to university?" Stephanie asked.

"Towards the end of high school," Kathy answered. "Owen was a bit upset, he had hoped that I would do something local."

"Is he okay about it now?" Stephanie queried.

"Mostly. I know he misses me and counts the days," Kathy said. "It's not quite so bad for me, because I have so much company at university."

Their next stop was the fabric store. Stephanie bought some fabric, because she thought she might be able to make a dress during the holidays. It had bright yellow sunflowers scattered across a white background.

Kathy wanted some artificial flowers, and some ribbon to plait through her hair for the Computer Tea, so they visited the small department store.

"You will look lovely," Stephanie said, "But why would you bother if Owen is not going to be there?"

"I can dream can't I?" Kathy said. "He is always here in my mind, and if any photos are taken I usually show him."

"You have got it all worked out," Stephanie said.

"Not quite, but I have made some compromises," Kathy said. "What about you - are you suddenly flying solo? I haven't seen Jeffrey around today."

"Jeff's gone to Sydney," Stephanie said, "And I have been bullied into letting the computer match me with someone."

Stephanie told Kathy about Dylan and Garry, and she laughed.

"It sounds as if you have some good mates there!" she said.

"I'm not sure," Stephanie demurred. "I don't know how I will explain it to Jeff."

"Tell him the truth, that always works best," Kathy said, "Anyway, it was him that went off and left you."

"True," Stephanie said. "Let's go to the chemist and look at cosmetics. I need some flesh coloured Clearasil or something, I have a couple of spots coming up."

They browsed through the chemist, and then visited the general store. The township surrounding the station was small and countrified, and the girls soon exhausted the places of interest. By three-thirty they were waiting for the university car to return.

Their Education class had a special weekend workshop set up in the Education hall with children from the local pre-school. The teaching students were required to ask the children whether a tall thin glass, or a short fat glass had more water in it. Piaget's theory predicted that the younger children would be fooled by the water level and identify the taller glass as fuller, even though the volume of water in the two glasses was identical. The same theory also suggested that an elongated row of lollies, would be infinitely more impressive than the same number of lollies all piled together.

Most of the children did give answers that tallied with Piaget's findings, but there were an interesting number of variations. A couple of children chose the fat glass over the thin and one child almost deduced that the two sets of lollies were identical. However, even the shrewd children couldn't stick to their conclusions in the face of repeated questioning. On the whole, Stephanie had to conclude that Piaget appeared to be right in his conclusions, given that the questions were asked in a particular manner.

Stephanie told Andrew Grosvy all about this at lunch, and he had to laugh despite his predominantly devout manner.

Suppressed excitement reigned throughout the weekend, as everyone valiantly tried to concentrate upon observing the days of rest. The Inter-denominational praise service provoked some heated discussion, and the Reform Church service caused a bit of excitement as one of the second year Theology students made his debut as a preacher.

Most of the students began to feel free to let their hair down about five o'clock in the evening. Being winter, and in a situation where they were shielded by the surrounding mountains, the sun set and darkness arrived quite early.

The Computer Tea was designed to be a formal occasion, so Stephanie wore the black taffeta dress that she had bought during the mid-year break. The bodice was a slim fit, and the full skirt rustled as it swung around her legs. It left her shoulders bare, so Stephanie wore her black cardigan across to the cafeteria.

Once there, Stephanie felt that she would be warm enough, and slipped the cardigan off. Collecting her ticket, Stephanie crossed to the table to find with whom she had been matched. To her amazement, Garry was sitting in the seat that corresponded to hers.

"Hello, Stephanie," Garry said as Stephanie approached. "You look very nice tonight."

"Hello Garry," Stephanie said. "What does your ticket say?"

"A21," Garry said innocently. "Apparently we are a perfect match."

"You trickster!" Stephanie exclaimed. "You must have filled my form out exactly the same as yours. Admit it, you did this on purpose."

"Yes," Garry said with a grin, "The mood you were in, I thought you would prefer to be with someone you knew."

"You were right, you know," Stephanie murmured. "I am pleased that I don't have to make polite conversation and explain that

I have a boyfriend who is away for the weekend. However, you didn't have to make a martyr of yourself."

"I am not making a martyr of myself at all," Garry said. "I didn't feel like being stuck with someone strange either. All of the girls that I have asked out have been from our little group, and I prefer to be with a friend."

"I see," Stephanie said. "Go on."

"You were looking pretty unobtainable," Garry said with a laugh, "But while the cat's away..."

"By the rules we play!" Stephanie said firmly.

"I was afraid you would see it that way," Garry said. "Nevertheless, I am finding this quite amusing. It is time someone took you out and treated you decently for a change. We can talk about Life Science all evening if that makes you more comfortable."

"I don't want to talk about Life Science all evening," Stephanie said. "Let's act like this is a date, within limits."

"Good!" Garry said. "Can I pour you a drink then, my lady?"

"Thank you kind sir," Stephanie replied.

Stephanie relaxed and began to glance around. Most of the established couples had managed to get themselves assigned to each other. Everyone else seemed to be placed more or less randomly. Height did not seem to be amongst the determining factors, because Stephanie could see the tallest girl on campus paired with what must have been the shortest guy.

Appetisers and soup were delivered, and Stephanie busied herself with the task of eating. Garry was telling her all about his favourite foods. He seemed to like most things, including the food being served that night.

Stephanie nodded and agreed as Garry talked. It was a pleasant change from sitting beside someone who complained about the food. Stephanie had always held the theory that people who liked their food were good natured by temperament. Garry seemed to prove that hypothesis right.

Between courses Phoebe dropped by her chair and stopped to chat. "What are you two doing sitting together?" she exclaimed. "Don't tell me that the computer did this. It couldn't possibly be so logical."

"No," Stephanie said. "Garry did it on purpose. The naughty boy has tricked me into a date."

"You look like you are having a good time," Phoebe said.

"Yes", Stephanie said, "It has worked out all-right. Who have you been paired with?"

"Tom," Phoebe said. "Actually, I am a bit disappointed. I can see Tom any day in English class."

"Don't tell Tom that," Stephanie advised.

"I wouldn't dream of being so rude," Phoebe said. "He is my date for the night after all".

"Did you happen to see who Kathy was with?" Stephanie asked curiously.

"Larry Forbes," Phoebe replied. "They appear to be getting along pretty well."

"That's nice," Stephanie said.

The main course arrived and Phoebe went back to her seat.

Garry claimed her attention again, and began to talk about his hobbies. With the exception of bushwalking, they were very different to hers, but Stephanie was pleased to hear that he liked to make things out of wood and metal.

When the meal was finished, Garry walked her across to women's hall, and behaved like a perfect gentleman.

"Thank you for the company," Stephanie said.

"You are welcome," Garry said. "I hope that we are still comrades. I didn't mean to complicate things for you with Jeff."

"I'm basically flattered," Stephanie said. "Except that Jeff manoeuvred me into a relationship without ever officially asking me. I'm determined not to let anything like that happen another time."

"Point taken," Garry said. "It's not my intention to be anything like Jeff. If the situation ever arises again I will ask properly."

"Of course this conversation would have more relevance if I were currently single," Stephanie said carefully.

"That goes without saying," Garry said. "I will see you in class Monday."

"Good night," Stephanie said. Garry left, and Stephanie went back into the dormitory. It had been a surprisingly pleasant evening.

CHAPTER NINE: ASSAULT

Stephanie spent the morning after class cleaning women's assembly area, and the afternoon reading a couple of novels by E.M. Forster for English Literature. Stephanie found the novels incredibly sad, and wondered however the author came to develop such a dismal world view. No matter how discouraged Stephanie became, her belief in God usually helped her look forward to a more positive future. She speculated that perhaps Forster did not have that.

In the evening Jeff arrived back. Stephanie ran into him outside the recreation area after tea, and asked how his weekend had gone. He said that he didn't want to talk about it, so Stephanie let him go back to his dorm.

In English Literature that morning, Bradley took a very interesting tutorial on *Three Cheers for the Paraclete* by Thomas Keneally. He compared it to several of the author's other novels and identified trends in the writing.

Stephanie was especially fascinated to hear that Keneally was a contemporary Australian author. The English Professor was also impressed, and she overheard him tell Brad that he had gotten eight out of ten for the tutorial.

Phoebe and Stephanie waited around after class to congratulate Brad on his presentation. He was pleased, and asked Stephanie if she was thinking of coming to watch him play basketball that afternoon.

"I guess I could," Stephanie said.

"I'll come and keep you company," Phoebe said. "I wouldn't mind seeing Brads play."

When Phoebe and Stephanie arrived in the gymnasium that afternoon, they noticed that Jeff was watching the basketball as well. They went to join him, but he turned away and made it clear he was trying to ignore them.

"What's wrong with him?" Phoebe whispered.

"I don't know," Stephanie said. "He hasn't been quite this bad before. Do you reckon we should leave?"

"No," Phoebe said. "It's our gym too, and Bradley is playing."

The girls stubbornly sat through the match, and congratulated Brad at the end, because his team won. Jeff got up and left, without saying a word to any of them.

Stephanie sat by Jeff in combined assembly, and although he had saved a space for her, he displayed the same sullen manner that he had for the past couple of days. When assembly was over, he resisted all her attempts to make polite conversation, and marched her outside.

"I have to talk to you Stephanie," Jeff said, grabbing her by the elbows and pulling her towards him.

"Sure Jeff," Stephanie said. "What do you want to talk about?"

"You have to stop following me around like this," Jeff said.

"What?" Stephanie exclaimed.

"Everywhere I've been this week, I've run into you," Jeff

complained. "You've been chasing me."

"I most certainly have not!" Stephanie said, shaking free of his hold. "I've been going to my own classes and worships."

"So why were you watching basketball yesterday?" Jeff demanded.

"Bradley was playing," Stephanie answered.

"He's nothing to you," Jeff said. "You must have been hoping I was there."

"No, it was a coincidence," Stephanie declared, "And so what if it hadn't been? We are in an established and negotiated friendship. I should be able to approach you."

"It still doesn't mean that you can follow me around, crowd me and stalk me," Jeff said.

"I was doing no such thing," Stephanie protested. "Something is wrong with your mind. You have come back from Sydney paranoid."

"No, I haven't," Jeff said. "It's you. Trailing after me all the time."

"I'll stay right away from you then," Stephanie said huffily.

"No need to go that far," Jeff snapped.

"We will both take some space then, that suit you?" Stephanie asked.

"Yes," Jeff said, "I had better go now." He lent over her glowering for a minute, and then walked off.

Stephanie went inside and went straight down to Kathy's room. Stephanie sobbed bitterly as she told her friend the story.

"I don't like the sound of that at all," Kathy said.

"Nor do I," Stephanie said. "I think that Jeff and I are breaking up."

"No, no," Kathy said, "I meant something more dangerous than that might be developing".

"What could be worse than breaking up?" Stephanie asked naively.

"It sounds as if Jeff is becoming obsessive," Kathy suggested gently.

"He has always been like that," Stephanie said, "There were patterns and habits he could never change."

"However did you put up with it?" Kathy said.

"It wasn't actually that bad," Stephanie reported, "At least he became predictable."

"Well, it would be nothing compared to the position you would find yourself in if Jeff's paranoia began to centre around you," Kathy warned.

"That would never happen," Stephanie assured her. "I am simply not important enough to attract anything like that to myself."

"Take care," Kathy said, "Too much modesty could get you into trouble."

"I always have been prudent," Stephanie answered. "And I always will."

"I hope that will be enough," Kathy said.

Garry and Stephanie were paired together to do a research

project on animal behaviour for Life Science. They decided that they would work on it in the library that evening.

"I have a Chemistry lab all afternoon," Garry said, "and I won't have much time to prepare my notes. Do you think that you could come over to men's hall immediately after worship in the evening?"

"Okay," Stephanie said, but she was secretly very nervous. With everything that was going on with Jeff, she was rather inclined to avoid the boys' dormitory.

"Don't worry," Garry said, seeing her face, "Just get me called over the public address system and I will come straight down to you."

Stephanie arrived at men's hall at the appointed time, and approached the Student Dean on the desk.

"Would you please page Garry Merton for me?" Stephanie asked.

"Sure," the guy on the desk said, and announced that Garry was wanted at reception.

Stephanie stood in the corridor, feeling a bit self-conscious on this alien turf. She was busily hoping that Garry wouldn't take too long to respond, when she noticed Jeff coming down the main stairs towards her.

Jeff marched straight up to her, and stood in front of her expectantly.

"Jeff," Stephanie said in puzzlement, "I didn't get you called."

"Why else would you be here?" Jeff said.

"I am looking for Garry," Stephanie said. "Did someone tell you that I was here, or did you see me through a window?"

"It doesn't matter," Jeff said. "So you don't want me for anything?"

"You are not involved in my errand tonight," Stephanie said diplomatically. "Would you please go back to your business?"

Garry arrived just then. "What's this?" he exclaimed. "Stephanie is here to work on an assignment with me, Jeff."

Garry and Jeff stood facing each other. Jeff was taller, but Garry had the more muscular build.

Jeff lifted an arm, and for a moment Stephanie thought that he was going to hit Garry, but then he backed off. "I must be going," he said, and went back up the stairs.

"Phew," Garry said, "What is eating the fellow?"

"I don't know," Stephanie said, "The other day he told me to get lost."

"He wasn't wanting to lose you tonight," Garry said. "If you had looked happy about it, I wouldn't have bothered to interfere."

"I'll talk to him sometime," Stephanie said, "And see if I can sort it out."

"Are you sure you want to do that?" Garry inquired.

"Yes," Stephanie said. "I'm still fond of Jeff, or I would be if there weren't so many problems involved."

Stephanie was gathering her books together to go to her Life Science laboratory, when Joelle came into their room.

"Hi," she said, "We are both here at once for a change!"

"It's pretty rare, isn't it?" Stephanie commented. "How are you this afternoon?"

"I'm good," Joelle reported. "How are you?"

"As good as I can be," Stephanie said. "Don't jump down my throat with advice, but Jeff has been worrying me lately."

"What has he been doing?" Joelle queried.

"Well, ever since he got back from Sydney, his moods have been more extreme than usual," Stephanie said. "And he seems to think that everything I do is connected to him. I can't go to the gym, or men's hall without him noticing; I can barely even go to the cafeteria without stirring him up."

"You can't let him rule your life. He's always been a bit that way inclined," Joelle remarked. "There is something that I've never told you Stephanie, but now might be the time."

"What is that? I only have a few minutes," Stephanie said.

"Well, when he took me to the Champagne Breakfast, Jeff was really rude," Joelle said, "Much ruder than Arthur was to you at the Reverse Tea."

"What do you mean?" Stephanie inquired.

"He was obviously only interested in your reaction," Joelle explained. "Once he saw that you had dressed up and gone with Andrew Grosvy, he ignored me altogether."

"What did you do?" Stephanie asked.

"Talked to other girls," Joelle said. "I had never felt so used in my life."

"I am sorry to hear that, I observed. "But I can't say I didn't warn you at the time."

"What are you going to do about it now?" Joelle said, "I reckon that his behaviour has only ever been half-way acceptable because he was interested in impressing you."

"I don't know," Stephanie said. "I will try talking to him, and get to the core of things quite soon. Tomorrow at vespers seems like a good time." Stephanie glanced at her watch, "You will have to excuse me. I have to go now, I'm due at the lab."

"Have a good afternoon," Joelle called after her.

"You too," Stephanie called back, "See you at tea".

Stephanie arrived at women's assembly area for the Uniting Church vespers, and picked her way through the congregated students carefully until she found Jeff.

"Hello, Jeff," Stephanie said, being careful not to presume because it was impossible to tell what mood he would be in tonight.

"Hello Stephanie," Jeff said.

So far so good.

"May I sit down?" Stephanie asked circumspectly.

"Suit yourself," Jeff said non-committedly. "The seat is there."

"Thank you," Stephanie said. "I just wanted to be sure."

"I guess you will be wanting to talk to me later," Jeff muttered.

"I would like that," Stephanie said carefully, "Except that I was under the impression you were the one that wanted to talk to me yesterday."

"Well, wait until everything is over," Jeff said. "Then I'll give you a bit of my time."

The vespers program passed quickly and closed with a session of prayer. After the prayer session, everyone sat reverently for a few minutes. Eventually a subdued hum of chatter arose.

Jeff stood up. "Are you coming?" he said. "We'll go somewhere quiet for this."

Stephanie followed Jeff out of the women's assembly area, and along the path onto the veranda of the campus meeting hall, which had been locked for the evening. Some flowering bushes screened them from the path.

"How's that?" Jeff said.

"It's fine," Stephanie said. "It has been quite a week, hasn't it?"

"Yes," Jeff agreed, "It has."

"It seems like you came back from Sydney pretty stressed out," Stephanie said.

Jeff shrugged. "I might have," he said.

"The week has been rough on me too," Stephanie said.

"So now you are blaming me for everything?" Jeff began defensively.

"Not really," Stephanie said. "I am just thinking that you need to find a way of defusing that stress without taking it out on me."

"Don't tell me what to do," Jeff snapped.

"I'm not!" Stephanie said taken aback.

"Don't contradict me either," Jeff said heatedly.

"But Jeff," Stephanie said, reaching a hand out to him imploringly.

"You shut up," Jeff hissed, "And keep your hands off of me!"

Jeff pushed her away from him roughly. Stephanie stumbled against the railing, and fell down the step onto the asphalt.

"Don't bother telling anyone," Jeff snarled, "They will just laugh." He rushed past her and ran towards men's hall.

Stephanie sat there winded and stunned, until Milton, who was coming along the path from women's assembly area, stopped and helped her to her feet.

"Whatever was that all about?" Milton exclaimed.

"How much did you see?" Stephanie said.

"Enough to know it was Jeff who did this," Milton said. "You have grazed your knee Stephanie. Whatever got into Jeff?"

"I don't know," Stephanie said. "You won't tell anybody will you Milton?"

"I really ought to," he said. "You are injured."

"No," Stephanie said, "I couldn't bear people knowing."

"Well, at least let me help you back to women's hall," Milton said.

"Take me to the back door," Stephanie requested, "I don't want to be seen like this."

"If you insist," Milton said. "But I don't like it one bit."

Stephanie went in the back door of women's hall, up the fire stairs and down the corridor to the room.

Joelle was there. "Whatever happened to you?" she exclaimed.

"I fell over," Stephanie said.

"Sure you did, Stephanie," Joelle said disbelievingly. "You fall over by yourself every day! Did Jeff help you back here?"

"No," Stephanie said, "Milton did."

"Milton did?" Joelle echoed. "Whatever happened to Jeff? You went off with him."

"I am going to take a shower now," Stephanie said fiercely, "This has nothing to do with Jeff."

"If you say so, Stephanie." Joelle looked sceptical, but she let her room-mate go.

Stephanie collected her soap and towel, and went to the bathroom. Once safely in a shower cubicle Stephanie took a long shower, letting the warm water run soothingly across her grazed and bruised limbs.

Stephanie allowed herself to cry there too. No one could hear her sobs, or see the tears that ran down her face, and she was glad of the privacy. Stephanie did not want to become the subject of malicious gossip because her boyfriend was losing interest in her, and had chosen to show it in a noticeable manner.

In the morning Stephanie pretended to sleep-in until Joelle had left the room. She did not feel like talking to her, or going to the cafeteria for breakfast. In fact, all Stephanie wanted to do was avoid being amongst people.

Stephanie dressed in a blue and white striped jumper, and a denim skirt, and covered the scabs forming on her legs with ribbed stockings. Then she went for a walk down girls' way alone.

Stephanie wasn't exactly brooding, more like licking her wounds and trying to sort things out. Jeff's behaviour puzzled and frightened her. Stephanie racked her brains trying to work out why he had turned upon her, when it was not so long ago that he had told her he still liked her.

Stephanie couldn't think of anything that she had done wrong, in fact she had made every effort to be nice to him. However, Jeff was attractive and important, so the fault must rest with her somewhere. Stephanie must have lost his respect in some way.

Perhaps Stephanie had come across as weak and clinging, or perhaps she had not been as bright and cheerful as Jeff wanted. It had been very hard to behave in a vivacious manner once Stephanie knew that he wasn't happy with her being the way she was naturally.

It was quiet and peaceful amongst the trees, and Stephanie circled around the track several times. She had always found being out amongst trees and grass soothing. Stephanie then returned to campus in time for a late lunch, and spent the afternoon shut away in her room.

The next day she also avoided the Inter-denominational and Reformed Church Services and spent the time reading the *Bible*. She was grateful that religion could be such a comfort in times of trouble. Stephanie read Genesis, and the poetic parts of Psalms and Proverbs. Then she prayed that God would lead her the way he led the patriarchs of old, and would help her understand what had happened.

Stephanie fixed her sights solidly on her studies. She was determined that whatever upsets Jeff might cause, her academic record would not suffer. Moreover, it gave her something absorbing to think about.

In the afternoon, Stephanie settled down to write her journalism essay. She was particularly puzzled by the criterion, but felt that it was time to make a start on the project.

The essay was meant to be something that could be accepted by a popular magazine, so after much thought Stephanie decided to write a piece on how to plan a camping trip. Stephanie hoped that this would fit the requirements of an outdoor magazine.

Joelle was in the room, working on her journalism essay as well. Stephanie was glad of the company by now. They had a short talk, and her room-mate seemed to have accepted that she wanted to forget all about her 'accident' the other night.

What Joelle said she found hard to understand though, was the emotional dynamic that Stephanie's relationship with Jeff had developed.

"From what I have seen Stephanie," she said, "You have become accustomed to accepting bad behaviour from Jeff so slowly - that you are unable to get angry at him - even when his behaviour is obviously ungentlemanly."

"It's not that simple," Stephanie said. "Anger was always forbidden in my family. I sometimes wish that I could get angry, but I can't. I have never been able to get angry when I should. I just get sad."

"You must be able to see when people treat you wrong," Joelle said.

"I can see when something is wrong," Stephanie said. "I just can't feel anything but sorrow and I cry. Besides my relationship with Jeff had an emotional depth that makes it hard to break off."

"Whatever do you mean?" Joelle inquired.

"Well, Jeff understood my insecurities," Stephanie explained. "There were simple things that I had confided to him: like my fear of failing subjects if I did not study hard, my grief at the death of my Grandmother and my frustration at being two-to-three years younger than the other first year students. It really meant a lot to me that Jeff was willing to listen."

"Those were serious things for you," Joelle observed.

"Yes," Stephanie said. "I haven't been able to tell just anybody."

"You could look for someone else who was empathetic," Joelle said. "Someone who had less hang-ups of their own."

"Well, understanding is one of the things I want from a guy," Stephanie said. "I haven't figured out exactly what else."

"There is a lot to find out about yourself then!" Joelle said. "Try to keep your head up until mid-semester. We will have a week's break then."

"I am looking forward to it," Stephanie said. "I am going to stay with a dear Aunt."

Stephanie saw Jeff at lunch, and was surprised to find that the original appeal (and whatever else that had drawn them to each other) was still there. Despite the memory of being shouted at and pushed, Stephanie wanted nothing more than to go and sit with him.

Jeff appeared to feel the connection too, because he turned, and stared at Stephanie where she was sitting with Cara and Phoebe.

Phoebe noticed Jeff's gaze and said: "Jeffrey is watching us."

"He is too!" Cara said. "Aren't you going to wave or something Stephanie?"

"Another time maybe, girls," Stephanie said. "I am eating now."

Joelle, who was on Stephanie's other side, put a hand on her arm: "Don't worry about him!" the room-mate whispered discretely.

Stephanie turned so that she could no longer see Jeff, and talked to Joelle and Milton.

Stephanie got up early, and went down to the Education building to prepare her blackboard presentation for Teaching Practice. The assignment was designed to help them develop their board writing and presentation skills. They were required to select one of the large boards along the wall, and fill it with the notes and diagrams required for a sample lesson.

Stephanie chose a Life Science topic, and wrote out a section of theory in her neatest handwriting. It was totally unlike writing in a book because the surface was at a right angle to her. She also had to use larger letters, and keep all the lines straight and even.

When Stephanie had finished writing out a description of the circulatory system, she drew some schematic diagrams from the text book. Stephanie was grateful that the Biology Master had forced them to learn to draw during lab.

Stephanie was proud of the finished product, and went to find the Practice Teaching Tutor. He promised to come and inspect the work as soon as possible, so Stephanie sat down to wait for him. It took him about five minutes to arrive, and she spent the time checking her work from different angles. It appeared to be clearly visible throughout the entire room.

The Practice Teaching Tutor was impressed, and gave her eight out of ten for her effort. He said that Stephanie could leave the presentation on display until the board was needed by another student.

Stephanie had three tests. The first test was for Fundamentals of Computing. She got up very early and reviewed her notes before class.

The next test was Life Science. This was the biggest, and most serious test to her mind. Stephanie had studied solidly all yesterday afternoon, and skipped convocation to fit in a review of her notes.

The last test was for Child Development. Luckily, Stephanie had kept up with her regular reading reports for the subject, and there wasn't too much she didn't already know.

Stephanie believed that she did well in all of the tests, but it made the day seem very heavy.

Classes were winding up for the break, and Stephanie was relieved to find that their Life Science lab was a short one. They had some specimens to draw and identify, and then they were allowed to go up to the library to work on their research reports.

Garry and Stephanie had nearly finished their papers. Stephanie had chosen to do animal communication, because it had interesting psychological implications. Garry was doing hunting and survival, and was focusing on the concept of instinct. The projects were meant to be linked, so they had created an interesting area of discussion and overlap between the two.

In the evening, May invited Stephanie to her room for another game of scrabble. Bethany was not there. Apparently, she had gone over to the recreation area with Grace.

Remembering how easily May had beaten her last time they played scrabble, Stephanie put her thinking cap on and drew on her extensive vocabulary in an attempt to create challenges for her. She improved her tally, but May still won by an amazing number of points.

Melanie dropped by to wish them all a happy holiday.

Stephanie thanked her, and asked how her wedding plans were going. She said that she would be spending the break in Sydney with Jonathon's family.

"Wow!" May said. "Meeting the in-laws, I've heard that can be stressful."

"Yes," Melanie said, "I hope that I get along well with his Mother. I've heard that is most important for a new daughter-in-law."

"She is sure to love you," Stephanie said. "You are a very sweet person. Don't let yourself be intimidated in any way."

"Thanks," Melanie said. "I wouldn't be worried at all, but it became obvious in July that my family and Jonathon's were very different."

"How do you mean?" May asked curiously.

"My Dad is a minister," Melanie said. "He was even a missionary for a while. He has never really worried about material things. Jonathon's family are in business. Their attitudes are very different."

"I see what you mean," Stephanie said.

"Jonathon got on with your family didn't he?" May queried.

"Oh, yes," Melanie said, "They loved him. They are a very loving group."

"I am sure that Jonathon's are too!" Stephanie said. "They will just show it in different ways."

"I hope so," Melanie said. "Talking of differences, what is happening with you and Jeff, Stephanie? I haven't seen you two together all week."

"Jeff hasn't been himself since that visit he made to his family in Sydney," Stephanie said.

"Oh!" Melanie said, "I've noticed a bit of something myself. He was grouchy with Jonathon the other day. But they have been friends for a long time, so Jonathon forgave him."

"Jeff was more than grouchy with me," Stephanie said. "His behaviour really hurt, but I don't know what to do about it."

"That is a pity," May said. "I have seen that Jeff still looks around for you."

"Maybe he does," Stephanie said. "But not consistently enough for the established friendship we were supposed to have. I am going to stick to my other friends for a while. I know exactly where I stand with them."

Stephanie had a huge day. She had been booked to catch a bus from the local Northcoast station to Brisbane at six-ten am. The university car dropped her off and left. Stephanie found the area out by the Motorway very confusing, with a lot of traffic rushing past her in both directions.

Stephanie didn't have a clue which direction led to Brisbane, and initially stood on the wrong side of the road. However, she managed to hail the bus when it came, and it waited for her to cross the road.

When Stephanie arrived at Brisbane Central Station, the Greyhound bus to which she was meant to transfer was standing ready to leave for Melbourne. The driver helped lift her luggage across, and they got under way immediately.

Stephanie had a fairly good trip to Melbourne. The girl sitting next to her turned out to be a Primary Teacher, and was interested in hearing about her studies. They sat together at meal stops, and the woman wished her luck when it came time to get off the bus.

The bus dropped Stephanie in Melbourne the next day. Auntie Sonia was there to meet her, and took her to her place. Auntie Sonia was not a blood relative, but the best friend of her real Aunt Moira. However, she was very kind and Stephanie loved her very much.

Auntie Sonia had a lovely house, with a lot of books. These books were 'best sellers' that her parents wouldn't have bothered with at home, so Stephanie was thrilled and tempted by their covers. Stephanie fell asleep over the first chapter of *The Thorn Birds*.

Stephanie had a week's holiday, in which she read and ate some wonderful lemon coconut slice that Auntie Sonia made. They went shopping once or twice, and Stephanie found some cream wedge heeled sandals that looked like they would be comfortable enough for walking around campus.

Auntie Sonia's wonderful collection of books included titles by Victoria Holt, and other popular authors her strict parents considered too sensational to buy. Stephanie read late each night, savouring the broadening effect each book had upon her point of view.

Auntie Sonia did not like the radio much, but they watched *Sale of the Century* hosted by Tony Barber and checked out the costumes worn by Delvene Delaney. The Saturday night movie was a Carey Grant classic reviewed by Bill Collins, and Stephanie thought the hero was very gallant.

In the second week of the break, Stephanie had an assigned practicum at a Victorian Secondary Academy to complete. She had a full program of classes, ranging from senior Biology, to junior Science, and English at all levels to teach.

Stephanie found the hands-on classroom teaching quite challenging, and it took a great deal of courage to give instructions and commandeer the senior classes. She was only seventeen, and was very much aware that in the eastern states, it was not uncommon for young people to be eighteen or nineteen before they finished high school. This meant that a high proportion of her 'students' could actually be older than her. However, Stephanie reasoned that they had no way of knowing this if she did not tell them, and behaved in as mature a manner as possible. This got her through most challenges.

Stephanie was pleased to find that Bradley had also been assigned to the Victorian Academy. They fell into the habit of eating their lunch together and comparing notes. Brad was having slightly more trouble adjusting to teaching than Stephanie was. Being a naturally easy-going, sensitive guy, he told her that he found the position of teacher and disciplinarian uncomfortable.

Amongst other things, Brad had been assigned to teach Mathematics, which was his third study area. He reported that the students disliked this subject, and requested that he complete numerous examples on the blackboard. Whatever Bradley did, the students still complained that they "couldn't understand".

Stephanie sympathised with him, and advised patience and perseverance. She remembered from her own high school days that they preferred to watch the Maths Teacher than do their own work, and warned him to be alert for deliberate 'go slow' tactics from the students.

The week drew to a close, and Stephanie drew up her reports and prepared her teaching folder with a sense of achievement. Stephanie felt that she had developed and matured a lot over the break.

Stephanie had also come to appreciate being free of the expectations and restrictions that Jeff constantly placed upon her. This led Stephanie to the conclusion that she would be vastly better off without him. She resolved to take the first possible opportunity to tell him to consider whatever remained of their relationship finished.

Stephanie knew that this would be easier said than done, but she was resolved to win her emotional freedom back before the end of the year.

CHAPTER TEN: A DIRTY TRICK

Stephanie was extremely tired after arriving back late that night. She slept past her alarm, and had to rush off to Fundamentals of Computing without going through her full morning routine.

After the class finished Stephanie had an hour free, so she hurried back to the dormitory to shower and change. The cafeteria had ceased serving breakfast, so Stephanie purloined an apple to keep her going until lunch. Stephanie had a lot to do if she wanted to get on with her assignments, so she went across to the library.

Jeff was there, talking earnestly to Bethany. The young girl was staring up at him, as if fascinated by everything he was saying. Stephanie briefly wondered what on earth they could have found to talk about. As far as she knew, they did not have anything in common.

Stephanie was going to pass them by quietly, but Jeff noticed her and said: "Hello, Stephanie."

"Hello, Jeff," Stephanie said.

"Can you wait a minute, Stephanie?" Jeff said, "I am not quite finished here."

"Okay," Stephanie said, unable to ignore a direct request.

Stephanie stood by while he finished a very mundane sounding conversation about campus life with Bethany. It did not sound very important, and Stephanie half suspected the purpose of the exercise was to keep her waiting.

Bethany finally said "Goodbye" to Jeff, and left without speaking to Stephanie.

Jeff turned to her: "How are you Stephanie?" he said.

"I am well Jeff," Stephanie said. "What was that all about?"

"Nothing much," Jeff said, "Just encouraging the girl to get involved in stuff."

"Oh!" Stephanie said blankly. "Bethany seemed to be doing all right without your help. She had made some good friends, including me."

"What are you doing now?" Jeff asked.

"Studying and going to classes," Stephanie said, remembering her resolution. "I have decided to concentrate on my studies for the rest of the semester."

"Will I be seeing much of you this term?" Jeff queried.

"No," Stephanie said, "Probably not."

"What a pity," Jeff said nonchalantly. "Still it can't be helped."

He ambled off out of the library and across towards men's hall, while Stephanie was left staring after him in confusion.

Stephanie was in their room after lunch sorting through her folders when Joelle came in. "Is it my imagination," her room-mate said to her, "Or is Jeffrey Mannington acting a bit stranger than usual?"

"What has he done now?" Stephanie asked. "I haven't seen him at all today."

"I was just walking across campus, and he stopped and said hello to me," Joelle reported.

"What is strange about that?" Stephanie asked.

"It is unusual for Jeff to talk to me at all," Joelle said. "I felt really uncomfortable, like I was being buttered up for something."

"Yes," Stephanie agreed, "I saw something similar happen yesterday between him and Bethany. Apparently he has been strutting around pretending to be the biggest man on campus."

"Jeff has to be up to something," Joelle said. "He is not the type to socialise indiscriminately."

"I've never thought of him as calculating before," Stephanie said. "I saw him as a nice quiet guy. Odd and abrupt at times, and a bit of a loner."

"Jeff may have been more genuine around you than with others," Joelle said. "But I reckon he directs his attention where he wants it to be. This reminds me of the time that he asked me to the Champagne Breakfast, and I don't want to be dragged into the middle of your relationship again."

"Don't worry about it," Stephanie said. "I have dropped him."

"Oh!" Joelle exclaimed. "That would explain everything."

"I don't see how," Stephanie said puzzled.

"Well," Joelle said, "Jeff must be taking some sort of face saving action."

"Like what?" Stephanie asked.

"Either giving everyone the impression he did the dropping," Joelle said, "Or trying to make you jealous."

"As if that would work!" Stephanie exclaimed.

"You would be surprised," Joelle said. "You had some pretty serious feelings for Jeff didn't you?"

"Yes," Stephanie admitted with a sigh.

"Those feelings can't all be dead yet," Joelle said. "He will try to use them against you somehow."

"I am much stronger since my holiday," Stephanie said, "He will find it pretty hard to get to me."

"For your sake," Joelle said, "I really hope so."

Having said that she was going to concentrate on her study, Stephanie settled down to researching material for her Child Development essay. The topic that she had chosen was centred on the influence of the family on personality. The material was fascinating, and Stephanie couldn't help applying it to her own life.

There were three basic parenting styles described in the literature. The first was 'authoritarian' in which the parents laid down strict rules for the children, the second was called 'authoritative' in which the children were taught guiding principles, but were not necessarily forced to conformity.

The last parenting style was 'permissive', in which the parents allowed the children to do absolutely anything that they pleased. It sounded great, but apparently was not. The end result was often insecurity, and slower moral development.

Her parents, although well meaning, would best have been described as 'authoritarian'. Stephanie had grown up with a certain fear of authority which inhibited her ability to take risks - like being more playful in social situations. Stephanie loved a joke as much as anybody else, but was worried about making a mistake, and being shown up in public as 'wrong'.

Stephanie also had a lot of rules running around in her head, which she found really confusing when she faced a decision which did not exactly conform to any of their edicts. For example, Stephanie had chosen to study Teaching, because she was interested in the subjects. Stephanie could just as easily have chosen Nursing, and none of the rules she had been given helped her make that decision. Such decisions were not based on morals, but related to aptitude and feelings, and her heart was relatively untrained.

Thursday was also a very full day. They had been studying genetics in Life Science. In their afternoon laboratory, they had a number of exercises to complete, and spent some time calculating the probability of a child inheriting certain genes from specific parents.

After they had completed the pen and paper work, they were assigned some statistical research. Garry and Cara were sent out around the campus to survey the students randomly, and bring back an account of the proportion of students with either blue or brown eyes. (For the purpose of this exercise, green and grey eyes were considered to be 'blue'.) The subjects' hair colour was also recorded and discussed.

Dylan and Stephanie had the bizarre task of testing those students unlucky enough to be strolling through the Science

Department corridors, for their ability to roll their tongues and taste PTC. (Phenylthiocarbamide, which actually, is not very nice.)

Stephanie elected herself secretary for this exercise, and allowed Dylan to do the talking. He made the exercise sound extremely amusing, and encouraged a high degree of participation.

After an hour 'in the field', they all met back in the laboratory, and compiled a profile of the student population. Like most of their Life Science labs, this one ran overtime, and they all arrived at the cafeteria extremely late.

Jeff was walking out of the cafeteria as they came through the door. He stopped opposite Cara, and said "Hello" to her in a cheerful manner.

Cara said "Hello" back to Jeff.

"How are you today Cara?" Jeff inquired.

"Oh, I am very well thank you," Cara said, sounding slightly baffled. "How are you Jeff?"

"I am good," Jeff said. "You are late for tea today."

"Yes," Cara said, "Our Life Science lab often runs late, as I am sure Stephanie has told you."

"Oh yes," Jeff said. "Well, I had better be going."

Dylan cleared his throat to remind Jeff that the rest of them were standing there. Jeff nodded briefly to him and left.

"Whatever was that all about?" exclaimed Dylan when they were sitting down. "It looked for all the world as if Jeff had been waiting for us. Then he began practically chatting Cara up in front of me."

"What I noticed," Garry said, "Was that Jeff didn't even speak to

Stephanie, or us guys. It was pretty rude."

"Jeff plays these little games sometimes," Stephanie said resignedly. "Don't worry about it."

"Even so," Garry said. "You two were an item. He could have been politer."

"And," Dylan reiterated, "He didn't have to come on to Cara in front of me. I haven't given up hope of winning her."

"I am sure you can look after yourself Dylan," Garry said. "I am more concerned about the fact that felt he had to do it in front of Stephanie. It was like he was interested in seeing Stephanie's reaction."

"Please try to overlook Jeff's behaviour, guys," Stephanie said. "You are embarrassing me far worse by talking it over."

Stephanie was crossing the campus going from the Life Science lab to lecture theatre one, when she saw Jeff standing talking to a group of giggling girls. Stephanie quickly scanned their faces, and made the cynical observation that a large number of them were Nurses who were new on campus and therefore not yet 'campus smart'.

Between Jeff and the girls, they completely blocked the main concourse outside the union building, and Stephanie had to say "Excuse me" to get through.

Jeff threw Stephanie a quizzical glance as she passed by, and casually placed a hand upon the shoulder of one of the girls. Although the girl shrugged his arm off, and moved away from his side, Stephanie recognised this as another instance of his theatrics.

Stephanie concentrated upon her class for the next hour and tried to tell herself that Jeff's behaviour didn't bother her. However, by the end of lunch, when Stephanie had to listen to him and his mates laughing loudly throughout the cafeteria, she had to admit that he was getting to her a bit.

Joelle was not in their room, so Stephanie went to visit Kathy. Kathy was designing a poster for a Practice Teaching presentation, and asked Stephanie how she thought it looked.

"It's excellent!" Stephanie said. "I love some of the things that you Primary Teachers make."

"I think it is a much more fun job than Secondary Teaching," Kathy said.

"I can see that," Stephanie said, "But I did want to get the four year Bachelor degree, so I chose Secondary Teaching."

"That is probably very wise for you," Kathy said, pushing her poster aside. "And how are things for you in general?"

"Well," Stephanie said, "Jeff is going around campus chatting up as many girls as he can."

"Ah, yes," Kathy said. "I suspect he is looking for a new sucker. Someone who will let him use them the way he used Joelle at the Champagne Breakfast."

"Joelle said something similar," Stephanie remarked.

"She is wise to him this time isn't she?" Kathy asked with some concern.

"Yes, she is quite cynical about him nowadays!" Stephanie

replied.

"Good," Kathy said. "He won't be able to get to anyone really close to you then."

"I tried to ignore it at first," Stephanie said, "But it isn't really pleasant to watch."

"It's not meant to be," Kathy said wryly. "Don't worry too much, anybody with any sense will turn him down."

"What do you think Jeff is going to do?" Stephanie asked.

"Act up a bit. Make a macho show and a fuss," Kathy said. "It will soon blow over."

"I will keep ignoring it then," Stephanie said.

"Good girl," Kathy said. "Tomorrow is the weekend. Wear something nice, and have as good a day as possible. You never know, someone else may even ask you out."

It was a beautiful spring morning, and Stephanie wore the pink georgette dress that she bought for an important function last year. It had soft draped sleeves that sat wide on the shoulder and created a really feminine effect, which seemed just right for the Inter-denominational praise service. Stephanie did not see Jeff as he rarely attended Inter-denominational services, which maintained an order of service eschewed by the Reformed Churches.

Outside on the lawn, a couple of the guys complimented her with soft whistles (not the crude wolf-whistle kind), and the girls said that Stephanie looked very nice.

In the afternoon, Stephanie went for a walk with Debbie and

David, Joelle and Milton, Phoebe, Kathy and May. The girls were picking the wildflowers that had sprung up along the sides of the bush tracks, and Stephanie ended up taking a sizeable bunch back to the room.

At four pm, there was an afternoon meeting, which lasted for about an hour. It included a presentation of slides taken by one of the Lecturers while travelling overseas on a "fly and build", in which a group of Australians volunteered to erect a church building in the South Pacific Islands. It was wonderful to see how much good could be done by someone donating just a week or two of their time, although the tasks involved did sound most suitable for men.

Stephanie spent the morning doing some more work on her Child Development essay. She was reading some interesting material about the influence of the position one occupied in the family. Stephanie was the oldest in her family, and as a consequence, was inclined to take responsibility, and be exceedingly law abiding.

Stephanie described her findings to Joelle, and she said that she could identify with the position of the middle child, who seemed to get sandwiched somewhere between the eldest and youngest. Both of them thought that the position of the youngest child sounded great, as they were commonly the one that got all the favours.

Stephanie decided to take a break in the afternoon, and wandered into the television room to see what was on. The afternoon movie was an old western. Bradley was sitting there looking a bit bored, but he brightened upon seeing her.

Stephanie sat down, and they talked a bit about their studies, and watched the movie until it finished. Then Bradley asked Stephanie whether she wanted to walk over to the canteen on the side of the cafeteria, and check if it was open.

Stephanie was surprised to hear there was a place on campus that sold junk food. Apparently it only operated certain days and certain hours, but they were in luck, and Bradley bought a packet of salted cashews which he shared with her.

The next day was routine until just after the evening assembly, when Stephanie was surprised to be called to the foyer. She was even more surprised to see that it was Jeff who had sought her out. He asked her to go somewhere and talk, and Stephanie agreed, provided that they stuck to the lighted areas.

They went across to the Humanities building, and sat down in one of the classrooms. Jeff was fidgeting, and seemed very tense.

"I have something to tell you," he said.

"Oh," Stephanie said half hoping for some sort of apology, "And what would that be?"

"I have asked Grace out," Jeff said.

Time stood still, and Stephanie could hear herself breathing. She had thought that she could get over Jeff, and had tried to ignore everything he was doing, but this was a fairly extreme form of provocation.

"I am confused," Stephanie said. "I thought that you might be going to say we had things to work out."

"That was all one big mistake," Jeff said. "I didn't ever mean to tell you that I liked you. I have been trying to get rid of you ever since."

Her head started to spin. Stephanie was pretty sure that Jeff was lying about something somewhere here. It appeared he felt better about denying their relationship altogether, than dealing with it being over. The opposite was true for her. Stephanie felt like he was telling her that her life, outside of her study, had been based on a lie for the past few months.

"I didn't think that you liked Grace much," Stephanie stammered. "You haven't taken any notice of her before now."

"Well, I have just gotten to know her," Jeff said.

"I am still confused," Stephanie said. "I don't believe that I have seen you anywhere near Grace all weekend. And you were all over a hundred and one girls last week."

"Nevertheless," Jeff said. "Grace is the one for me now."

"It is very sudden," Stephanie said, "Whereas there had been stuff going on between us for months."

"I wouldn't hurt you for all the world," Jeff said, "That is why I am telling you like this."

"But you did hurt me," Stephanie said puzzled. "Over by the meeting hall."

"No, Stephanie," Jeff said, "You brought that all on yourself."

"I don't see how I could have," Stephanie said puzzled, "But I think I had better go now. I hope you and Grace will be very happy."

Stephanie returned to the dormitory in a state of absolute

turmoil and confusion. She had been steeling herself for the break-up with Jeff, but had not envisioned that it would be anything like this. Stephanie had thought that he would be sad, and she would be sad; and they would give the friendship a decent burial, so as to speak.

Instead, he had served her with a total parody, and made a mockery of something to which Stephanie had been deeply committed. A finger of doubt crept into her mind, and Stephanie asked herself what fatal flaw within her had caused her to be treated in such a manner. Stephanie couldn't think anymore, and she spent the rest of the evening crying.

Luckily Joelle was practicing the piano in the women's assembly hall and didn't come in till late. Then she mercifully refrained from asking any questions.

Stephanie washed her face with cold water a number of times in the morning before she dared go down to the cafeteria for breakfast, and even then, she suspected that her eyes were red and swollen. Her friends were too kind to comment, and tried to talk to her as if everything was normal.

Stephanie chose not to linger in the cafeteria, or any common area where she could conceivably run into Jeff and Grace. Her timetable was fairly light on a Tuesday, so Stephanie spent an hour or two cleaning the women's assembly area, and then retreated back to her room.

Joelle came in after lunch, and hovered around uncertainly for a few minutes. She looked pretty concerned, so Stephanie forced herself to speak.

"Have you heard?" Stephanie said, the tears threatening to start again.

"That Jeff and Grace claim to be going out together?" Joelle said. "Yes, I have heard."

"Does everybody know?" Stephanie said.

"Hard to tell," Joelle replied. "Jeff and Grace are both telling the story, but they don't act as if they are particularly together."

"I don't think that either of them knows what together is," Stephanie said forlornly.

"You are probably right," Joelle said. "Jeff didn't treat you decent, and this thing with Grace is not based on any sort of friendship."

"Still," Stephanie began to cry, "I can't help ask myself, why Grace? Why not someone nice that I could at least feel attracted him with her exceptional qualities?"

Joelle sighed. "Because Grace is the only girl desperate enough to go out with him, given the amount of unfinished business he has with you."

"That somehow makes it worse," Stephanie sobbed.

"I was afraid that you would feel that way," Joelle said crossing the room to hold her in a loose hug. "I wouldn't like it either, if Milton tried to lie and flirt his way out of his relationship with me."

"Why is Jeff doing it?" Stephanie cried.

"He is weak," Joelle said. "Jeff is a complete weakling, and Grace is a girl who has no sense of ethics."

"At the moment all I can think of is how much I cared about him," Stephanie sobbed, "And how we will never be together again."

"That is probably another reason why Jeff has done what he has," Joelle said. "Jealousy has made you forget all his faults, and think about his good points."

"I don't know what to do," Stephanie cried.

"Concentrate on looking after yourself," Joelle said. "And try to remember why you wanted to leave the relationship. You had good reason."

"I'll give it go," Stephanie said drying her eyes. "Thank you so much for being here."

"That's my job - I am your room-mate," Joelle said. "Why don't you sleep for a while? And then shower, and wear something nice to worship."

"Okay," Stephanie said, "I do feel pretty lethargic."

It appeared to be a nice spring morning, so Stephanie spent a few extra minutes styling her hair, and wore the tiniest hint of make-up. She was sitting next to Phoebe, Bradley and Cara during Fundamentals of Computing, and made sure that she walked into convocation with them.

The meeting itself was taken by the student union members, and was very lively. There were several skits and comical songs, and the committee promised the students at least two more social events before the end of the year. Stephanie sneaked a look around, but could not see Jeff and Grace anywhere near where they were sitting.

She assumed that the couple were together somewhere else.

After convocation Stephanie had Life Science and Child Development, both of which were interesting enough to get her thinking about study once again. She spent the afternoon reading her Life Science text book as she figured that they would be sure to have another test soon.

Stephanie was leaving the cafeteria after lunch, when she passed alongside Tony and Roger. The boys were mates of Jeff's, so Stephanie tried to give them a wide berth. However, Roger called out to her and told her to stop for a minute.

"What do you want?" Stephanie said.

"We aren't seeing much of you now that Jeff is with Grace," Tony said.

"I think that is understandable, don't you?" Stephanie said.

"You can figure out why he left you," Roger said. "Grace is a real goer!"

"I am not interested in hearing about it," Stephanie said.

"It wouldn't be any good trying to get Jeff back," Roger continued. "He's on to a good thing now."

"Excuse me guys," Stephanie said. "I am not finding this conversation particularly useful."

"Don't you want to know what they have been doing?" Roger jeered, placing a hand on her arm.

"No," Stephanie said, "Why-ever would you want to tell me? Is this another one of Jeff's set-ups?"

"Oh, come on mate," Tony said, "She is no fun!"

Roger let go of her arm, and Stephanie hurried back to girls' dorm. She was shaking when she arrived there. Stephanie collected her books for Life Science, and began to walk towards the lab.

Stephanie met Cara on the pathway, and they walked the rest of the way together. Cara was very friendly, and Stephanie felt herself begin to relax.

The atmosphere in the lab was calm and matter of fact. Dylan made a number of jokes, but they were not directed at anyone in particular. Stephanie had forgotten her calculator, so Garry offered to share his with her. They only needed it for a few minutes towards the end anyway, when they compiled the population statistics.

When the lab finished, the class all went up to the cafeteria together. They sat and talked until it was almost time for the evening meetings. Stephanie didn't join in the conversation as much as she usually did, but the others gave no indication they minded. It was good to be amongst such tranquil friends and colleagues.

Stephanie dressed for the Uniting Church vespers in her cream skirt and embroidered jumper. This outfit made her feel comfortable and confident. Debbie had offered to drop by her room, and pick her up for vespers. Debbie knew that it would be awkward for Stephanie to come up to the room in case she ran into Grace.

Stephanie arrived at the women's assembly area along with Debbie and David, and sat down in a pew. Milton was with them, because Joelle was off playing the piano.

Jeff walked into the women's assembly hall alone, and Stephanie was surprised when he crossed over to where she was sitting.

"Hello Stephanie," he said.

"Hello Jeff," Stephanie said, not moving from beside Joelle.

"How are you doing, Stephanie?" Jeff inquired.

"I am fine Jeff," Stephanie said, bending the truth a little in self-protection. "How are you?"

"I am good Stephanie," Jeff said, "Sorry I can't sit with you, I have to go and find Grace."

Jeff moved off across the interior of the women's assembly area, and finally sat down with Roger, Tony and some of his other mates. Grace arrived a few minutes later, with Bethany and May following her. They sat down in the pew directly in front of the one that the guys had chosen. Grace turned around, and handed something to Jeff, and then vespers commenced.

David let out a deep breath: "Why can't that guy just leave Stephanie alone?" he said under cover of the singing.

"I don't know," Debbie said, "Jeff seems to have some sort of axe to grind."

"How could he when they are broken up?" David questioned.

"I think Steph is actually doing too well for Jeff's taste," Debbie said. "He wants her to be miserable. And he probably enjoys the attention."

"Doesn't Grace mind?" Milton asked.

"I don't think that she has worked it out yet," Debbie said. "And she probably wouldn't care if she did. It is not easy being her room-mate."

"Will you excuse me?" Stephanie said. "I think that I will go back to the room. I agree with most of the things you are saying, but I don't relish being talked about."

"Don't go," Milton said, "You are safe enough with us."

"I don't want to have to watch Jeff and Grace carrying on," Stephanie said.

"Swap with David then," Debbie recommended. "The view is pretty well blocked from there."

"Thanks," Stephanie said, and the friends did a reshuffle.

As it turned out, Stephanie was glad that she stayed throughout vespers. The presentation was interesting, and the atmosphere worshipful, once she could no longer see Jeff out of the corner of her eye.

The weekend was unusual, in that a regional youth rally was being held on campus. The Reform Church service was held over in the gymnasium, which was employed as a worship venue whenever it was expected the congregation would outstretch the capacity of the campus meeting hall.

Half-way through the service, Kathy began to feel faint. Stephanie helped her out through the crowd, and sat her down outside. She was sweating and appeared to be developing a fever, so they continued on to the dormitory.

When Kathy was safely in her room, Stephanie volunteered to

get the university Nurse, who administered some aspirin and suggested that Kathy have a jug of fruit juice by her bed.

Stephanie went across to the cafeteria, and arranged for the loan of a plastic jug and a cup. She filled the jug with the red juice which was the universal favourite around campus, and began to make her way back to the dormitory.

Stephanie was part-way there when she ran into Grace and Jeff. They were just standing around the rear of the dormitory, where they really had no business to be, given that there was a service taking place. Indeed, Stephanie could have sworn that she had seen them seated together in the gymnasium, just before Kathy and she left.

"Hello, Stephanie," Grace said.

"Oh, hi," Stephanie said, not really knowing how she should act. This was the first time that she had faced them as a couple.

"We were wondering how you were doing now that you are alone," Jeff said.

"I am fine," Stephanie said, "But I'm not really alone, I have all my friends."

"But none like Jeff anymore," Grace said coyly, leaning up against him.

"No, none of them are like Jeff," Stephanie said as calmly as possible, but Stephanie had to admit that they were getting to her. "I think of that as a good thing nowadays."

"I don't believe that," Grace said. "I know that you miss him."

"Think what you like," Stephanie said shortly. "I have my own interests."

"We just wanted to know that there were no hard feelings," Grace cooed. "You haven't been very friendly to me since I got together with Jeff."

"I don't see you that often," Stephanie said, desperately trying not to let her voice quiver. "Jeff always had his own friends."

"And now I am one of Jeff's friends," Grace cooed. "I told you that I could get him off you anytime I wanted."

"Oh that," Stephanie said. "I wasn't taking you seriously."

"Perhaps you should have been," Jeff said nonchalantly.

"You can see why he chose me," Grace said, tracing a hand across the front of Jeff's shirt.

"No not really," Stephanie said. She was beginning to have to concentrate on the jug, as her hand was shaking and it was threatening to spill. "You have been together for a few days, and you think that is a serious relationship."

"Maybe we have been together for longer than that," Grace said suggestively. "Maybe something was going on already last semester..."

"That's a lie!" Stephanie said, suddenly feeling hot all over. The anger she had spent a lifetime repressing rushed to the surface and she lifted the jug of juice, up-ending it all over the other girl.

Jeff, who had been watching Stephanie closely, stepped aside so that no more than a few drops landed on his suit. He burst out laughing.

"Of course it was a lie!" he exclaimed. "She really got you there!"

"Stephanie got me too," Grace said, shaking herself in dismay. "I was wearing a white dress too, what a bitch!"

"I am terribly sorry guys," Stephanie said. She was crying now, because she hated scenes and was horribly ashamed of her part in this one. "I don't know what came over me."

"I do," Jeff said. "You are pretty transparent Stephanie!" He was still laughing, "Come on Grace, your dress will wash or something."

Jeff and Grace left, and Stephanie continued on into the dorm, and went to Kathy's room.

"I am sorry," Stephanie said, "But I have spilt your fruit juice."

"Fill the jug with water then," Kathy said. "And tell me what is wrong."

"I have just had a fight with Jeff and Grace," Stephanie sobbed.

"Pretty embarrassing - if it was in public," Kathy said.

"I don't think that too many people saw," I said. "But that is not the point. I am not used to losing my temper, and I did something aggressive."

"Self-expression is a skill that you should cultivate," Kathy said. "We have all been wondering when you would give Jeff a good verbal blast."

"Unfortunately," Stephanie said, "It didn't occur to me to give anyone a verbal blast. I gave Grace a jug of juice instead - all down her front."

"That was a bit over the top!" Kathy said. "But drenching her in red fluid does represent a great deal of poetic justice."

"Jeff certainly thought so," Stephanie said. "He laughed."

"Jeffrey thought it was funny you poured the juice over Grace?" Kathy exclaimed. "That guy is weirder than I thought!"

"Anyway, I apologised," Stephanie said, "To both of them."

"You apologised?" Kathy exclaimed. "Now that does worry me."

"Why?" Stephanie said, "I thought it was the right thing to do."

"Under normal circumstances, yes," Kathy said, "It is good to apologise. But who was provoking who here?"

"Jeff and Grace did seem to be lying in wait for me," Stephanie said.

"And did they apologise for that?" Kathy asked.

"No," Stephanie said. "Grace called me a rude name, and Jeff went away pleased with himself."

"So, let me see if I've got this right," Kathy said. "They did not apologise, but you did?"

"Yes," Stephanie said.

"That will just encourage them to do something similar again, now they know it works!" Kathy said.

"I can't do anything about that," Stephanie said. "Although I don't think Grace was happy."

"Well, we will see what happens," Kathy said. "I had better have a rest now."

Stephanie went back to her room somewhat calmer than she had been before talking to Kathy, but she was still burning with shame. It was unlike her to express anger in any way, and this time Stephanie had noticeably lost control. She could sense that the incident was one which would leave its mark upon her for some time.

CHAPTER ELEVEN: CONFUSION

The Cafe Proprietor had organised a barbecue for tea. It was designed to be a casual event, with two long trestle tables of food under the trees, and large dispensers of drink set up on the pavement in front of the cafeteria.

Stephanie arrived and looked around for her friends, intending to join them immediately. May, Phoebe and Brad were already settled down and eating. Jeff was sitting on the edge of the stone wall quite near them. There was no sign of Grace anywhere.

Jeff beckoned to her saying, "Come here Stephanie."

Stephanie collected a plate full of food, and somewhat timorously walked across to Jeff.

"What do you want?" Stephanie asked.

"Sit down next to me," Jeff said.

When Stephanie hesitated, Jeff reached his hand out, and closed it on her left wrist just above the joint. He tugged on her arm until Stephanie gave in and sat beside him.

"How are you today Stephanie?" Jeff said.

"I am fine!" Stephanie said, "Considering."

"You are not going to do anything silly are you?" Jeff said.

"Wasn't yesterday silly enough?" Stephanie said.

"I meant silly like killing yourself," Jeff said.

"Of course not!" Stephanie said. "I was upset, but I am hardly likely to get suicidal over you."

"I wouldn't be surprised if your emotions overcame you after everything," Jeff said.

"You are right out of luck there," Stephanie said firmly.

Stephanie tried to stand up again, but Jeff tightened his hand around her wrist, grinding the flesh against the bone.

"I want to get a drink," Stephanie said.

"Will you come back here?" Jeff said.

"If it is that important to you," Stephanie said.

Jeff released her arm, and Stephanie rubbed it carefully. A bruise was beginning to form already. Stephanie went and got herself a drink. Stephanie considered making a run for it, but Jeff had followed her across to the dispenser.

"Let's go somewhere away from these people," Jeff said. He took possession of her arm again, and walked her along the path to one of the seats beside the gymnasium. Stephanie noticed that he chose a bench that was sheltered by some flowering bushes.

"You have to understand some things," Jeff said.

"I am listening," Stephanie said.

Jeff began speaking very fast. "My family, they were not like the ideal family. When I was a kid, there was a lot of yelling and shouting. Even hitting and punching - and some of it is still going on."

"I am sorry," Stephanie murmured, not knowing what else to say.

"My father came and went when it suited him," Jeff continued. "When he was living with us he was very strict. He had these ideas about who we should be, and what we should all do. We were punished if we didn't measure up in the slightest detail."

"Oh," Stephanie said. "That is very severe."

"I have never been able to please him," Jeff said. "I know that I am not any sort of man in his eyes."

Jeff sounded like he was going to cry, and whatever he had done to hurt her, Stephanie was now feeling sorry for him. Stephanie put an arm around his shoulders.

"A couple of years ago, things suddenly got even harder for me," Jeff said. "I can't really explain it. It was like everything got on top of me. I couldn't stop stressing out. Anxious thoughts whirled around in her head, and I couldn't get them to stop."

"What did you do?" Stephanie asked.

"I had just finished high school, and home seemed to be the problem, so I came up here," Jeff said. "It helped to be in a structured environment, and I built up a routine that I could trust."

"That's good," Stephanie said, "I think, I'm not an expert."

"I was comfortable here until things began to go wrong with you," Jeff cried. "Now, I want to leave here too."

"I haven't really done anything that bad," Stephanie said. "I am ashamed of what happened yesterday, but it is not as if anyone were really hurt."

"You are okay Stephanie," Jeff admitted. "Sometimes I know that, and sometimes I don't."

"That's pretty complicated," Stephanie said.

Stephanie didn't bother asking about Grace. She didn't seem to be anywhere in the equation at the moment. It was obvious that it was only Stephanie who had got seriously under his skin.

They sat out there with the twilight closing around them. It got dark and the moon rose. Jeff curled against her as if he was a child, despite the fact that he was twice her size.

At last Stephanie said: "It is cold. I came out here without a jacket."

"Better go in then," Jeff said, "I'll see you tomorrow."

Her wrist throbbed, and showed some blue and purple blotches. Stephanie covered them up with a smear of foundation. She felt instinctively that by preventing comment and protecting Jeff, she could also protect herself. Besides, Stephanie felt obliged not to betray his trust in confiding family matters to her.

Stephanie was trying very hard to get her studies organised once again, but she had been given an emotional burden to carry. Stephanie believed that getting back together with Jeff would be a mistake, even if that was what he wanted, but feelings had been admitted and expressed once again.

When Stephanie tried to go to the university post office, and discovered that it was a public holiday off campus, but they were having classes anyway, she felt restless. Stephanie wanted some stamps and writing home was one way she maintained her extra-curricular interests. It also highlighted the fact that it had been a long time since she had been home.

Stephanie sat down with an English novel and made herself read the entire thing through again. It kept her busy, and surely would help her in preparation for the exams, which were not so far away.

One of the women's deans came to her room, and asked Stephanie for an explanation of the scene on the weekend. The Dean had obviously been told a story that made Stephanie sound like the aggressor. Some of the embellishments to the story sounded suspiciously like the sort of thing that originated from Roger, who would have got a sketchy account from Jeff himself.

The Dean would not say who had told her about the weekend's incident. The older woman gave Stephanie the impression that it had come to her through 'general gossip'. The Dean did agree, however, that it was unfair that such gossip should be spread about her.

Stephanie gave the Dean a very literal account of the interaction between Jeff, Grace and herself. Stephanie also explained something of the history of her relationship with Jeff to the Dean. Stephanie told her how Jeff ran hot and cold on her, embarrassed and criticised her all the time.

Stephanie did not mention to the Dean that she had spent Sunday evening with Jeff. Nor did she mention the push earlier in the year, or the bruises currently on her arm. Those things were buried far too deep in her soul by the confusion and shame they triggered.

The Dean was sympathetic, and talked to her about taking pride in herself. It was obvious that the Dean did not know what else to do, given her responsibility to all parties, and the conflicting stories she had been told.

The morning was reasonably full of classes. Stephanie sat with Garry and Cara in convocation, and walked down to Life Science with them almost immediately afterwards.

The Biology Master dictated notes to them at top speed. It was a while since things had been quite so fast paced, but the semester was at least two thirds of the way through, and they had several more topics to complete before the finals. Her hand was aching by the end of class.

Child Development was more relaxing, as the Lecturer screened a film on trends in adolescence, and the influence of "peer pressure". The film had been made in the seventies, and was a little dated in appearance, otherwise it was quite interesting.

Apparently, if a number of subjects were told that their friends had enjoyed completing some extremely dull wooden puzzles, they would also report a high degree of enjoyment associated with the activity. Stephanie couldn't imagine being fooled to quite that extent herself, but then, Stephanie prided herself on her originality.

After lunch, Stephanie went downstairs to clean the women's assembly area. It was exceedingly difficult to hear the public address system from there, and Stephanie normally didn't bother trying to listen, but at one time she thought that she could just hear her name being announced.

Stephanie went up the connecting stairs, and into the foyer.

"Was that a call for me?" Stephanie asked.

"Oh yes," said Gloria who was on the desk, "You have a telephone call."

Stephanie went into one of the private booths, and picked up the receiver. "Hello", Stephanie said.

There was some giggling, hooting and laughing at the other end, and the call was disconnected.

"Yuk," Stephanie said to Gloria, "That was a prank call."

"It came from men's hall," Gloria said, checking the switchboard. "Someone using one of the internal phones. Maybe I didn't switch you through properly."

"Maybe, but I doubt it," Stephanie said. "I am going back down to women's assembly area. I will be vacuuming, and it will be absolutely impossible for me to hear the PA, so if anyone calls back for me, take a message."

"Sure I will," Gloria said, "And I will get a name for you."

"Thank you," Stephanie said. "It might just be a joke, but I appreciate your assistance."

"That's okay," Gloria said. "A trick is only funny when you are in on it."

Stephanie had to present her Child Development tutorial, and hand in her essay. She had decided to write up a couple of sample case studies, and get the group to discuss the families represented.

Stephanie borrowed one case from a Psychology text, and located another in an Educational magazine. She was obliged to adjust them a little, and hand-write the examples out on an overhead projection sheet, to avoid problems with copyright.

The Lecturer was impressed with the discussion, and liked her duplicated summary sheet. Stephanie got nine out of ten for the tutorial itself, and eagerly awaited the mark on her essay.

The Uniting Church vespers program was conducted by a group of travelling actors known as "The Nazareth Players." They performed a series of short skits, designed to make them think about their attitudes and behaviour.

Everyone enjoyed the performance, and clapped lightly between the acts, despite being in a place of worship. At the end of the announced program, the players asked whether they had enjoyed the presentation, and would like an encore performance. This appeared to be designed to increase audience participation, because they had a few more mimes already prepared.

When the program finished, Stephanie stood up to leave, and finding there was a fair crowd at the back door of the women's assembly area, she exited through the side door.

Jeff was standing there, leaning up against the brickwork. Stephanie almost walked past him in the dark, and jumped when he called: "Over here Stephanie", to her.

"Hello, Jeff," Stephanie said, "What are you doing just standing there?"

"Getting some fresh air," Jeff said. "Are you going straight back inside?"

"I was going to," Stephanie said.

"I have to talk to you," Jeff said. "It is important."

"Okay," Stephanie said. "Most people are still gossiping anyway."

"Come away from here," Jeff said.

"Oh, I don't want to go too far," Stephanie said, "And I don't want to be too long."

"That's all right," Jeff said, "It will probably be a bit more peaceful around the back of girls' dorm, and you will be almost home."

Jeff led her around the side of girls' dorm, and stopped in the concave section formed by the steps leading down to the laundry.

"People have been talking about us since last week," he said.

"I wish they would just forget it," Stephanie said. "I certainly haven't given them anything to talk about since."

"I have been trying to protect you," Jeff said.

"Funny that you should say that," Stephanie said. "I have noticed that it is mostly guys like Roger and Tony doing the talking. They are your mates, and you must have some influence over them. Why don't you just ask them to stop?"

Jeff looked annoyed. "I can't do that," he said, "You had better take my word for it Stephanie."

"I don't see why not," Stephanie said puzzled.

"You are in no position to tell me what to do," Jeff snarled, "Absolutely everybody here despises you now."

"Not everybody, surely..." Stephanie faltered. She was shocked and intimidated. The prospect of living on campus for the next few months was beginning to look mighty unpleasant.

"All the guys at least," Jeff asserted, "You won't find anybody else willing to date you. You had best do things my way from now on."

"I'll live it down," Stephanie said. "Fires always die if there is nothing more to fuel them."

"There are some things that you still don't understand," Jeff said roughly. He reached out, and grabbed her by the shoulders, pressing the bones uncomfortably, and yet at the same time, drawing her towards him.

Stephanie squirmed in Jeff's grasp, but that really hurt, so she relaxed and leant against him. It would have been a pleasant embrace, if Jeff hadn't been holding her there by force. They stood like that for a few minutes, and the tears began to roll down her cheeks.

"You are hurting me," Stephanie sobbed. "How can you be so cruel?"

Jeff let her go, and stood there panting. "I am going to lose control," he said. "Oh...why do you hang around me Stephanie?"

"I don't know," Stephanie murmured. "I liked you once, when I thought you were just a simple guy."

"Well, get over it," Jeff said. "Get over it at once, before I make you real sorry."

Jeff strode off into the dark, and Stephanie turned and made her way back into girls' dorm. Stephanie didn't dare think too much about what had just happened, so she went straight to bed, and mercifully, fell asleep immediately.

When Stephanie woke up in the morning, some of the impact of what had happened last night began to impinge upon her. Jeff had laid hands upon her again, despite her insisting that they stay close to the dormitory.

He had forced body contact on her, in a manner which was both violent and sexual at the same time. Stephanie was young and inexperienced, but she was still sure that the two were not meant to go together.

And finally, Jeff had uttered something which constituted a threat. It had been unclear whether he was threatening her with sexual acts or violent ones, but given his attitude, it would probably be a combination of the two.

Joelle got up and showered, and went to play the piano for the Reformed Church service. Stephanie just laid there in bed. She reached out, picked up her *Good News Bible*, and began reading it, turning to passages and texts that she had always found comforting.

After a while, Stephanie went and had a leisurely shower. Knowing that if she went to lunch before the Reformed Church was finished, there would be less people to confront, Stephanie hurried across to the cafeteria.

Once safely fed, Stephanie went back to her room and picked the *Bible* up once again. Stephanie began to read through some of the less well known books of the *Bible*, hoping that they would contain some answers for her. She found one text that seemed significant, and read it through several times:

"Who can understand the human heart? There is nothing so deceitful; it is too sick to be healed. I the Lord, search the minds and test the hearts of men. I treat each one according to the way that he lives, according to what he does." Jeremiah 17:9-10

The text didn't promise her any cures, but it seemed to explain the disappointment Stephanie had found in committing her feelings to Jeff, without being critical of his behaviour. He was a fallen human being after all, and God was the only one that could be trusted completely.

It appeared that was all the revelation God had for her that day. Stephanie put the *Bible* down again, and laid her head on the pillow. Stephanie must have fallen asleep, because she woke to Joelle shaking her gently.

"It's time for tea," her room-mate said, "Are you sick or something?"

Stephanie dressed, and obediently followed her.

Stephanie woke up early, and dressed without showering. She grabbed herself a quick breakfast and then went down to clean the women's assembly area. Because it was isolated from the rest of girls' dorm, Stephanie was able to run the vacuum cleaner without disturbing anyone.

Weekend clean-up usually took a couple of hours. When Stephanie was finished, she went back upstairs, and prepared to take a shower. Stephanie spent half an hour in the bathroom and then returned to her room.

Joelle was awake, but still lying in bed, and Stephanie modestly turned her back upon her room-mate while dressing.

Stephanie was startled when Joelle suddenly said: "What is that

Stephanie?"

"I don't know," Stephanie said. "What are you referring to?"

"There is an oblong mark on your back," Joelle said. "It could be a bruise."

"Where on my back?" Stephanie asked puzzled.

"Under the shoulder strap of your bra," Joelle said, "Running down across your back."

"Oh that!" Stephanie said, "I must have bumped into a door."

"Not unless doors have fingers," Joelle said getting out of bed and coming towards her. "That looks like a man's hand."

"It couldn't be!" Stephanie exclaimed.

"It is!" Joelle pronounced. She gave Stephanie a stern look. "If I didn't know better, I would think you were still dating Jeffrey Mannington."

"No," Stephanie said, "That relationship has been over for some time."

"What were you doing with Jeff then?" Joelle demanded.

"He wanted to talk to me," Stephanie admitted slowly.

"Tell him to use his vocal cords, not his fingers next time," Joelle said. "That is shocking! You should report him."

"No," Stephanie said. "They wouldn't believe me. And too many people know that I liked him, enough to almost fight with Grace over him."

"That effectively disguises the real state of affairs," Joelle said. "But this is getting serious."

"Don't worry, I won't let it happen again," Stephanie said. "I have learnt my lesson."

"I will let it go this time then," Joelle said, "But if I see any more marks on you, I will be reporting them herself."

It was a relief when classes commenced for the week. Stephanie threw herself into the routine, and spent as much time as possible with the classmates that she had come to trust.

Stephanie had been finding trust increasingly difficult lately, because there were several groups of guys who sniggered and jeered whenever she was unfortunate enough to pass by them. One group was composed of Roger, Tony and a variety of Jeff's basketball mates; while the other group was headed by Arthur and Michael, who had been mildly unpleasant ever since the Reverse Tea, way back at the beginning of the year.

Stephanie held her head high, and tried to take as little notice of the harassment as possible. She needed to get about her business as usual; dropping out and going home was not an option, because her parents had struggled to pay the deposit on her fees, and would be bitterly disappointed by such an outcome.

Stephanie had a great morning. It revolved around a Practice Teaching presentation that she was required to perform. It was meant to be a ten minute sample section of a forty minute lesson, and it was quite a challenge to create just the right segment for an interesting demonstration.

Stephanie made a verbal presentation of some theory about the fruit bat, and included some diagrams. Then she asked a series of questions. This format was designed to demonstrate her mastery of a variety of teaching techniques, and encourage participation so that Stephanie did not have to do all the talking.

Stephanie had tailored the questions to match the presentation, so that her classmates would not be stuck for the answers. Nonetheless, it was quite amusing to watch them pretend to be school students. Some people went over the top, and put their hands up a lot, saying "Miss Lowood, Miss," all the time.

The Practice Teaching tutorials often required fellow trainees to help each other along. Stephanie was glad to be in a small group with people who had demonstrated their ability to be extremely good sports, and left the class feeling quite cheerful.

However, in the afternoon, things took a down-turn for her. Stephanie had just returned from having lunch in the cafeteria, when she was called to the foyer. Melanie, who was on the desk, said that there was a phone call for her.

It was nearly a week since that other prank call, so Stephanie picked the receiver up unsuspectingly.

"Hello," Stephanie said.

There was a moment's silence and then someone began to speak in a hoarse whisper.

"I have to see you as soon as possible," the voice said. "Will you meet me outside the library in ten minutes?"

"Err - who is this?" Stephanie said.

"You know who," the voice said.

"I'm afraid that I don't know who you are," Stephanie said. "I am going to hang up now."

Stephanie put the receiver down, and sat down hard on the nearest chair.

Melanie looked concerned. "Whatever was that?" she said.

"A whisperer," Stephanie said.

"It sounded normal when I put it through," Melanie said puzzled. "I half thought that it might be Jeff."

"They weren't being normal when I came to the phone," Stephanie said. "Whoever it was tried to spook me."

"What did they want?" Melanie asked.

"To meet me at the library," Stephanie said.

"Are you going over there to meet them?" Melanie asked. "You would see who it was then."

"I doubt it," Stephanie said, "They would watch to see that their trick had worked, and then make themselves scarce."

"Oh, dear," Melanie said, "I am sorry that I paged you for something like that."

"You weren't to know, Melanie," Stephanie said. "I've been getting a bit of that sort of thing lately. It is like everybody has suddenly decided I am ripe to be teased."

"You had an unfortunate break-up," Melanie said. "That makes people mean. I haven't liked that Grace since the beginning of the year. She was always out to get one of our boyfriends."

"I rather think that Grace is being used herself this time," Stephanie said.

Melanie gave her a long look. "Surely not," she said. "I still have to think of Jeff as one of Jonathon's friends."

They had a great discussion in English Literature. The Professor was encouraging them to write their own poetry, and there was an annual poetry competition administered by Brisbane University that was open to all students. The Professor wanted his students to have a go, and even promised that he would read what they had written, and give them pointers in his spare time.

Phoebe, Milton and Stephanie were fascinated by the idea. Milton had a series of lyrical poems already written, and he had a way with rhyme and rhythm that Stephanie admired. Phoebe had a few simple pieces she had attempted in the past. Her verse was quite passable, if a bit prosy.

Stephanie felt that her poetry was inclined to be a little baroque for the modern taste. The love poetry was stylised, being copied from Shakespeare and Wordsworth, and certainly not ready to hand in to anyone. She resolved to polish her writing, and aim for next year's competition.

The best poem Stephanie had written so far was a modernised piece about her fear of being hurt. She had produced it during the mid-year break, when she was meditating on her situation with Jeff. She showed it to the Professor, and he said that she had talent, but her subject was a bit cryptic.

Stephanie asked Bradley whether he was interested in writing poetry and he said, "I think I am more of a factual person, but you never know with the right inspiration."

They continued talking for a few minutes, and he suggested that Stephanie might like to come and watch him play basketball that afternoon. "It is getting pretty close to the finals," Bradley said, "The competition is hotting up."

Stephanie looked doubtful and he added, "I haven't seen you in the gym for ages. You mustn't let Jeff scare you away, you know."

"Okay, Stephanie said, "I'll be there about four."

Stephanie had been sitting in the gymnasium for about ten minutes, when Bethany and Grace came in with Roger and Tony. They started to laugh and joke when they saw her, and Stephanie attempted to ignore them. Eventually they came right up to her.

"Sitting there in the hopes that Jeff might come along," Roger said. "That's really pathetic Stephanie."

"He is still my boyfriend you know," Grace said, "There is no way you are getting him back."

Bethany looked a bit doubtful about all this, but it was obvious that she was going to go along with the others.

"Go away," Stephanie said. "I have nothing to say to you."

"How will you make us?" Tony said. "None of us are afraid of a bit of cordial."

"That's good," Stephanie said, "That wasn't intentional anyway. I just happened to be holding a jug."

"What are you holding today?" Roger jeered.

"Nothing!" Stephanie said, "Shall I throw that at you?"

Stephanie got up and walked off. She wasn't sure if Brad would notice her go, but she would explain it to him later. No one wanted disruptions in the gym during a game, even if they were warranted.

They had a particularly long Life Science practical, and ended up going to the cafeteria as a class. The Proprietor was beginning to pack up, but Garry spoke to him, and he brought out the last remaining tray of savoury. Between them, they completely cleaned out the salad bar, and sat down at a table.

The internal phone rang, and the Proprietor answered it. He came across to her and said, "It is for you Stephanie."

"Oh", Stephanie said, suddenly suspicious, "Ask them who it is."

The cafe Proprietor returned to the phone, and requested that the caller provide identifying details.

"It is Bradley Parker," he said, returning to the table.

Stephanie thought that highly unlikely. If Brad had wanted to get hold of her he would probably have come in person.

"Tell him that I will see him in English tomorrow," Stephanie said, "And tell him to bring a protractor."

The Cafe Proprietor relayed the message, and gave her a nod. "He says that he will."

Cara, Dylan and Garry were very curious.

"That was weird," Cara said, "What would you need your protractor in English for?"

"I don't," Stephanie said. "It was just a test. I don't think that was Bradley at all. I think that it was some weirdo. But I will see Bradley in English, and if he doesn't have a protractor, I will have my proof."

"Very clever," Dylan approved.

"It is a pity that it is necessary," Garry said. "You should have told us you were having trouble, Stephanie."

"And what would you have done?" Stephanie said. "If this is coming from Jeff or his mates, they are way senior to you."

"Ugh," Dylan said. "I wouldn't want to take on Jeffrey Mannington. He's a real despot around the gymnasium, and a grouch in the dorms."

"You see," Stephanie said. "Even you guys wouldn't like to be in my position. I had no idea that he was that bad though."

"He didn't used to be," Dylan said, "He started getting snaky around about the time he broke up with you, Stephanie."

Stephanie looked alarmed. "Do you think it is my fault?" she asked.

"Don't see how it could be," Garry said, "Jeff is over twenty-one. He should be responsible for his own actions."

When Stephanie saw Brad in English, he did not have a protractor. He looked exceedingly puzzled when she asked him for one.

"Do you need it for a Life Science write up?" he said. "I would have to go back to the dorm to get mine. I only occasionally take it to Geography when we do map making."

"That's all right," Stephanie said, "I might be able to find mine."

Stephanie smiled reassuringly at Bradley, but a hard knot was forming inside her. Someone was spreading rumours about her, someone was setting people onto her, and someone was playing silly tricks with the telephones. That someone was sounding suspiciously like Jeff.

Stephanie decided to bead the lion in his den, and marched across to men's hall about half an hour before vespers was due to commence. It was still light outside, and Stephanie felt relatively safe.

The guy on the desk paged Jeff for her, and Stephanie stood there waiting for him. Several guys sniggered as they passed her, and Stephanie wondered for a minute or two whether Jeff might refuse to come down and talk to her.

Stephanie was turning to leave when he arrived. "This is a surprise Stephanie," Jeff said.

"Yes," Stephanie said, "I need to speak to you about something major."

"Okay," he said, "I don't care much about assembly."

Jeff led her out of men's hall, across the grass and down to one of the less frequented areas behind the gymnasium. They stood facing each other.

"Jeff," Stephanie began, "Some strange things have been happening lately, and I have reason to believe that you might be behind them."

"That's nonsense, Stephanie," Jeff said. "I have no interest in you nowadays, and indeed, it was always you who made all the moves."

"Hear me out for a minute," Stephanie said.

Jeff planted his feet firmly on the ground, and folded his arms.

"I have done nothing!" he said. "I hardly ever even speak to you."

"Some of those nothings are pretty significant," Stephanie said.

"You are nuts, Stephanie," Jeff said. "You can't make a complaint about nothing."

"Jeff," Stephanie said, "It is always your friends who harass me; it is your friends who talk about me; I have received numerous messages through your friends, and I have reason to believe that you could be encouraging someone to make prank phone calls to me. Whoever it is knows my routine really well, and who all my friends are."

"Nonsense," Jeff said, "You can't prove a thing."

"Maybe I can't," Stephanie said. "But listen to this Jeff. I am holding you responsible for those things happening to me. If you do not speak to the culprits and ask them nicely to stop, it is you with whom I will be angry."

"That is unreasonable Stephanie," Jeff said angrily, "You can't hold me responsible for things that other people do."

"I want those things to stop Jeff," Stephanie said. "Right now! You are a guy, you have a lot of influence, you could get them stopped - whether they have anything to do with you or not."

"I don't have to do anything you say," Jeff snapped. "I've spoken to you about ordering me around before."

Jeff stepped forward, seized Stephanie by the upper arms, and gave her a slight shake. Then he slid his hands under her arm pits, and pinched her soft skin cruelly.

Stephanie was shocked at how easily Jeff could hurt her and she couldn't seem to engage her muscles to gather the force required to twist away.

Jeff held her immobile for a minute or two. "If you don't stop bothering me, I will do something that really hurts you," he said.

Another long minute passed, and Jeff finally let her go. "I think we have that all sorted out now", he said.

Jeff turned and walked back to men's hall. Stephanie sat down. She was trembling, and her legs wouldn't hold her up; finally, fear of being locked out of girls' dorm made her get up and stumble back there.

As you might have guessed, the incident left no bruises or scrapes for Joelle to remark upon. However, the psychological trauma ran pretty deep. It so happened that particular Saturday was marked as the girls' dormitory "open night". It was the one night in the entire academic year when the men were allowed to enter girls' dorm and look around.

Girl's dorm had been a safe haven for her up till now, and Stephanie could not bear the thought of it being invaded. Despite having helped Joelle clean the room on Friday afternoon, she did not want any guys to come inside.

Stephanie got very shaky and frightened thinking about the guys that were constantly teasing her around campus. She was also plagued by Jeff's statement that all the guys despised her, and after last night, she was convinced that they were all in league with Jeff to hurt her.

Stephanie began the evening quite bravely, with the bedroom

door just slightly ajar. However, she thought that she heard familiar chuckles and guffaws coming down the corridor. There was the sound of running feet.

Stephanie had no idea where Jeff was. She thought it unlikely that he would come into her room himself, but he could easily send Roger or Tony to do his dirty work for him.

Stephanie crossed the room, locked the door, and sat cowering on her bed. There was an insistent knocking at the door. Visions of Roger, Tony, Arthur, and maybe even Michael coming to get her crowded through her head.

Someone called out. It was Joelle, and she was getting quite annoyed with her.

"Stephanie," Joelle said, "Open the door. What is wrong with you?"

"I don't want any guys to come into the dorm," Stephanie replied.

"I want to show Milton our room," Joelle retorted.

"Please don't make me let any guys in," Stephanie said.

"Come on, Stephanie," Joelle said, "It is only David and Milton. You know them, they are okay."

Stephanie opened the door and retreated to her side of the room. Joelle brought the guys in, and they stood there for a few minutes looking as if they felt awkward.

Joelle suggested that they might like to go down to the lounge. They said goodbye and left, thoughtfully closing the door behind them.

Her level of panic decreased as the noises in the corridor slowly subsided and Stephanie could no longer hear any voices that sounded like those of Jeff's mates. The rush of visitors was obviously finished.

Joelle returned to the room an hour later looking perplexed. "That was embarrassing," she said. "Whatever has gotten into you Stephanie?"

"I'm sorry," Stephanie said, "This thing with Jeff is making me nervous. I am starting to expect trouble from all sides."

"You can't live that way," Joelle said, "I hope that it soon starts to sort itself out."

"Just give me some time," Stephanie said. "I am sure that there is an answer around somewhere, if I can just find it."

CHAPTER TWELVE: CLARITY

Stephanie went across to the library as soon as it opened in the afternoon. Early though she was, Milton had arrived before her. He was sitting at a table writing some of his own poetry.

Milton gestured to invite her to sit down. "How are you today?" he said.

"Good," Stephanie said, "Much better than last night. I am sorry about that by the way."

"That is all-right," Milton said. "It was obvious that there was something upsetting you."

"Yes," Stephanie said, "There was."

"Do you want to tell me about it?" Milton asked, "I'm not an ogre, you know."

Thanks," Stephanie said, "You are very understanding. It was a combination of the things that have been happening to me lately. Guys poking fun at me around campus, people being rude right to my face, Jeff getting agro once or twice, and of course the phone calls."

"What phone calls?" Milton queried.

"Some guys from men's hall are ringing me in the dorms, and being silly if I take the call," Stephanie said.

"How many of these calls have you had?" Milton asked.

"I don't know, I haven't taken them all," Stephanie said, "At least four or five."

"That's quite a pattern developing!" Milton said. "We had better put a stop to it at once."

"How would we do that?" Stephanie asked.

"Simple," Milton said, "The next time that you get one of those calls, don't take it straight away. Instead, go to one of the other internal phones and get me paged. I will come down to the foyer and see who is using the phone booth there."

"Wow," Stephanie said, "You would really do that for me?"

"Yes sure," Milton said, "What are friends for?"

"It could mean falling foul of some of Jeff's mates," Stephanie said, looking Milton up and down. He was a wiry little fellow, not someone that you would pick out as being inherently brave. "They are big guys."

"That doesn't bother me," Milton said. "They are insensitive sporting types, and petty bullies. They are also all several years younger than me. I have seen much worse thugs out there in the world."

"Oh really?" Stephanie said fascinated. "And it has given you this strength?"

"This strength and a few weaknesses of my own," Milton said wryly. "Sometimes the bad things come back to haunt me."

"Does Joelle know about this?" Stephanie asked.

"Some, but not all of it. She knows that my brother got heavily involved in the drug scene," Milton said. "I will tell her that I continue to worry about him when the need arises. To a large extent,

Joelle and I are still at the just-good-friends stage."

"I thought that you two had gotten much further than that," Stephanie remarked.

"I like Joelle, but I have been holding back in case I can't be the way a Christian girl expects her boyfriend to be," Milton admitted. "I dated some pretty fast girls that I met in hotel bars in the past. I don't want to shock Joelle with all that and you can never be too cautious about commencing a long term relationship."

"You are telling me!" Stephanie commented, reflecting on her own experience. "So you weren't just shy about asking Joelle out at the beginning of the year?"

"No," Milton said. "I had my reasons. Most guys do when they don't go ahead and ask a girl out. That is why it isn't always a good idea for the girl to rush along and do the asking herself."

"Do you think that is where I made my mistake with Jeff?" Stephanie asked.

"Jeff had given you a heap of signals that he wanted to go ahead," Milton said. "And then he stuffed up. You should stop trying to find a way to blame yourself."

"Oh!" Stephanie said, "But I am still confused. Do you think that a girl should avoid calling a guy even after the friendship is started?"

"Only if the girl has doubts about the guy's sincerity. If you had been more alert to the bad vibes Jeff was sending out, you could have practised a bit more self-preservation," Milton said. "Otherwise, guys appreciate return calls. A relationship would die really quickly, if the guy was obliged to make each and every one of the moves."

"It is so hard to work out," Stephanie mused.

Milton laughed. "You are very innocent Stephanie," he said. "A nice guy would value that quality in you. The other sort would see it as an excuse to eat you alive. Jeff was obviously the wrong sort."

"Interesting!" Stephanie said, "Well, I want to get some study done. Thanks for the chat."

"That's okay," Milton said. "Remember, the next time that you get one of those prank calls, I am going to help you nab the culprit."

"Yes," Stephanie said, "It will be good to put a stop to that sort of thing. It has really disrupted my life recently."

Milton and Stephanie did not have to wait all that long to catch the perpetrator of the prank calls. In fact, an opportunity presented itself almost immediately.

Stephanie dropped by the dormitory about nine-thirty to get rid of the folders from her earlier classes. It got very tiring carrying excess books and folders around all morning. Stephanie had some unexpected free time due to her Standard English class being re-scheduled and replaced by a communication workshop to be held in the afternoon. (They would be practicing assertion and 'I statements' in smaller groups than the regular class.)

Stephanie had barely entered her room when she heard her name called over the public address system. The timing was uncanny, and gave her the feeling that someone was watching her every move. It seemed pretty suspicious.

Stephanie hurried down to the foyer. "Hi," she said, "Was that a phone call for me?"

"Yes," said Melanie, who was on the desk once again. "I have switched it through to booth one."

"Internal or external?" Stephanie queried.

"Internal," Melanie said, "From men's hall. You don't think it is one of those creepy ones again, do you?"

"You never know!" Stephanie said. "Here is what I want you to do: page Milton Short, and ask him to come to the foyer. Then speak to the caller on the other line, and tell them that I am on my way. Don't let them hang up."

"Got you," Melanie said. She lifted the receiver, dialled the desk at men's hall and asked for Milton. She sounded very calm. Then she spoke to the other caller, "Stephanie will be with you in a minute, please hold on."

Stephanie grabbed the phone that Milton was going to be answering, and prayed that he would be in the boys' dorm. He had the same tutorials as her, so she knew that he would not be in class.

The receiver crackled and Milton answered: "Milton here".

"Oh I am so glad you are there," Stephanie said. "It is Stephanie. Whoever the prankster is, he is on the other line."

"Good," Milton said. "I will go and see. Then I will call you back."

He put the phone down, and Stephanie was left listening to the spacey sound of an empty line.

Stephanie hung up and turned to Melanie, "I will take the other call now."

Stephanie went into booth one, and picked up the receiver. "Stephanie Lowood speaking," she said. There was a gasp on the other end. It sounded like the receiver was dropped, but not hung up. Stephanie listened curiously, but she could not tell what was going on.

It was a few minutes before any of the phones in girls' dorm rang. Melanie answered, and then beckoned to her. "It is Milton," she said, "And it really is him, he sounds the same as he did a couple of minutes ago, except maybe puffed."

Stephanie grabbed the phone and spoke into it: "Who was it? What happened?"

"I have some good news, and some bad news for you Stephanie," Milton said. "The good news is that the person is unlikely to do it again. I spoke to him, and told him that I would support any complaint you chose to make to the discipline committee about him. He slunk off like the coward he is."

"What else?" Stephanie asked anxiously.

"The bad news is that it was Jeffrey Mannington," Milton said, "With one of his mates - Roger Faraday by his side."

Stephanie gasped.

"I am sorry Stephanie," Milton said, "I suspect you were hoping that it wouldn't be the man himself."

"I did hope to keep a few of my illusions intact," Stephanie said. "It was easier to blame some creepy friends."

"Well, it was best that you knew," Milton said, "You won't go letting him back into your life now."

"You wouldn't just say that to make sure I do the right thing, would you Milton?" Stephanie asked.

"No way," Milton said, "Joelle would give me heaps."

"Well thanks," Stephanie said, "I guess that is one problem sorted."

Melanie looked at Stephanie curiously when she got off the phone. "Well, who was it?" Melanie said.

"Milton says it was Jeff," Stephanie said.

Melanie looked shocked. "Did Milton actually see Jeff?" she asked.

"Yes," Stephanie said, "There was very little room for error."

"I am so sorry," Melanie said. "I will get Jonathon to talk to Jeff if you like."

"No. Stay out of it," Stephanie said. "I want to forget it, and I don't think Jeff will do it again. Milton gave him quite a shock."

Melanie looked relieved. "Yes, we all make mistakes," she said, reverting comfortably back to her forgiving world view.

"Some of us more than others," Stephanie said ironically. "Thank you for your help Melanie, I have classes to go to now."

Stephanie had maintained a cool face to Melanie, but she had been more upset than she admitted by the discovery of Jeff's perfidy. Stephanie tried to do as she had told Melanie, and "forget" the whole thing, but she found herself continually putting her books down, and pacing the room.

When night fell, Stephanie was no nearer achieving a relaxed state. She went to bed around ten as usual, and found herself lying awake all night with confused and regretful thoughts running through her head. Consequently she had large dark patches under her eyes in the morning.

This would not have been a huge concern to Stephanie, except that she had a Life Science test coming up on Friday. Like all their Life Science tests, it was very important, and put the whole class under some pressure.

Stephanie spoke to the Dean just after lunch, and she said that if the sleeplessness continued, she would send Stephanie to the doctor to see whether he thought sleeping tablets would be helpful.

After another restless night, Stephanie was sent to see a doctor. The university car dropped her off at the local Northcoast Medical Centre. Stephanie registered her name with the receptionist, and filled out a form, writing down the new Medicare card her mother had insisted she apply for at the beginning of the year. Then she took a seat, and settled down to wait for the doctor.

At last her name was called. Stephanie followed the Doctor out of the reception area, down a corridor and into a private room. He invited her to sit down.

"What seems to be the problem?" the Doctor asked.

"I am having a bit of trouble sleeping," Stephanie said. "I don't really want to go on sleeping tablets, but one or two good night's sleep might help me get through my tests and exams."

The Doctor grunted, and proceeded to listen to her heart and chest, and take her blood pressure. He asked her about a range of symptoms, from fever to headache, none of which Stephanie suffered.

"Well," he said, "I can't find anything wrong with you, and I do not like proscribing sleeping tablets to young people. Have you been under any extra stress lately? You did mention some exams."

"Oh, I cope with exams all-right," Stephanie said, "I just haven't been able to sleep since the boy I was involved with turned nasty towards me, but that wouldn't have anything to do with my physical problems."

"You would be surprised," the Doctor said. "Tell me about this boyfriend of yours."

Stephanie explained that Jeff had mood-swings, and seemed to take his aggression out on her. Stephanie described the campaign of jealousy and humiliation that had been waged upon her, and how Jeff had been found to be the perpetrator of the prank phone calls. Feeling protected by the Doctor's obligation to maintain patient confidentiality, Stephanie even told him about the push, the bruises and the threats.

The Doctor listened in silence. When Stephanie had finished, he spoke very seriously: "What you are describing qualifies as relationship violence. I don't think that there is anything wrong with you that getting away from this Jeff wouldn't fix."

"I've tried," Stephanie said. "There is no longer any relationship between us."

"But he has been able to draw you out and provoke you into

speaking to him again," the Doctor said. "I would advise you to guard against that. If leaving campus isn't an option for you, act as if he simply is not there."

"I will try that," Stephanie said. "I am partly this messed up because I can't understand why any of this happened. I try, and try to work out what went wrong."

"Some men hit their wives and girlfriends for no real reason," the Doctor said, "But in this case, it is possible there may be a real mental health problem underlying Jeff's behaviour."

"Oh dear," Stephanie said.

"I can't say without seeing the boy himself," the Doctor said, "But what you are describing sounds like the result of some emotional disorder."

"What do you mean?" Stephanie inquired.

"Well, the distressed thought patterns, the disjointed speech and the need to comfort himself with routine are all symptoms," The Doctor said. "This sort of condition often develops in the late teens, or early twenties. It can be very disruptive to the person suffering from it, and agonising for those who care about them."

"So, it is not his fault then?" Stephanie said. "He has this condition that makes him act the way he does."

"That is not completely true," the Doctor said, "I would say he does have some control over how, and when he acts out his aggression."

"How is that?" Stephanie asked.

"Well, Jeff has succeeding in handling his distress to the extent required to earn himself a degree," the Doctor said. "Tell me, if he went for a job interview, would he be likely to assault the panel of interviewers?"

Stephanie laughed: "Not likely! He would be very business-like and charming."

"Exactly - he would make an effort to control himself. But he does not feel the need to be as circumspect around you," explained the Doctor. "He has chosen to target his aggression, and make you a scapegoat for all his problems."

"That is a very sad thought all by itself," Stephanie said, beginning to cry.

"You are obviously very sensitive," remarked the Doctor, "And that might be why he was drawn to you. However, it in no way implies that any of the abuse you suffered was your fault."

"Could Jeff be helped?" Stephanie asked.

"He would benefit from seeing someone professional," the Doctor mused. "However, you must not make it your task to get him to seek help. It would be best if he did that voluntarily. Stay away from him, and concentrate on keeping yourself safe."

"Thank you, Doctor," Stephanie said. "I will try to avoid further contact with Jeff, and I do feel better knowing for sure that's what is necessary. Something inside of me always wanted to forgive him, and sort things out."

"Quite understandable in a normal friendship!" The Doctor said supportively. "Unfortunately, it's not possible to sort things out with someone who is not operating from a logical basis."

Stephanie woke up determined to get back into both her studies, and the university social life. Telling someone about the problem and receiving some sort of explanation had relieved her mind enough to allow her to sleep again, and Stephanie was feeling healthier than she had for days.

When Stephanie arrived at English Literature, Phoebe was talking about the Pancake Night. Stephanie was startled to realise that it was scheduled for the coming weekend, and quickly tuned into the conversation. Phoebe told Elisabet and Stephanie that Dylan had asked her to be his date for the evening.

"Dylan said he was getting tired of being turned down by Cara all the time," Phoebe explained. "He asked me whether I would take pity on him, and go along for a bit of relaxing company."

"And are you going with him?" Elisabet asked.

"I told him I would think about it," Phoebe said.

"Dylan is a lot of fun!" Stephanie said. "You would enjoy the evening."

"I know," Phoebe said, "It's just not the most gallant invitation I've ever received. That is why I didn't say yes straightaway."

"Dylan could learn some tact," Stephanie said, "He is too honest for his own good! I think that is why he isn't getting anywhere with Cara."

"At least you know where you stand with him," Elisabet said. "I wouldn't mind going out with a guy like that!"

"What about you, Stephanie?" Phoebe said. "Who are you going to go with, now that you are single?"

"I don't know," Stephanie said. "I hadn't really thought about it."

Bradley and Tom had just entered the room. They took the seats on the other side of her.

"Do you really not have a date, Stephanie?" Brad inquired.

"I don't," Stephanie said. "Don't make a big issue of it, okay? I don't know who would ask me out, with the break-up with Jeff being so recent and messy."

"You know, Steph," Bradley said, "You are a great girl. You are bright, and you take an interest in a guy's progress. A lot of guys would ask you out if they were sure they wouldn't have to fight their way through Jeffrey Mannington to do it."

"Jeff is definitely out of the picture," Stephanie replied.

"Are you sure?" Bradley said, "That is not the way Jeff tells it around the dorms."

"I don't care what Jeff is saying nowadays," Stephanie said. "I am not planning to take him back."

"How about going with me then?" Bradley suggested.

Phoebe, who a minute ago had been laughing at something Elisabet said, suddenly went quiet. Stephanie glanced over at her in concern. If Phoebe had shaken her head even slightly, she would have interpreted this as an indication of interest in Bradley, and turned him down. However, Phoebe would not look her in the eye. Stephanie reasoned that Phoebe was as good as fixed up with Dylan anyway.

"I would love to go with you Brads," Stephanie said.

"Great!" Bradley exclaimed, "I will pick you up at the girls' dorm half an hour before it commences."

The Professor arrived, and they fell silent in preparation for the upcoming lecture. It was about Tolkien, and Stephanie took careful notes, planning to check every word against what she had written in her essay.

Joelle was pleased when Stephanie told her that she had a date with Bradley.

"I am glad to hear you are getting back into things," Joelle said.

"I am surprised at how easy it is," Stephanie said.

"Well, you had never dropped your bundle completely," Joelle observed. "Listen, I had a message for you. May dropped by, and asked whether you would like to play scrabble with her."

"I guess so," Stephanie said, "I'll go by her room. I haven't done that for a while, for fear of running into Grace up there."

"You probably won't see Grace," Joelle said, "And if you do, just remember that nobody takes her that seriously."

"I'll try to remember that," Stephanie said, taking off down the corridor.

May and Bethany were both home. May got out the scrabble, and Bethany joined them for a quick game. May won easily, and Stephanie declined a re-match.

"I'll only get beaten!" Stephanie said, "Tell me how things are going for you."

"Okay," May said, "The study is quite heavy."

"How about you Bethany?" Stephanie queried.

Bethany shrugged, "The same as May," she replied.

"Do you have dates for the Pancake Night?" Stephanie asked.

"I don't," May said, "There is a group of us Nurses all going together. We are too new on campus to have found anyone, especially as half of the others are already going steady."

"What about you Bethany?" Stephanie said.

"I am not going at all," Bethany said.

Stephanie was stunned. Bethany was pretty, and she was outgoing. The girl had enjoyed the Computer Tea, and Stephanie knew that she had several lacy dresses in the wardrobe for other such occasions.

"Grace must have introduced you to a lot of guys," Stephanie said.

"I suppose she has," Bethany said. "But none of them have asked me to the Pancake Night."

"I am sorry to hear that," Stephanie said, "It should be a good evening."

"Yes," Bethany agreed listlessly. "I think I will go and have a shower now." She got up, collected a few of her things and left the room.

"What is wrong with her?" Stephanie said to May, after Bethany had left.

"I don't know for sure," May said, "I think there may be somebody in particular who hasn't asked her out."

"Oh, I am sorry to hear that," Stephanie said, remembering back to the time that she had found herself in that position. "But she must learn not to stay in and mope about it."

"That is exactly what I told her," May said, "I couldn't get through though."

Stephanie dressed carefully, enjoying the feeling of being on a date with a guy who appreciated her. Bradley was an easy-going guy, and she didn't have to fear the uncertainty involved in partnering Jeff at a function.

The Pancake Night was only semi-formal, so Stephanie wore a white knitted top that she had bought in Melbourne, and teamed it with her red and black skirt. The ensemble felt both comfortable and feminine.

Bradley picked her up from the dormitory about 6:00 pm. Stephanie could tell from the look on his face, that he liked what she was wearing. He said, "Wow," which was pretty flattering, if not particularly descriptive.

They walked across to the cafeteria, and selected a table to sit at. The table was equipped with a jug of maple syrup, and a bowl of cream. It was set for eight people, so they called Debbie and David, Joelle and Milton, and Warren and Gloria, across to sit with them.

Bradley took their plates and went across to the centre of the room to collect a stack of hot pancakes. Tubs of ice-cream were also set up over there, and he waved at Stephanie to determine what she wanted.

Stephanie began to get worried that Bradley wouldn't be able to carry everything. She was getting up to go across and help him, when he managed to bring the two over-flowing plates back to the table with all the finesse developed defending the ball on the basketball court.

"Thanks," Stephanie said, "That was impressive."

"You are welcome," Brad said. "I think I saw some lemonade amongst the drinks. I will see if I can get us some before it all goes."

"That would be nice," Stephanie agreed, "Soft drink is pretty rare around here."

Bradley went off, and was back a few minutes later with a bottle of Schweppes. "I got some for everyone at the table," he said, "Do you guys want some?"

Everyone was pleased, and thanked Brad profusely.

When they had eaten, Brad and Stephanie started talking about study, and then went on to explore their other interests to determine what they might have in common.

After a while, they began talking about basketball. Stephanie was interested to hear about the A grade competition from Brad's point of view. A number of his opinions differed to those that Jeff had always expressed. Stephanie filed the differences away to think about later. Warren joined in this conversation, and they were still talking after most of the other couples had left.

At last Warren and Gloria announced that they had to go. Brad turned to Stephanie:

"I will walk you across to the dorms," he said.

"Thank you," Stephanie said, "I appreciate that gentlemanly

stuff."

"That is good to hear," Brad said, "A guy barely knows whether to do it or not nowadays."

"Oh, it is a definite do around me," Stephanie said.

They had reached the back door of women's hall, when Brad touched her lightly on the shoulders, and turned her around to face him.

"Did you have a good time?" he asked.

"Lovely thank you Brad," Stephanie answered.

"Would you like to do something next weekend?" Bradley queried.

Stephanie hesitated. Brad was every bit as tall as Jeff, and possibly a great deal cuter. He could be amusing when he got going, but he was predominantly quiet natured. That was the problem - in some ways he reminded her of Jeff. Stephanie was sure that he wouldn't have the same problems, but he probably would leave most of the communication up to her. It was enough to put her off.

"You are a good friend Brad," Stephanie said, "But that is all I am looking for at this very moment."

Brad looked disappointed, and a vision of Phoebe ran through Stephanie's head. Phoebe had attended the Tea with Dylan, and sat several tables away from them. Stephanie had caught the other girl looking wistfully towards Bradley and her several times.

"You know what Brads?" Stephanie said. "I think Phoebe likes you."

Bradley looked surprised. "Oh!" He said, "Oh, oh! I had her

marked as the friend, and you as the girlfriend."

"Maybe it was meant to be the other way around," Stephanie suggested.

"I will have to think it through," Bradley said. "It is not exactly what I had planned."

"My year hasn't exactly gone to plan either," Stephanie said, "But I am sure it will work out." Stephanie thanked Bradley once again for the lovely evening, and retreated into girls' dorm.

Stephanie had set an alarm that night, because she had to get up early in the morning. The Biology Master waited for no one, and asked no permission to schedule a field trip.

They took off about eight am, and drove to one of the local Noosa beaches. Stephanie was surprised to see that this one was actually sandy! They walked for some distance, observing how tufts of coarse grass and creeping ground cover were beginning to grow some distance back from the ocean.

Apparently this was called "succession". The theory postulated that plants able to survive on the sea front secured the sand, thus preparing the way for trees and more complex plants to grow.

The class left the beach and began to walk inland towards a sparse scrubby area. The main feature of this area was some scraggy trees which the Biology Master identified as "angophora". The Biology Master was particularly interested in the circumference of these trees, and kept sending Dylan and Garry out into the scrub to run a length of rope around their trunks.

After a while, they reached the beginning of the rainforest area. Here the Biology Master pointed out the variety of trees and plants. Some pre-historic looking ferns called "cycads" came in for a special mention. There were a number of seed pods on the ground that the Biology Master explained would only germinate after they had been cracked open by a fire.

Around two o'clock, they stopped to eat their packed lunch. Some of the class had been becoming alarmed in case the Biology Master would not let them eat at all. There was always another thing that he wanted to see first!

They pushed a little deeper into the forest after that. There were one or two plants that the Biology Master was keeping a regular watch upon, and he wanted the students to help him with his observations.

It was almost tea time when they returned to campus. Stephanie was hot and very tired, but she felt that she had a fun day in an exhausting type of way.

Stephanie had a full morning of classes, and arrived at lunch quite late. After Stephanie had finished eating, she began to walk back to the dormitory. Melanie, who had been sitting chatting with Jonathon, fell into step beside her.

"How are you going Stephanie?" she asked.

"Pretty good Melanie," Stephanie said. "How about yourself?"

"I am fine," Melanie said. "But it is hectic doing my final assignments, and organising a wedding all at once."

"How is that going?" Stephanie asked.

"I have picked the bridesmaid's dresses, and booked a church in Melbourne," Melanie said. "Mum and Dad are taking care of the rest."

"What about your dress?" Stephanie asked.

"I am having something made," Melanie said. "It is much cheaper that way, and I can have exactly what I want. I have bought some really lacy material, and I think I will have several rows of frills around the edge."

"It sounds lovely," Stephanie said. "Does Jonathon know anything about his job yet?"

"Oh yes," Melanie said, "His was one of the first placements out. He has got something down in Sydney."

"That is good," Stephanie said. The mention of Sydney made her think briefly of Jeff, but she wasn't going to ask about him.

"I have some news for you," Melanie said.

"What would that be?" I asked.

"Jeff and Grace have split up," Melanie said. "He marched her out of the Pancake Night half way through, and read her the riot act."

"Whatever for?" Stephanie exclaimed.

"Being over-possessive, flirting around with Roger - all the things that Grace does," Melanie said.

Stephanie shrugged. She was surprised at how cool her reaction was. "Grace is an easy target if you are determined to be critical; and those things suited Jeff less than a month ago," Stephanie said. "I was supposed to be too quiet, and too emotionally attached to him."

"I think he preferred you," Melanie said. "You were probably right about Jeff using Grace. I think he wanted to make you jealous, and when that stopped working, he got rid of her."

"Either way it is not a pretty picture," Stephanie said.

"No, it's not," Melanie said thoughtfully. "Although Jeff is free now, if you are interested in having him back."

"Not really," Stephanie said. "There are the other things that he has done - remember?"

"Oh," Melanie said, "I thought that you might be able to forgive him those. He must have been pretty confused at the time to do them."

"I can believe that!" Stephanie said, "The problem is, I can't see any sign of him getting un-confused."

"You may be right there," Melanie said. "His vision of the future seems fairly monotonous. I thought that a good woman could change that."

"I don't see it as my job to fix Jeff up," Stephanie said.

"You have made your decision then," Melanie said.

"Yes!" Stephanie said, "And I am determined to stick to it."

The Biology Master pinned a giant contour map of the region they had hiked through on Sunday up on the wall near his office. He put coloured drawing pins in the different areas to help the class orient themselves as they did their write-ups.

Stephanie had already begun work on her field trip report, and raced upstairs to consult the map as soon as she heard about it. Garry was up there too, making notes. He suggested that they get together in the library that afternoon to exchange observations, in case one of them had recorded data that the other missed on the day.

The *Silver Spring University Year Book* came out just after Assembly. The publication contained a small square "mug shot" of every student and staff member, and a number of pages of coloured photos of group activities. As soon as it was known to be available, the students all rushed to the student union office to collect their personal copy. Then they spent ages searching for candid shots of themselves, and inviting friends to autograph their photo for them. (Apparently this was a long-standing tradition.)

Stephanie was pleased with the messages most people wrote in her year book. It seemed that she had been more popular than she realised.

CHAPTER THIRTEEN: A NEW LOVE

The English Professor was screening a series of BBC productions of Shakespearian plays. The film nights were primarily for the benefit of the second year students, on whose curriculum the texts appeared, but the Professor suggested that some first year students might also like to attend.

The Professor was planning to screen *As You Like It* this week, and *Twelfth Night* the following week. Displaying a merry disregard for the commercial world represented by the late night shopping shuttle to Northcoast, he had chosen Thursday evening for the activity.

Stephanie found herself sitting with Garry at lunch, and she mentioned the film to him incidentally. Stephanie thought it unlikely Garry would be interested in attending because he appeared to be a pure Science person, but he surprised her by saying that he could enjoy the Arts without studying them.

"I would love to go along," Garry said, "It is something different to do in the evenings. I could especially use the break after the Life Science lab. That always makes me sick of study!"

"Meet me outside of lecture theatre one just after the dorm meeting then," Stephanie said, "That is when the Professor plans to start."

When Garry arrived at theatre one that evening, he had a packet of Fantails, which he insisted on sharing with her.

"We might as well treat it as a real movie," Garry said, selecting a chocolate and unwrapping it. Stephanie looked around to see if the Professor had any objections to this behaviour, but he was far too busy in the projection room to notice.

They went into the theatre, and sat down a couple of rows ahead of Bradley and Phoebe, who appeared to have arrived together.

Stephanie turned around and said "Hi" to Phoebe, and nodded to Brad. They both looked quite satisfied.

Then the Professor poked his head in the door to check that all his second year literature students were present. He turned the lights off, and the film commenced.

As You Like It had been acted in period costume and on location, which Stephanie always enjoyed. It portrayed a series of romantic mix-ups with people running around in disguise, not even realising that the person they were courting was out in the forest with them. It was amazing how much more honest people were about their feelings when they thought that the object of their affection was not present!

At the end of the play, everyone was lined up and married off to the right person. The multiple wedding ceremony made her sniff a bit, and Stephanie was surprised to discover that her romantic sensibilities were still intact. It was evident her heart, despite its experience with Jeff, thrived on happy endings.

Stephanie didn't have much time to think about this discovery, because Garry began talking to her.

"That was quite good," he said. "I was surprised that I could follow the words."

"The gestures help," Stephanie said. "And I sometimes suspect that they edit or abbreviate the text in the film version."

"Could be!" Garry said. "Here let me walk you back to women's hall."

"Thanks," Stephanie said falling into step beside him. "You don't have to, you know. This was just a friendly occasion."

"It's dark out there," Garry said, "And you never know, you could run into Jeffrey Mannington."

"That guy is history as far as I am concerned," Stephanie said. "Why do I have to keep telling people?"

"Jeff could still be lurking in a dark corner," Garry remarked, "That seemed to be how he operated."

"You're telling me!" Stephanie said with a shiver, "I don't even want to think about it happening again!"

"Let your friends do the worrying for you then," Garry suggested. "We all want to see you get over him."

"Yes," Stephanie said. "I appreciate that. Well, we are back at girls' dorm now."

"Just before you go," Garry said turning to face her, "This Friday night is going to be a special program with music and candles. Would you consider making it a date?"

Stephanie took a deep breath, and regarded Garry carefully. He was pleasantly blonde in appearance, and had a practical approach to life that she liked. Up till now, their friendship had been completely free of romantic overtones. However, Stephanie sensed that might be about to change.

"I am happy to go along with you," Stephanie said, "If we can leave the dating part till a bit later. When I start a relationship with someone new, I will want to take things slowly and carefully."

"That is fair enough after what you have been through," Garry said. "I will see you tomorrow." He turned and walked back across the campus whistling softly under his breath.

The weather was warm, and somewhat sticky. Stephanie found herself breaking out into a sweat as she vacuumed. The women's assembly area was being decorated with white flowers and tall candelabra; several deaconesses were scurrying around, and while they said little more than "Hello" to her, Stephanie enjoyed the company. Cleaning was usually solitary work, and it was nice to have a change of pace.

After Stephanie had finished work in the women's assembly hall, she went to have a shower and neaten herself up, before going to the cafeteria for tea. As the Uniting Church vespers would follow soon after tea, Stephanie put on a light cotton dress that would be suitable for both.

The frock was one Stephanie had made herself using the white fabric spotted with yellow sunflowers. It was sleeveless and had a square yoke, while the body of the dress was attached just above the chest-line. Stephanie clinched the waist with a white leather belt and it gathered in quite nicely.

Stephanie had a quick tea with Joelle and May. Joelle left to have a last minute practice of the evening's songs, and May invited

Stephanie back to her room for a while. They were sitting chatting when the call came over the public address system for her to go down to the foyer.

Stephanie was suddenly extremely nervous. "That's my summons down to worship," she said to May. "Why don't you come along with me?"

"I would love to," May said, "If you are sure that I won't get in the way."

"Of course not," Stephanie said, "Garry will be pleased to see you."

"What happened to Bradley?" May exclaimed in surprise.

"Otherwise engaged I hope," Stephanie said cryptically.

"Don't you mind?" May asked.

"Not in the least," Stephanie answered. "We were just friends."

"Is it you and Garry now, then?" May inquired.

"No," Stephanie said, "It is going to be me and me for a while."

"Until Garry manages to change your mind," May commented.

"Something like that!" Stephanie said.

Garry greeted Stephanie as soon as she arrived in the foyer. "You look very nice," he said.

"Thank you," Stephanie said, "I made this dress myself during the break. Auntie Sonia let me use her machine."

"It was well worth the effort," Garry said. "I am lucky to have two such lovely ladies to take to vespers."

Garry led the way out around the side of the building. It was dark inside the women's assembly hall when they arrived. The only light, other than the spot trained on Joelle to allow her to read the sheet music, came from the candelabra up the front, where the white flowers and the faces of the choir members gleamed in the dusk.

The choir sung a number of African American Spiritual pieces including "This train is bound for glory", and "Do Lord". The highlight of the evening was "This little light of mine", during which each and every choir member held a white candle.

Stephanie loved the program. It took her all the way back to the sing-alongs she had in primary school. Garry and May also said that they enjoyed the performance. Afterwards, Garry walked May and Stephanie around to the foyer, and said "Goodnight" politely.

The weekend news bulletins were full of the shocking assassination of Indian Prime Minister Indira Ghandi. Mrs Ghandi had been a popular leader serving her country for a number of terms. However, she had sent the army to quell a Sikh uprising at Amritsar earlier in the year and a number of citizens were killed. It appeared that her Sikh bodyguards had killed Mrs. Ghandi in revenge for their fallen comrades. The political unrest continued with several violent assaults against the Sikhs.

As with many forms of overseas violence, the students at Silver Springs University in peaceful Australia found the news difficult to comprehend. A special prayer vigil was held in the evening and attendance was voluntary. The participants silently thanked God for the Australian constitution which ensured their freedom to participate freely in Christian, Buddhist, Muslim, Hindu,

Sikh or other religious groups. They prayed for the welfare of those who were unfortunate enough to live in countries where such civil rights were less well established.

Stephanie woke up early on Sunday and put on her blue crepe suit. It was raining outside, and she tripped quickly across to the cafeteria under the shelter of her umbrella. Even after almost a year in Queensland, Stephanie was still surprised by the summer rain. It continued to pour throughout the morning, and Stephanie was glad that the Inter-denominational praise and Reformed Church services kept her busy and dry.

Stephanie sat with Debbie and David in the Reformed Church service. They arrived early, and Stephanie discretely made sure that the seat on the other side of her remained empty until Garry arrived. Stephanie was pleased to see that he looked around for her immediately upon entering the campus meeting hall. Then he crossed the floor to sit at her side. Reciprocity had become important to her, and Stephanie was ensuring that it was in operation.

After lunch the sky cleared, and David suggested that they risk going for a walk. He invited Joelle and Milton, Phoebe and Bradley to join them. They changed into casual clothes, and carried their Parkas just in case of another down-pour. However, the blue sky held, and they enjoyed sloshing along the bush path, watching the sun play upon the pools of water.

"This is the life," David said, stopping beside the creek to observe its swollen waters. "I love walking after a storm."

"So do I," Stephanie said, "Although I have rarely seen rain as heavy as this."

"It happens quite often here in Queensland," David said.

"Hey," Debbie said pointing at Phoebe and Bradley, who had chosen to walk some paces ahead of the general group, "Look at those two holding hands!"

"That is another couple in our midst," Garry said, "Funny how things work out." He looked slyly at her, but Stephanie decided that this was a good time to go and walk the other side of Debbie.

"Shall we catch up to them?" Debbie queried, "Or shall we pretend that we don't notice what they are up to?"

"Oh pretend, by all means!" Stephanie said, "It is such fun - and besides, they will tell us all about it in their own time."

"I think that we should mind our own business," David said somewhat pompously.

"Wishing our friends well is our business," Stephanie retorted, "But I don't expect you blokes to understand...it's a girl thing."

"Let's change the subject," Debbie said. "Tell us about the far north, David."

The rain returned with a vengeance in the morning. Stephanie had to be careful not to make wet tracks in and out of women's assembly area as she worked.

Stephanie spent several hours working in there, because the Dean had asked her to clean all the wax spots off the carpet. The Dean had suggested a neat trick, whereby Stephanie could remove the spots by placing an absorbent paper towel over the target area, and heating it up with an iron. The wax melted easily, and soaked into the paper.

In the afternoon Stephanie settled down to some serious study. She spent half of her time reading an English novel, and the other half underlining the main points in the most current chapter of her Life Science text.

Stephanie had a full morning of classes, and spent her one free period analysing a poem for English Literature. She had resolved to analyse one poem a day, with the intention of getting her mind into good analytical shape for the English exams.

Garry and Stephanie had arranged to meet in the library after lunch to put the finishing touches on their Life Science field trip write-ups. Stephanie arrived there about 2:00 pm, and at first she thought that Garry might have forgotten, because he was not there. However, she chose a table near the Science section of the library and settled down to study.

Garry arrived about two-fifteen, and apologised profusely, explaining that he had been held up by someone asking to borrow his Chemistry text. Stephanie thanked Garry for making the effort to explain his absence. It occurred to her that Jeff would never have bothered to apologise, or account for his behaviour in any way. Garry was turning out to be a more courteous companion all round.

The Life Science assignment took them longer than they expected, and it was almost tea time before they packed up. They had both written different things, but they were confident of getting reasonable marks.

Garry asked Stephanie whether she would like to go for a walk down to the bridge in the period between tea and worship. He spent the time they were walking explaining the plot of a book he had read. Garry and Stephanie were both very fond of reading, but their taste in books was vastly different, as she liked the 'classics' and he liked futuristic fiction. He offered to lend one or two books to her, and Stephanie promised to try reading them during the holidays.

Stephanie hadn't seen Kathy outside of class for several days, so she decided to go downstairs and drop by the other girl's room. Kathy called out: "Come in", in response to her knock on the door.

Stephanie entered and was surprised to see that Kathy wasn't looking very happy.

"What is wrong with you?" Stephanie said, dropping down on the bed beside Kathy. "You are usually so full of life."

"I have a really big decision to make," Kathy said. "Owen has asked me to marry him."

"That is wonderful!" Stephanie exclaimed. "Why aren't you over the moon about it?"

"He also wants me to give up my studies, and settle down straight away," Kathy said.

"Oh no!" Stephanie said, "I thought that you were talking about a long engagement."

"No," Kathy said listlessly, "Basically, Owen has given me an ultimatum. Now or never, be mine tonight, sort of thing."

"What happens if you won't marry him straight away?" Stephanie inquired.

"He wants to start seeing other girls," Kathy said.

"Ouch!" Stephanie said. She felt absurdly sad hearing about this. Kathy and Owen had been one of the most romantic-seeming couples she had ever known. "I can see the problem, but it would be a real pity if you two broke up."

"I can't give up my chance to get a degree just to please a guy," Kathy said dejectedly.

"Of course not," Stephanie returned emphatically, "That is a form of blackmail Owen has laid on you. He could be a bit more understanding."

Kathy sighed. "I know that all he really wants is an end to the loneliness of us being separated all the time," she said.

"It comes at too high a price though," Stephanie said. "You would waste all the study you had done this year, and you might never get a degree."

"I could change universities," Kathy said, "But it wouldn't be the same...my mind is made up. I will have to set him free to see other girls."

"I think that you are right," Stephanie reasoned. "If Owen really wanted to marry you, he wouldn't be able to talk about seeing other girls. Either he is sure - in which case he will want to marry you now or in two years' time; or he is not certain - in which case he is not ready for marriage at all."

"I'm not holding out any hopes he will come back to me," Kathy said. "But I am not going to let myself get depressed either. There are plenty of guys I could have gone out with here, if I had not been so disgustingly faithful to Owen."

"Next year will be another year, and you will be able to go out with those guys then," Stephanie said. "It's a pity that this has come up so near to the end of the academic year though. You would have been off to Armidale for the summer in a mere month's time."

"It made sense to Owen, he thought that we could start planning the wedding over Christmas," Kathy said. "However, it is going to be awkward now that he has forced my hand."

"If things get too tense up in Armidale, you could come to Adelaide and visit me," Stephanie suggested.

"Thank you Stephanie," Kathy said. "It is nice to have the option. However, I think that there will be plenty to do over Christmas, Owen or no Owen."

They were shown a very thought provoking film in Child Development the next day. It was on the topic of moral development, which apparently continues right on throughout adulthood. In the film, a group of university students were asked to deliver a series of electric shocks to the 'subject' of the experiment. These shocks were punishment for failing to answer questions correctly. Whenever the 'subject' got the question wrong, the student was asked to increase the voltage, until it became quite lethal.

Towards the end of the film, the audience was told that the real experiment was being performed upon the university students, not the so-called 'subjects', who were actually actors and not hooked up to the electricity.

The point of the exercise was to demonstrate that very few people are capable of refusing to obey an instruction perceived as coming from a legitimate authority figure, even when the consequences are potentially harmful. Hence, the ability to make independent moral judgements is thought to be the very last stage of moral development.

Stephanie found the idea fascinating, and spent the afternoon discussing it with Phoebe, who had come up to her room to copy out notes from a few classes she had missed.

The film had touched upon a developmental milestone for her. Stephanie was probably the least rebellious person on campus, but she had begun to feel a growing need to question whether the guidelines they lived by were ethically based, or merely derived from custom and habit. There appeared to be a confusing mixture of the two behind both individual motivation, and the way they lived as a society. It made for some tough decision making, especially about friendships and relationships.

They had a particularly interesting Life Science practicum. Several work stations were set up around the laboratory. At one, they were working with torches, and recorded the contraction and dilation of their partner's pupils, as the torch was moved around. They also that found their eyes would continue to see a bright point of light for a few seconds after it had been turned off.

Then they did a complex test designed to determine colour-blindness. There was a chart on the wall, and a heap of coloured pins. The subject was required to follow instructions, and make a pattern with the pins.

Cara, Garry and Stephanie had no difficulty completing the pattern, but Dylan turned out to be chronically colour blind. His placement of the pins varied wildly.

Stephanie asked Dylan why this disability was not obvious on a daily basis, and he said that he had two main methods of compensating. One was to note the position of an object: for example, the red traffic light is placed at the top of the signal post throughout Australia. The second coping mechanism involved learning what textures were referred to as a certain 'colour' by everybody else.

After Life Science was finished, they went up to the cafeteria as a group. Dylan was joking around as usual, and made a lot of rude comments about the spaghetti and "mystery balls". Stephanie laughed, because she thought the bolognaise was delicious, even if it was made from left-overs.

After tea, Garry walked Cara and Stephanie across to the dorms. He said that he would be back to pick Stephanie up immediately after their respective dorm meetings, if she still wanted to go and see *Twelfth Night* in lecture theatre one.

Stephanie said that she would love to do that, so Garry returned in about an hour's time. The film turned out to be a delightful light comedy, with the action centring upon the antics of the actress Felicity Kendal, as she ran around disguised as a boy.

Stephanie was sitting eating her lunch with Joelle and Milton, when Jeff shuffled up to her. He put his tray down and began to pull out a chair.

"Hello Stephanie," Jeff said.

"Uh, hi Jeff," Stephanie ventured reservedly.

"Why don't you come and watch basketball anymore?" Jeff asked. "Even when Garrick Merton is playing?"

"I'm busy," Stephanie said. "Anyway, the season is over."

"It's a pity," Jeff said.

"Oh?" Stephanie said.

"I've missed you," Jeff mumbled. "You should have come."

Stephanie wasn't sure that she had really heard Jeff right. He seemed to be trying to act as if nothing had ever gone wrong between them. Moreover, he appeared to be trying to create the impression that whatever had parted them, it had not been of his doing.

Stephanie gave Jeff a long hard stare, and deliberately plastered a stern look upon her face. It was one of the most painful things that Stephanie ever had to do.

"I am not interested anymore Jeff," Stephanie said firmly. She picked up her tray and moved several tables across to join Garry and Cara.

"Whatever did Jeffrey Mannington want?" Garry demanded as soon as Stephanie sat down.

"Just to talk," Stephanie said.

"You blew him off pretty quick," Cara commented.

"I felt it was necessary," Stephanie said. "I believe in forgiveness, and I would forgive Jeff in an instant if it would do any good. But he isn't looking to be forgiven."

"What is he looking for then?" Garry asked. "Free absolution?"

"More than that," Stephanie said. She had been thinking very hard, and applying some of the things that she had learnt in both their Child Development and Theology classes. "Jeff is not sorry. He merely wants me to condone what he did, and maybe even let him do it again."

"You don't want that," Cara said. "He was an oaf."

Stephanie shuddered: "You don't know the half of it." She was silent for a minute. "It is not like I wish him any harm. I don't hold a grudge or anything."

"It is simply not safe for you to forgive Jeffrey Mannington, if he is incapable of repentance," Garry said.

"Thank you Garry," Stephanie said. "I couldn't have put it better myself."

"It wouldn't be good for Jeffrey himself, to be allowed to carry on that way either," Cara observed.

"Probably not!" Stephanie said dryly. "But let's not get all noble. I am simply looking after myself here."

"I for one, am glad to hear that!" Garry said firmly. "I was worried for a minute or two there, when Jeff came up to you."

It had been raining on and off all week. Debbie and David, Joelle and Milton, Kathy, Garry and Stephanie had finished lunch, and were sitting around a table in the cafeteria watching the rain.

"What shall we do this afternoon?" David asked the group in general.

"We could play card games or do quizzes," Debbie said unenthusiastically. "But we have done that several times already."

"Yes," Stephanie said, "I think that we must know the answers to the questions in David's quiz book off by heart by now."

"We could get our umbrellas and walk in the rain," Milton said, "But only if we wanted to get really wet."

"Why don't we all go back to the dorms, collect our quietest indoor activities, and meet back in the recreation area?" Joelle suggested.

"Good idea!" David said, "See you all across there in fifteen minutes."

Their group took over television room number one. It was the one with the rows of carpeted blocks around the outer perimeter. These were designed to be used as seats, amphitheatre-style. The television overlooked their proceedings, sitting strangely quiet and lifeless. David flicked a switch and the commentary for a minor sporting event began to drone quietly in the background.

Stephanie had collected her good best set of pencils, and a scrapbook. She was attempting to record her most significant dressmaking creations over the last couple of years. Garry sat down beside her with a map of the local area that he enjoyed consulting.

Joelle was reading one of the C.S. Lewis "Narnia" fantasy series.

Debbie had a letter from home to read. She told them that it contained the news that her older sister was expecting a baby. They were thrilled, and somewhat surprised to hear that Debbie was going to be an aunt. It started them all talking about their ages and relative maturity.

Kathy had a sketch-pad, and offered to do pencil portraits of each of them with their partner. She offered to do Garry and Stephanie separately, as they were not yet an official couple, but Garry said that he would like them to be together. He draped an arm loosely around her shoulders for the purpose of the picture, and Stephanie tried not to look too self-conscious about the contact.

Kathy was a remarkably good artist, and despite the stylisation and shading, Stephanie could almost recognise herself in the picture. Stephanie decided to put it in a frame to treasure as one of her positive memories for the year.

Milton and David had both brought their *Bibles* across, and they fell into a deep theological discussion. David was a great believer in grace. He argued that Jesus sacrifice was sufficient to ensure their salvation, if they repented and accepted it as a gift.

Milton said that he was uncomfortable with the idea of receiving forgiveness so easily. He felt that some degree of punishment and self-sacrifice should be necessary. Milton argued that he would feel more secure of his salvation, if he were able to earn it through prayer and fasting.

"David won't be able to get Milton to change his mind," Joelle whispered to her. "He often talks like this."

"It sounds as though he would be happier elsewhere," Stephanie whispered back. "He is angry at the campus churches."

"I think it is something to do with his brother," Joelle whispered, "Milton would like to be able to force God to save him."

"If only it worked that way," Stephanie whispered back. "Sometimes it is hard to let go and live by faith."

"It is a pity Milton thinks the way he does," Joelle said, "I am afraid it has begun to limit our friendship."

"I am sorry to hear that," Stephanie said sympathetically.

"Don't be," Joelle said, "It has been a nice friendship for my first with a guy."

Stephanie was pleased when she woke up that morning, because the weather was clearer than it had been for the previous week. Stephanie took a walk by herself immediately after breakfast, going down to the suspension bridge, and observing how quickly the river subsided back to its normal flow.

Cleaning the women's assembly area took her several hours, as Stephanie had to literally scrape the dried mud off of the carpet. Luckily, the plastic mats by the doors had taken the worst of the punishment.

After lunch, Garry took Stephanie down to the workshop behind the gymnasium, to show her the raft that he and Dylan were building for the raft race coming up on Tuesday. It was made out of planks and old tires, and looked like one large, flat platform.

"You are really going out on the river in that?" Stephanie said.

"Yes," Garry said, "Although we could do with a few nice fine days first."

"It looks sturdy!" Stephanie said.

"Yes, it is solid. I hope it is not too hard to propel along," Garry said. "But we are determined to make it to the finish line, while some of the others might not!" He indicated several other hulks hidden under tarpaulin. They were all in various stages of completion.

"Good luck," Stephanie said, "I hope you win."

"Either way, it will be a lot of fun," Garry said. "Will you come and watch the race? There will be a picnic afterwards."

"I would like that," Stephanie said.

"You will have to come down to the river by yourself though," Garry said, "I will be busy lugging this monster across."

"I will bring Kathy," Stephanie said, "She needs to get out and about a bit more now she is single."

"That sounds good," Garry said. "You two can be my cheering squad!"

Stephanie returned to her room to concentrate on study for the afternoon. This time it was Fundamentals of Computing and Standard English Language that were taking most of her attention.

Bradley told Stephanie that most of their essays had been marked, and were available to be picked up from outside the Lecturer's offices. Stephanie eagerly began making the rounds. The marks that she had received were excellent, and given that she was confident she would do a good solid 'eight out of ten' exam performance for most of her subjects, Stephanie could almost predict her grades. She could see the potential for doing even better in one or two of her subjects, and resolved to put in an extra special effort.

The day dawned bright and clear. Stephanie breezed through her classes and cleaning in the morning, because she was really looking forward to watching the Adventure Club raft race. It was one of those crazy things that students would do in-between periods of intense study.

Stephanie persuaded Kathy to go down to the suspension bridge early, so that they could get a good position near the starting line. Stephanie wanted to get a good look at all the rafts, before any of them disintegrated as Dylan and Garry assured her they surely would.

The teams arrived slowly. Each group was carrying their raft between them. The rafts had been completed in somewhat fantastic fashion, and decorated with plastic flags. The guys put their creations down on the river's edge and launched them carefully onto the water. The home-made craft all floated, and the spectators cheered.

They held their breath as the teams attempted to board their rafts. Several people fell off immediately. One raft began to sink into the water, and two of the team clambered off to join the spectators. Thus lightened, the raft hovered shakily on the water's surface.

The raft that Dylan and Garry had built was holding steady. Cara was also a member of Adventure Club and had been persuaded to join Garry's team. Stephanie steadied her friend from the side as she clambered on board. Cara was wearing bathers and a life jacket.

"I hope you don't need them," Stephanie said, wishing her luck.

"Oh, I am sure I will get wet," Cara said. "Even if we don't sink, someone will throw water at us. It is all part of the fun."

"Better you than me then," Stephanie said. She had almost joined the Adventure Club once, until they had explained to her that they actually meant back-packing and abseiling, when they said "bushwalking". It was just a bit too arduous for her.

Someone fired a starter pistol, and the rafts attempted to take off. Dylan and a couple of other guys had long poles, and were heaving the raft through the water.

Kathy and Stephanie left the starting area, and hurried down to the water hole that had been declared the finishing point. Despite being weighed down by several people's beach towels, they arrived well ahead of the contestants.

Six rafts had commenced the race. Three rounded the bend, and headed towards the winning post. They were told that the others had tipped up at various points, and had to be hauled across to the edge by the ropes attached to their sides.

Kathy and Stephanie were pleased to see that Dylan and Garry were still upright. Garry was now helping pole, and Cara was clearing debris away from the edge of the raft. They weren't quite first, but they were very close to it.

The largest raft was coming towards them at the greatest pace. It had at least ten guys poling away like crazy, but it had developed a list. They pulled ahead of Dylan and Garry, passed the finish point, and stopped abruptly. Most of the contestants fell off into the water, but they were officially declared the winners.

Dylan, Garry and Cara carefully circumnavigated this hazard, and tied their raft up against the diving tree. They were awarded second place, although many people considered them the real winners because they had actually managed to stay on their raft!

The last raft was sinking below the surface. The guys poling it were ankle deep in water, but they kept valiantly moving towards the finish line. Everyone cheered resoundingly when they reached the diving tree, and they were awarded third place.

The contestants who had ended up on the wrong side of the river were collected by row boats, and transported across to join them. Stephanie gave Garry and Cara their towels. They had gotten pretty wet, and were glad to dry off.

Kathy had the bag which belonged to Dylan and the other two boys from the team. She handed it over with her congratulations.

The guys laughed and joked as they collected their gear from Kathy, and Stephanie noticed that Kathy looked brighter than she had for weeks. Two red spots appeared in her cheeks.

The proprietor of the cafeteria had gone to all the effort of packing sandwiches into eskies, and transporting them down to the river-side for them. The students fell upon the food hungrily, because the open air and the excitement had stimulated their appetites. The tropical punch that had been mixed up in huge buckets was also very welcome.

CHAPTER FOURTEEN: TESTED

The last convocation of the year was conducted by a selection of graduating students. They each spoke about what their degree meant to them, and what they hoped to achieve in their work next year.

It was interesting to view the graduands, and Stephanie found herself wondering how often she would run into them in later life. It would be curious to find herself attending a church where the minister was someone who had been a student along with her, or doing business with a firm whose manager had studied accounting at Silver Springs. It would be strange for her too, if Stephanie ended up working in a school her peers chose for their children.

Stephanie spent the afternoon organising her notes, and drawing up a study timetable, which she meant to follow immediately classes ceased and study-vacation commenced on Friday. The exam timetable had already been posted, and it looked as though Stephanie would have a very intense couple of weeks ahead of her.

Stephanie was surprised to find herself sitting with Grace in the cafeteria at lunch. Stephanie had come in with a group comprising Phoebe, Bradley, Kathy and herself. They sat down at a relatively empty table and commenced eating. May had arrived, with Bethany and Grace following closely behind her. The amiable girl saw them, and approached their table.

"Do you mind if we join you?" May inquired.

"Sure," Stephanie said, "Take a seat."

May sat down next to her.

Bethany sat over to one side. She appeared to be looking around for someone else, but could not find them. "They're not here," she whispered to Grace.

"We'll find them later," Grace said. She sat down immediately opposite Stephanie, who blinked at her in surprise. The friends all fell silent, watching to see what Grace and Stephanie would do.

"How are you Stephanie?" Grace asked in an appealing tone.

"I am good, Grace," Stephanie said feeling puzzled. "What do you want?"

"This seat wasn't saved for Garrick Merton was it?" Grace asked slyly. "You sure found someone else quickly after Jeff."

"I might have been expecting Garry," Stephanie said. "It is hard to say. We haven't got quite to that stage yet."

"Garry is really very nice," Grace said. "I saw him win that raft race yesterday."

"He actually came second in the raft race," Stephanie said.

Grace shrugged. "Whatever," she said, "But he is a nice guy isn't he? I've seen him come up to the dorms to pick you up, and a lot of other things Jeff wouldn't do."

"Garry is a gentleman," Stephanie said. "What is your point here Grace? Are you collecting information for Jeff or something?"

"No way," Grace said, "Jeffrey Mannington is a coward. Fancy relying on women to fight his battles for him!"

"I am glad you have worked that out," Stephanie said, "And I hope that you are suffering no ill effects from your encounter with him."

"I'll get over it," Grace said. "I have amazing powers of recovery."

"Evidently," Stephanie said dryly. "I took what happened a great deal more seriously than you did."

"That is your problem Stephanie," Grace said, "You are so sensitive about everything."

"Better than being callous," Stephanie said.

"Whatever that means," Grace said dismissively. "I thought I had better tell you, that if you are not interested in Garry, there might be others who are."

Phoebe let out a hissing breath, and Kathy coughed.

Grace stood up. "You obviously don't want me here," she said huffily, "Come along Bethany."

Bethany looked around helplessly, picked up her tray and followed Grace. The girls went to sit with Roger and Arthur, who had just come into the cafeteria.

May turned to the rest of the group apologetically. "I am sorry about Grace's behaviour," she said uncomfortably. "I thought that they were just being friendly when they decided to come with me."

"Don't worry about it," Stephanie said. "We have known Grace longer than you have."

They continued eating their food in silence for a few minutes.

"Stephanie should have hit Grace!" Phoebe finally burst out. "The wretched girl is after Garry now."

"So what?" Stephanie said. "She is always up to something."

"Owen had no ideas about seeing other girls before Grace butted in," Kathy said ominously. "You never know what will happen when another girl puts the pressure on."

"I feel a bit weird sitting here listening to all you girls talking like this," Bradley said. "However, I think you should know that not all the guys are vulnerable to Grace's inducements. I have never fancied her myself."

"Thanks Brad," Stephanie said, "I think I can trust Garry too." She glanced at her watch, "I have to go to Life Science now. See you all later."

"Good luck," chorused the girls.

Despite Stephanie saying she trusted Garry, she found the idea of him being pursued by Grace was not a pleasant one. Garry and Stephanie had not yet discussed exclusivity, although she hoped that if he was determined to pursue a friendship with her, he would not be easily distracted from his course.

Stephanie was afraid, however, to bring the topic up out of the blue, in case she did half of Grace's work for her. Stephanie was also afraid to change her own behaviour too much, in case she spoilt the delicate dynamic of their friendship by coming across as possessive. That left her with only one option, watch and wait and try not to get too insecure.

It seemed that wherever Garry went, even if he was with Stephanie, Grace was not far away. She sat in front of them in any classes they shared, and she walked behind them to the cafeteria. When Garry had a free period and Stephanie had English, Grace followed him into the library. Stephanie tried not to think about what the girl might be up to in there without her.

Grace was always laughing and talking, and attempting to draw attention to herself. The louder Grace became, the quieter Stephanie felt. The quieter Stephanie felt, the more convinced she became that Garry would begin to notice Grace in a romantic sort of way.

Some of the things that Jeff and his mates had said came back to haunt her. Consequently, Stephanie began to doubt her own self-worth and attractiveness; she developed a headache and was unable to attend the Uniting Church vespers that evening.

Garry inquired about her health when he picked her up from the dorm in the morning. He was very thoughtful and concerned. Stephanie said that she felt much better, and thanked Garry for his attention.

Stephanie crossed her fingers and hoped that Grace had forgotten her inexplicable interest in Garry. It seemed the girl had, because she left them alone lunch time too.

About two o'clock in the afternoon, however, there was a special program which featured a visiting brass band. Stephanie was keen to go, because she had always enjoyed brass band music. The rhythm, the marches and the enthusiasm inherent in the music had always appealed to her.

The concert was being held on the grassy expanse between

men's hall and the library. Half way through Stephanie began sneezing. She was prone to hay-fever, and the grass in early summer always affected her the worst.

"I am just going back to the dorm to get a handkerchief," she told Garry.

"Let me come with you," Garry said.

"That would be silly," Stephanie said. "Stay here and save my place for me."

"Okay," Garry said. "I will do that."

Stephanie left the concert area, and hurried across to women's hall. She collected her handkerchief quite quickly, and started back towards the lawn.

For a minute or two Stephanie could not see Garry, and she thought that he might have moved. She started walking around the outside of the area.

Then Stephanie noticed Grace, right where she had been sitting. The cheeky girl was gazing up at Garry as if he was the only guy in the world. "What guy could resist such a look?" Stephanie thought. Grace could turn her flirtatious looks on and off at will, whereas Stephanie could not put on an insincere smile to save her life.

Grace laughed and drooped her head a little. Her hair brushed Garry's left shoulder, and Stephanie gasped in horror. She had never really got that intimate with Garry herself.

Stephanie was turning to leave, when she saw something else. Garry raised his right hand, and pushed Grace upright very gently and firmly. Then he said something in a low voice which made

Grace's face crumple. Grace curled herself up into a sulky ball.

Garry stood up and began to walk purposefully towards women's hall. Stephanie realised that he was looking for her, and began to wave.

"Over here, Garry," Stephanie said.

"Oh, there you are Stephanie," Garry said. "I thought that you had been away a long time."

"What was that all about with Grace?" Stephanie asked. She had a fair idea what had expired, but still wanted to hear Garry's explanation.

"Grace tried to get all over me," Garry said. "She tried it last night too, after you went to bed. I had to go and deliberately wedge herself between Milton and David to get away from her!"

"What was it that you said to her?" Stephanie asked.

"Just that spot was saved for you," Garry said. "And that you were the only girl on campus in whom I was ever going to be interested."

Stephanie would have fallen over, if Garry had not caught and steadied her.

"Sorry if I came on a bit strong," Garry said.

"It's just that guys are not usually so forthright about their feelings," Stephanie murmured.

"Well, I've seen what happens to guys who give in to pushy girls like Grace," Garry said. "They get chewed up and spat out in no time."

"So, you didn't mean what you said about me?" Stephanie asked.

"Of course I meant that," Garry said, "I just thought this might not be the right time to discuss it."

"I want to discuss it now," Stephanie said.

"What about the concert?" Garry asked.

"Forget the concert," Stephanie said, "I think that we need to go for a walk."

Garry and Stephanie spent the afternoon sitting down by the suspension bridge, discussing what they wanted in a relationship. It turned out to be a lot easier than Stephanie expected, because they both agreed that they were at the beginning of something special.

The Inter-denominational praise service and Reformed Church programs both passed by uneventfully on Sunday and Stephanie spent the afternoon studying. Around five o'clock Garry came across to the dormitory and had her paged, so that they could go to the cafeteria together.

As they were walking along, Garry took her hand in his. It was virtually the first time that Stephanie had held hands with a boy, outside of playing a children's game like "ring-a-rosie" with a mixed group. The contact tickled, and Stephanie jumped, almost snatching her hand away.

Garry grinned, and squeezed her hand tighter. Holding hands in public was also the universal signal around campus that a couple were past merely 'going out', and were now 'going steady'.

Hand holding involved a degree of mutuality unsurpassed by other gestures. A touch on the back or arm could be administered by one person, and simply tolerated by the other. However, to hold hands, both parties had to reach out.

They kept on walking, knowing that their friends, adversaries and the general gossips were all noticing their gesture. Stephanie felt herself getting hot in the face and going red. It would be the talk of campus for a day or two, and then it would be old news. After a while, no one would take any notice any more.

Garry and Stephanie ate a quick meal, and then returned to their respective dormitories to study. Despite the excitement of their personal lives, they were both very conscious that it was the middle of the study-vacation, and the lead up to exams.

Although it was still study-vacation for most people, the Life Science class were scheduled to take the dreaded practical-exam. Luckily Stephanie had developed a greater familiarity with laboratory procedures than she had at the beginning of the year, and was able to approach the exam with more confidence.

Stephanie also had a flair for topics involving genetics and populations. There was some new material on ecology and succession, but Stephanie had researched the material thoroughly while writing her field trip report.

Stephanie left the practical exam sure that, while she hadn't performed outstandingly, she had passed comfortably. Stephanie would have lost a few marks here and there on her sketches and calculations, but she could approach the theory exam without any sort of handicap this time.

Having the practical-exam out of the way lifted a great weight off of her shoulders. Stephanie arranged to play a quick game of pool with Garry and Kathy, and then get back to the study.

Stephanie had the day completely free, and wholly dedicated her time to study. Stephanie had planned and developed this routine, where she would read for one subject for an hour or two, go for a walk or clean the women's assembly area, and then return to read her text for another subject.

Stephanie knew that twenty minute study blocks are recommended in the "how to" books, but she had never been able to feel she made any progress in twenty minutes. It seemed like a lot of getting up and down, and looking around again for her books, so her favourite study block actually consisted of two hours.

Stephanie was well into her afternoon study period, when there was a hesitant tap at the door. She opened it and found Grace standing there.

"Come quickly Stephanie," Grace said. "Something is wrong with Bethany, and I don't know what to do."

"Why did you come to me?" Stephanie asked puzzled.

"This is your floor, and I thought you might know what to do," Grace said. "You are smart in a sort of dull way, Stephanie."

"Thanks a lot," Stephanie said dryly. "I will come if you think it is serious."

Stephanie put her books aside, and hurried down the corridor. Bethany was in her room. She was sitting on her bed clutching her head. Her eyes were swollen, and her face was red.

"What happened here?" Stephanie asked.

"I don't know," Grace said, "I just found her like this. She isn't making any sense."

I sat down on the bed, and put an arm around Bethany. She barely seemed to notice her, and her forehead was clammy.

"I think she has a fever," Stephanie said, "Do you know where she keeps her wash-cloth?"

Grace picked up Bethany's vanity bag, and offered it to her.

"Thanks," Stephanie said, beginning to mop the girls' forehead with the still moist cloth. "Do you know if she was coming down with anything? Had she been out walking, could she have been bitten by anything?"

"I don't think so," Grace faltered.

Bethany stirred. "I think I'm going to be sick," she muttered.

"The bathroom is next door," Stephanie said, "Help me get her there."

Grace and Stephanie supported Bethany between them, and got her leaning over one of the sinks. Stephanie put an arm around her shoulders and braced the girl as she retched.

"Ugh," Grace said.

"There is something very wrong here," Stephanie said.

Bethany began to cry, dry wheezing sobs. "I took some pills," she said.

"Oh, no!" Stephanie said, "What sort of pills? Panadol? Aspirin?"

Bethany shook her head. "Sleeping tablets."

"How many?" Stephanie inquired.

"Half a bottle," Bethany said.

Grace gasped.

"I'll take care of this," Stephanie said. "You go and dial triple zero now. Then bring one of the deans back up here."

Grace hesitated, and Stephanie lost her cool. "Grace," she shouted, "Even if you have never taken anything seriously in your life before, go and dial triple zero NOW. Ask for an ambulance to be sent out here immediately."

Grace scuttled off, and Stephanie turned back to Bethany. "You will live," Stephanie said, "From what I understand, most of the sleeping pills available now are non-lethal. However, it is a good thing you are vomiting them up again. Whatever made you do it?"

"My boyfriend," Bethany whispered.

"Forgive me for saying this," Stephanie said, "But I haven't seen you around with any guy. You didn't even have a date for the Pancake Night."

"That was all his idea," Bethany said, "So that no one knew we were going out together."

"Why did he want to keep it a secret?" Stephanie asked.

"So that no one would guess that we had been doing it together", Bethany whispered.

"Was that what you wanted?" Stephanie asked.

"No," Bethany wheezed.

"Did you even want to have sex?" Stephanie queried.

"I would have preferred not," Bethany admitted. "I just wanted to go out like the other couples."

"Let me get this straight," Stephanie said, "You wanted a mutual relationship, and this guy merely wanted a sexual partner, so he refused to let anyone see you together?"

"That's exactly right," Bethany said.

"Which guy was this?" Stephanie demanded.

"Tony Dantean," Bethany sobbed.

"That figures," Stephanie said. She stood there thinking. Tony was one of Jeff's mates, and Bethany was maybe even a little naiver than Stephanie had been at the beginning of the year. Tony was twenty, and hanging around with the graduating class had made him far too fast for Bethany. If any of the girls had known what was going on, they would have advised Bethany against giving in to Tony. Which was precisely why he had not allowed them to know!

Bethany retched again, and shook all over.

"Those guys are not worth taking pills over," Stephanie said. "Believe me, I should know!" Stephanie wiped her forehead again with the sponge. "Bethany, you are a talented girl. You could do a lot with your life."

"I know," Bethany said, "I will if I get through this."

"Don't let anyone take advantage of you ever again," Stephanie said. "You don't have to do things you don't want to keep a guy."

"I thought I had to, or he wouldn't love me," Bethany said. "Don't you and Garry?"

"Certainly not!" Stephanie said, "We are waiting by mutual choice."

"But you hold hands...", Bethany said.

"That is step number one, out of about two hundred that all have to be taken in the correct order," Stephanie said. "A nice boy would be willing to move along at a pace that is comfortable for you."

"So Tony wasn't even a nice guy," Bethany murmured.

"It doesn't sound like it," Stephanie said. "You will do better next time if you keep your smarts about you."

Grace arrived just then, with the dean. "The ambulance has arrived," she announced.

"I will look after Bethany now," the Dean said. "Thank you Stephanie. See if you can get back to your studies. I know that it will be hard, but I will be with Bethany. She is in good hands."

Stephanie had been studying solidly since breakfast. She had both English Literature and Standard English Language examinations coming up shortly. Stephanie had combined her study for the two, as they were eminently compatible.

Around 10:00 am, the Dean sent for her. Stephanie went down to her office, which was situated opposite the reception desk in women's hall. She knocked on the door, and was invited to enter.

"There you are Stephanie," the Dean said. The woman was seated at her desk. "I thought that as you were involved yesterday, we would tell you what was happening with Bethany."

"I would appreciate that," Stephanie said, "I am still concerned about her."

"Northcoast Hospital decided to keep Bethany in overnight," the Dean said, "And we have made arrangements for her to be sent home to her folks. That seems to be the best place for her to begin re-building things."

"You are probably right," Stephanie said, "But what about her exams?"

"Bethany is in no state to sit her exams," the Dean said. "We wonder whether it was pressure from them that made her attempt suicide."

"Exam pressure might well be part of it," Stephanie said, "But Bethany did mention a boy, Tony Dantean."

The Dean frowned: "That does complicate things. However he couldn't possibly have done anything that would upset her that much."

"I beg your pardon," Stephanie said, "I have to disagree. It hurts to be used. Bethany did not mention any violence to me, but there was clearly a great deal of intimidation used to get her to comply with his sexual demands. If the age gap between the two had been any greater, or if Bethany hadn't so clearly given her consent, this would have been a matter for the police."

"Bethany did not tell me any of these things," the Dean said regretfully, "I would have done a lot more for her if she had." She frowned: "There is still very little I can do, if Bethany is unwilling to speak out against the boy."

"I think that a fair bit of persuasion went into keeping her quiet," Stephanie said.

"It is a great pity," the Dean said. "However, home is the best place for her now. There may be things that her parents ought to have taught her. This way they all get a second chance."

"I hope that they take it," Stephanie said.

"I think they will," the Dean said, "They sounded like very understanding people when I spoke to them on the phone. Maybe a bit busy - more inclined to buy their daughter things than set boundaries for her."

"That is a problem most of us would enjoy having," Stephanie said with a smile.

"I don't know," the Dean said. "You might not have brought the most expensive clothes to university Stephanie, but your working class background has made you very resilient."

"I know," Stephanie said, "Sometimes I really appreciate that."

The Dean was silent for a moment or two. Then she spoke: "You seem to have gained an understanding of the dangers of relationships that is quite beyond your age, Stephanie. Are there any things you should have told us about Jeffrey Mannington?"

"Quite probably," Stephanie said. "I told the doctor that you sent me to though. I would like to leave it that way, if you don't mind."

"Oh," the Dean said considering. "A doctor should know what to do." She sighed, "You may go if you like Stephanie."

Stephanie was relieved to hear that. She did not enjoy being questioned about Jeff and his mates, however deserving of punishment they might be.

Stephanie returned to her room and settled down to follow her study timetable. Garry came across to collect her for lunch, and they went for a short walk afterwards. Then she put in a substantial afternoon and evening's worth of study.

Stephanie had her Standard English Language exam in the morning. She wrote flat out throughout the entire three hours, and was satisfied that she did quite well.

Stephanie treated the news report they were given to analyse like a short story, and commented on its structure, language and composition.

Stephanie had done her essay on the poetry of Psalms, so she was required to choose the question on Song of Solomon in the exam. Stephanie focused on its structure, and the purpose of the writers for including a love poem in the Bible. She avoided Freudian interpretation of the imagery, because she found those too 'clinical', but there were plenty of other things she could say on the subject.

The poem they were given to analyse was one of the more inspiring ones from amongst the sample of Australian writers that they studied. Stephanie found that she could remember most of her thoughts about it, and wrote several pages of analysis.

The English Literature exam was in the afternoon. This allowed her to spend the morning revising, and drawing up lists of main points about the texts. Stephanie hoped that these would come in handy whatever question she was faced with.

Stephanie answered one question on Ezra Pound. Although he was not her favourite poet, there were a lot of features worth pointing out in his poetry, and she found that her pen absolutely flew.

The second question Stephanie chose to answer was on Oscar Wilde's *Lady Windermere's Fan*. Wilde had long been a favourite of mine, and she had acted out *The Importance of Being Ernest* in high school drama class. Stephanie found that she could easily locate the quotes that she wanted, and was able to draft a reasonable argument based upon on the question.

The other question Stephanie chose was on a fascinating little novel called *The Inheritors* by William Golding. It was written from the point of view of either a Neanderthal or Cro-Magnon man, and was quite puzzling to read, but very interesting to discuss.

The three hours seemed to absolutely fly, and Stephanie was only just finished when they were told to stop writing. She was relieved to have her English exams over, and looked forward to taking a break as the weekend approached. Stephanie knew that Garry had sat his Chemistry exam that morning, and he would be as exhausted as she was.

They had a quiet day. Most of the group had at least one exam already, so they were all happy to attend the meetings and fill in the rest of the time sitting around the cafe lounge.

Joelle and Milton, who had been a bit more energetic than the rest of them and gone for a stroll, noticed a poster announcing a screening of *The Karate Kid* at the Silver Springs mineral water bottling factory. It was scheduled for that very evening.

Milton asked whether Garry and Stephanie would join him and Joelle to make up a foursome. Stephanie was thrilled, because she rarely got to see a movie. Most of the films that came to the cinema did not pass the extra censorship laid upon them by the Christian community. Even *The Karate Kid*, which was rated PG, was criticised for promoting a martial art. However, it was also partially accepted for its themes of integrity and self-discipline.

Garry took very little persuading, and they found themselves walking into the factory around 8:00 pm. They went up a flight of stairs, past some offices, and into an assembly room of moderate dimensions.

The group settled down, the lights were turned off, and the film commenced. Stephanie let herself lean gently against Garry, and he reached out to take her hand in his. The sensation was still very new to her, and she felt her hand twitch sensitively once or twice before it settled down in Garry's grip.

The movie, which had been released in the cinema around June that year, was very dramatic, featuring an Italian boy who moved into a new neighbourhood. He met the local bullies, but was befriended by an Asian veteran who taught him to perform karate moves properly.

As they walked back to the dorms afterward, Stephanie noticed that Joelle and Milton were keeping a certain amount of space between them. They seemed very cordial with one another regardless, and they all had a lovely evening.

After cleaning the women's assembly area thoroughly, Stephanie settled down to study. She still had exams for Life Science, Child Development and Fundamentals of Computing coming up.

Joelle had set her books up on the other half of the desk, and they had to be careful not to bump each other as they worked. They had been studying like that for about an hour when Joelle put her pen down and stretched.

"Are you busy Stephanie?" Joelle asked, rubbing her forehead.

"Yes," Stephanie said, "I am making notes here. Just let me finish this sentence and I will be with you."

"I can't help noticing that things are moving along with you and Garry," Joelle remarked.

"It's not all that sudden," Stephanie said putting down her pen. "We have known each other all year."

"Sure you have!" Joelle said. "That is not what I meant. It is just that I wish things were that simple for Milton and me."

"Oh?" Stephanie queried.

"Milton is talking of leaving Silver Springs University," Joelle said.

"Not before he has finished his exams, I hope!" Stephanie exclaimed.

"Of course not!" Joelle said. "It is just that he won't be coming back here next year."

"Is that because of his disagreements with some of the Christian beliefs?" Stephanie asked.

"Partly," Joelle said. "He doesn't know what he will be doing, but he is not interested in remaining at our university."

"That is a pity," Stephanie said. "Where does that leave you two?"

"We will be keeping in contact," Joelle said, "But I don't expect anything exciting to happen."

"There would be a significant area of divergence between you," Stephanie mused.

"Exactly!" Joelle agreed. "I think that it is better to let him go. It is lucky that I was not looking for a serious relationship to develop this year, isn't it?"

"I suppose," Stephanie said, "Although, I must wonder whether you found exactly what you were looking for at the beginning of the year."

"What was that?" Joelle said, "Can you remind me?"

"An escort who would not try to tie you down and interfere with your music," Stephanie reported.

"You are right!" Joelle exclaimed. "I did think like that. It seems an age ago now. I have learnt since that half-and-half arrangements can be unsatisfactory in the long run."

"Oh - why would that be?" Stephanie asked, although she had a few ideas of her own.

"They don't encourage people to be honest with each other from the beginning," Joelle reported. "Milton and I have only just begun to cover the basics, and we don't like what we found."

"I guess there is a better chance of finding the right guy if you are looking for the real thing," Stephanie said. "Even if you make a mistake along the way, like I did with Jeff."

"Yes," Joelle said, "But you got hurt."

"I could have been more cautious, but I handled it," Stephanie said. "I think I learnt something. Some of your behaviour has been very self-protective though, have you been hiding from possible hurt?"

"Not consciously," Joelle said thoughtfully. "I just thought dating was a game and wanted to win a few rounds. I couldn't understand your taking things so seriously, that is, until I became fond of Milton."

"Do you regret having spent the year with Milton?" Stephanie inquired.

"No," Joelle said, "I will be sad to say goodbye to Milton, but I still have my music, and it really was too soon for me to settle down."

"That's good," Stephanie said, "I would hate to see you upset during exams."

Stephanie had her Life Science exam in the morning. When Stephanie arrived at the venue, she was a little disconcerted to see that they were sharing the room with a group of fourth year Mathematics students also doing an exam. This meant that Jeff was there, and he cast a significant glance in her direction.

Stephanie chose a seat well towards the front, so that she could not see Jeff at all. Stephanie said a little prayer, and steeled herself to concentrate upon her exam, and that only.

As soon as the "reading time" was announced, Stephanie checked through each question and made what notes were allowed upon the sheet. Once they were allowed to write properly, Stephanie began to push her pen at the fastest possible speed.

Stephanie had studied Life Science for many hours, and the information rushed back to her, almost faster than she could write. When Stephanie had finished all the questions, she went through and checked them once again. There were a few small details that Stephanie could add, and she did her best to be thorough.

The end of the examination period was announced, and Stephanie handed in her paper. She left the hall without looking back at Jeff, and marched up to the cafeteria.

Garry caught Stephanie on the way to the cafe, and asked her how she felt she had done. Stephanie said it had been "passable". Garry was quite confident himself, and assured her that she would have done well.

The Education exam was in the afternoon. Stephanie spent the morning making shorter and shorter summaries of the notes. At last Stephanie was able to identify all the theorists, and their theories using a few short words.

Stephanie was glad of her preparation once the exam commenced. There were a large number of multiple choice questions, which format Stephanie liked. There was also a series of true/false questions which she did not like much.

The true/false questions were designed to trick the examinee, and all sounded very plausible. The Lecturer was planning to deduct a half point for any wrong answers. This was supposed to compensate for guessing, but it made her nervous. Stephanie never guessed in exams, and hence felt that it was an unfair penalty.

The rest of the exam consisted of four short essays, which she found relatively easy to write. Stephanie seasoned her argument with facts and theorists, whenever she found an appropriate point.

Fundamentals of Computing was her last exam, and it was scheduled for the morning. Stephanie wrote as much as she could about each topic. Some of the questions were fairly broad, and it was a little hard to judge what to include, but Stephanie was confident that she would have passed quite well.

Tea time Stephanie met Garry up at the cafeteria. He had just finished his Standard Maths exam, and it sounded awful. Stephanie was very glad that she did not have to take that subject!

Standard Maths had been Garry's last exam, so they would be free to enjoy what was left of the academic year together. The coming weekend sounded particularly interesting, and Stephanie was looking forward to seeing her first graduation.

Stephanie stopped to listen to the music as she passed through the foyer into girls' dorm. The Christian community that sponsored the dorm did not usually allow contemporary popular music to be played, but an exception was being made today for the release of "Do they know it's Christmas?" recorded by *Band Aid* – a group of prominent musicians led by Bob Geldof, who had joined together to support aid efforts towards alleviating the famine in Ethiopia.

CHAPTER FIFTEEN: GRADUATION

After sharing a leisurely breakfast with Garry, Stephanie went back to her room to begin packing her belongings. The Deans had provided the girls with large cardboard cartons in which to store their things over the summer break, and a section of the basement area was filled with shelves that reached up to the ceiling.

Joelle was also sorting through her things, and the girls talked as they worked. Joelle and Stephanie had become fast friends during the year. The friendship had looked a bit shaky for a while, but they rallied to support each other through the ups and downs of their first relationships with boys.

They had both tackled (and they were pretty sure, conquered) the rigours of tertiary study, and faced classrooms full of high school students during practicum. They concluded that they would miss each other over the holidays, and promised to send each other a Christmas card.

About four o'clock in the afternoon, Garry came across to escort Joelle and Stephanie to the Tropical Pool Party. This was a gala event celebrating the end of the academic year, and promised to be a fun occasion.

Stephanie was wearing her hibiscus print bathers with a short denim skirt, and she used a bright scarf to tie her hair back from her face. Garry remarked that Stephanie looked "Very festive" in the outfit, and they set off across the lawn.

The Tropical Party was being held in the swimming pool area around the back of the cafeteria. Several tables were loaded with food in a buffet style, and a Caribbean flavoured instrumental was playing through the cafe sound system. Garry, Joelle and Stephanie located Bradley and Phoebe, and sat down.

Milton came up and said "Hello" to them all. He then went to sit with Debbie and David. Stephanie glanced at Joelle, but she made no move to follow him. Apparently the pair were easing themselves out of their friendship already.

Taking care not to lose their spot on the sunny bench, members of the group went up to the table in relays and collected plates full of food. There was a variety of salads, sausages and gluten-steaks which were pretty challenging to cut with the plastic knives provided. Stephanie checked what everyone else was doing, picked her vegetarian 'steak' up in her fingers, and nibbled at it discretely.

When he had finished eating, Garry put an arm casually across her bare shoulders. "I hope you are not getting burnt", he said solicitously.

"I don't think so," Stephanie said. She relaxed, feeling comforted and protected.

Phoebe was looking around the pool area. "Look over there Stephanie," she said, "Do you reckon those two will get together by graduation?"

Stephanie followed her gaze across to where Grace stood with Roger Faraday. "I don't know," Stephanie said. "They have spent more time with each other than with anybody else this year."

"Surely not!" Garry said, "Roger is single. Grace never goes for a guy who is not at least interested in someone else."

"There is a first time for everything," Phoebe commented.

"They are suited in a funny sort of way," Joelle said. "Roger is a cad and a prankster, but Grace is so manipulative that she might just outwit him."

"They would kill each other," Bradley remarked. "It would not be a pretty sight."

"It would be a volatile relationship for sure," Stephanie said soberly, "But some people think that is what love is all about. I hope that all of us know better by now."

"Grace couldn't bear to finish this year single," Phoebe said. "I say they will be together by tomorrow night."

"What do you bet they will be split up again by Christmas?" Bradley said cynically.

"You never know," Joelle said, "They might be married by the New Year."

"Then they will spend the rest of their lives fighting," Garry asserted.

"That is mean!" Stephanie protested from within his arm.

"Actually," Bradley said, "It is realistic. I am changing my bet."

"Let's go and get desert guys," Stephanie said to change the subject. "I see pavlova."

"You stay put Stephanie," Garry said, "I will go and get two bowls."

He scrambled to his feet, and Bradley got up with him.

"Fresh cream and no ice-cream please," Stephanie called after Garry.

"I'll do my best," Garry called back.

"That is all we ask, isn't it Stephanie?" Phoebe said.

"As there is no gentleman in my life I will have to get my own," Joelle said, "See you again in a minute ladies."

Garry and Stephanie went for a walk immediately after breakfast. They strolled hand in hand through the bushland, enjoying the feeling of being free during the morning hours when they would usually be occupied by classes.

When it got too hot outside, they turned their steps back towards campus. Garry dropped her off at girls' dorm, where Stephanie persevered with the job of packing up in her room until lunch time.

After lunch Stephanie went down to women's assembly area to help clean and decorate it with flowers for the weekend festivities. The ceremonial proceeding would be carried out in the gymnasium, but her little hall would be on display to family and friends throughout the weekend. That project kept her fully occupied until it was almost time for tea.

That evening, Garry came across and collected Stephanie in a formal manner to attend the graduation dedication. They walked across to the gymnasium, and sat quietly while the senior students walked down the centre isle in full gown and regalia.

The organist played a stirring march composed by Mendelson,

and Stephanie felt her heart swell within her chest. Then and there Stephanie made a solemn promise that she would complete her studies and walk down that same carpet in three years' time to receive her own degree. Stephanie whispered this to Garry, and he said that it was something he could understand and respect.

The service continued as the Chancellor prayed, thanking God for the talent and dedication of the graduands assembled before him. He prayed that the Lord would be with them wherever they went after graduation, and that God would grant them a work which would make a difference to the world.

It was dark when the ceremony finished, and Stephanie asked Garry to simply walk her back to the dormitory. They parted in perfect harmony, but with little conversation. Stephanie was still preoccupied by a sense of awe and praise for student achievement, some of which she was taking personally.

Stephanie had concluded the first year of her degree, and developed patterns that would enable her to complete projects throughout her entire life. In many ways, Stephanie felt that the graduation ceremony at the end of her first year, while officially dedicated to the students who were leaving Silver Springs University, constituted her own personal milestone.

Due to the crowds attending graduation the weekend church services were being held down in the gymnasium. Stephanie had arranged to walk across with Joelle and meet Garry just inside the main door of the structure.

The graduands were lined up outside the building, awaiting the cue for the processional. They all looked very impressive in their caps, gowns and coloured sashes. Joelle and Stephanie decided to take the opportunity to congratulate their friends as they passed. There were Melanie and Jonathon, standing with their respective Bachelor Degree classes, Warren and Gloria were together, with Roger hovering slightly off to one side. Grace was dressed in a plain black gown, and stood alongside all the other Secretarial Certificate students.

Jeff was standing on his own, with no visible family members or friends to support him. He looked intently at her, and Stephanie felt a sudden surge of compassion and stopped to speak. Joelle moved discretely on to talk to some of the Degree of Music students.

It felt strange to be facing Jeff in amicable circumstances after all that had happened between them. He was wearing a black suit under his robe, and Stephanie had to admit that he looked quite striking.

Stephanie took a deep breath and said, "Congratulations."

"Thank you Stephanie," Jeff said seriously. "It means a lot that you would speak to me today."

"I wish you well out there in the work-force," Stephanie said as neutrally as possible.

Jeff looked pleased. "I have been given a job in Brisbane," he said. "I may be able to drive out here next year, and visit you after all."

Stephanie shook her head. "I don't want you to bother with

anything like that," She said serenely, "You can make a new life for yourself. The life you always dreamed of." It was on the tip of her tongue to advise Jeff to get some counselling help, but Stephanie reminded herself that it was no longer any of her business.

"Is that because you are going out with Garrick Merton now?" Jeff asked intently.

"No," Stephanie said carefully. She recognised this as a trick question. While she did feel committed to Garry, he was not the fundamental reason for her break-up with Jeff. Moreover, if Jeff could blame another person for coming between them, he might never accept that Stephanie did not want to go out with him. There was a strong possibility that he would simply begin to focus on whether she appeared to be available or not, and come back to bother her if she appeared single again.

Stephanie decided to try to be as conclusive as possible. "It is not because I have a boyfriend that I don't want to see you Jeff," I said. "It is because of some of the things that you have said and done this past year."

Jeff looked confounded, but he was determined to put as good a face on things as possible. "I am sorry you feel that way," he said.

Stephanie smiled and nodded, although she suspected that his statement was insincere.

"Goodbye and good luck," Stephanie said with a deliberate air of finality.

Stephanie felt that it was high time to move on. She passed through the double doors, and found Joelle and Garry waiting for her. The service was lovely and lunch was nice, if a bit too crowded by family, friends and other visitors.

In the afternoon, they gathered together the members of their first year group and went for one last sentimental walk along the river-front. Debbie had her camera, and asked them to pose for several group shots. She promised to send them all copies for Christmas.

Stephanie awoke early, and ate a leisurely breakfast. Then she returned to her room and dressed in her blue crepe suit ready to attend the graduation ceremony. Garry came across to pick her up, and they crossed the lawn to the gymnasium.

The lawn was extremely crowded because visitors had been arriving all throughout the weekend. Both the graduands and lecturers were wearing full regalia, and they amused themselves by checking the outfits that the different Lecturers were wearing. Some of the lecturer's Doctoral robes were extremely elaborate, with purple and gold stripes. One or two Lecturers even had crimson robes that Stephanie presumed were from an overseas university.

Garry and Stephanie entered the gymnasium, and found themselves a seat alongside Phoebe and Bradley. It was not long before the graduation ceremony commenced, with the processional being even more impressive than it had been the previous days.

The Chancellor rose and gave a short speech, and then the graduands were called up one by one to receive their testamurs. Stephanie followed through the list of names given in the printed program, and tried to clap especially loudly whenever one of their friends was called to make the short walk onto the stage and back.

After all the degrees had been presented, the graduands marched down through the centre isle and out onto the lawn area. Garry and Stephanie waited a few minutes for the crowd to dissipate, and then followed them outside.

They found a number of photographers busily posing people into class and family groups. It was obvious that the event was being well recorded for posterity!

Stephanie was surprised to hear somebody calling out her name, and turned to see the Biology Master leave the official group to speak to her.

"Hello Stephanie," he said, "I wanted to be the first to congratulate you on getting a high distinction in Biology."

"I didn't know that the exams would be marked already," Stephanie exclaimed.

"We had to work fast because of graduation," the Biology Master explained. "You both did very well, but Stephanie's mark was outstanding. It has been several years since we last awarded such a high mark in this department."

"Wow," Stephanie said, "I don't know what to think, I just wanted to make sure I passed this semester."

"Well you did that, and more," the Biology Master said. He hailed a passing photographer, and requested that Garry and Stephanie pose either side of him for a photograph. Then he turned and left to re-join the faculty.

"What do you think of that?" Garry said.

"I am outrageously thrilled," Stephanie said, taking Garry by the arm and skipping towards the cafeteria.

After lunch Garry asked Stephanie to go for a walk alone with him. He led her down the main trail to girls' way, and across the little bridge. Then he steered her down one of the tiny tracks that looped down to the river bank and back.

When they were thoroughly enclosed by the leafy trees, Garry turned Stephanie to face him and pulled a slim package out of his pocket. "I have got something for you," he said.

"That is so sweet of you," Stephanie exclaimed, taking the package. Stephanie untied the gold ribbon, and parted the striped paper to reveal a matching watch and pen set. It was a novelty package that you could buy at a newsagent, but it made a fantastically romantic gift for all that.

"I noticed that your watch stopped half way through this semester," Garry said, "And you have been making do ever since."

"I can't believe that you actually saw that," Stephanie murmured.

"I like to observe everything about you," Garry said. "I hope you like the watch. I couldn't afford gold or anything, and I am not used to buying gifts for girls."

"It is perfect," Stephanie said. "It is slim, which is the main thing, and I just love the burgundy leather strap."

"Here", Garry said, "Let me do it up for you."

Stephanie stood obediently still as he buckled the watch around her left wrist.

"There," Garry said, "Now you can think of me all the time."

That was trite, but also very romantic. Stephanie looked up, and found herself looking straight into Garry's eyes. It was obvious that he wanted to kiss her. Suddenly shy, she turned her face so that his kiss landed on her cheek.

"Thank you for the watch," Stephanie said, looking down at the ground.

"It was my pleasure," Garry said. He lifted her chin so that Stephanie had to look at him again. "Why Stephanie, you are blushing!"

"I guess I am," Stephanie said, "I think that I should go back and finish my packing now."

"You are probably right," Garry said. "What time is your plane tomorrow?"

"About four o'clock," Stephanie answered.

"Well, I will come as far as Brisbane with you to see you off," Garry said.

"I would like that," Stephanie said, "It is going to be a very long summer."

"We will have to write every week," Garry said, "It will help the time we are apart pass quicker."

"Okay," Stephanie said. "I promise to write faithfully."

Stephanie taped up the last of her boxes, and transported them down to the storage area in the basement. Then Stephanie finished packing the things she had decided to take home in her suitcase, and locked that up.

Around eleven o'clock, Stephanie met Garry around the back of women's hall. The university car was ready to transport the students to the local Northcoast station, from there they caught the train to Brisbane Station and a bus to the airport.

Garry arranged for his baggage to go directly on to a plane to Sydney (from where he would catch a train to Wollongong) then he helped her carry her bags to the point where Stephanie could check in to an Adelaide bound plane.

"This is it, I guess," he said. "Take care."

"I will be all-right," Stephanie said, "I have made the trip before."

"But you are doubly precious now," Garry said. He leant down to kiss her, and this time Stephanie did not turn her head away. Their lips touched briefly and fleetingly, but with a definite sense of promise for the future.

"I will call you on Christmas Day to tell you that I love you," Garry said. "And perhaps, if your parents let you come back a little early in February, you can visit my family in Wollongong."

"It sounds like fun," Stephanie said, "I will see what I can do."

The boarding call for his flight sounded then and Garry gave her a quick hug, before turning and walking to the exit. Stephanie waved until she could see Garry no longer, then she faced the doorway leading to her own aeroplane. It was exciting to be going home for Christmas, and while she would miss Garry, writing over the long break would be an excellent test of the durability of their relationship.

Stephanie knew that she had developed the ability to maintain the core of her being despite challenges and external limitations; and had found a kindred spirit with whom to share her interests. Gleefully Stephanie congratulated herself on passing safely through the silver clouds of adolescence into the shining spring of young adulthood.

"To everything there is a season, a time for every purpose under heaven. A time to be born, and a time to die; a time to plant; and a time to pluck what is planted...a time to weep, and a time to laugh; a time to mourn, and a time to dance..."

Ecclesiastes 3:1-4 New King James Version

ABOUT THE AUTHOR

Cecelia grew up in the Barossa Valley, an area of South Australia predominantly settled by German immigrants. She remembers the struggle to learn to read and how reading was a slow process until one birthday, when she sat down with her new book, the mystery story was so exciting, she finished it in one session. She has wanted to write her own stories ever since!

Cecelia writes from the perspective of a Bachelor of Education and Master of Arts, and experience as an Accredited Counsellor for four years.

She is also the author of *Special Pictures to Talk About* (ISBN: 978-0-646-97235-0) which developed out of her work on language delay and speech development in Kindergartens.